THE PORTASS OF TARTAE

THE LAND WITH THE TWO MOONS

MARCIA SOLIGO

To my husband, Glaubert Queiroz

THE PORTASS OF TARSAE

THE LAND WITH
THE TWO MOONS

CHAPTER ONE

BOOKS AND STORIES

H er way to work was the same as always. Wide streets surrounded by trees, some leaves scattered on the ground and a faint breeze that seemed to always follow her wherever she went. And the sleepiness. The sleepiness was persistent; so was a pain in her right wrist.

Olivia Halin worked at an old bookshop, and she walked there every single day. At that odd store, one would find the latest releases and also dusty, ancient books. The kind that had a very distinguished scent of old pages and stories that had been told too many times. A scent that Olivia didn't even notice anymore, because she had spent too much time there, drowned in a sea of pages that were now discolored under the ruthlessness of time.

Olivia was seventeen years old, she was tall, and her hair was as brown as a chestnut. Her dark green eyes were big and always alert, maybe because she was trying too hard to avoid surprises. She didn't want to get caught off guard anymore.

On this early afternoon, Olivia felt as if she were being pushed by that familiar breeze. The day was bright, and the sun was warming her face softly, making the cold breeze quite agreeable. It was the last day of school before the winter break, and she had absolutely nothing special planned for that period. From now on, Olivia would be working full-time at Lucent Bookshop, and that was probably it. Some might find this dull, but for her, knowing exactly what would happen and being in a predictable routine was the best she could ask for.

As she walked along the streets of the City of Leve, a small town full of trees, white houses and unnecessary fences, the delicate breeze became a violent gust of wind. Olivia's hair flew all around, and the temperature suddenly dropped. The now very cold wind made the girl shiver as it touched her skin. "Maybe there's a storm coming," she thought to herself, and that thought was soon followed by the realization that she didn't have an umbrella, and if she had to venture the rain, she would probably freeze on her way back home. After fighting the strong wind for a couple of blocks, the girl arrived at the bookshop and had trouble closing the door, which kept swinging back because of the incessant blasts of air.

"Odd weather, huh?" said an old man with gray hair, crooked teeth, and huge round glasses, peeking outside through the glass window.

"Yes, Mr. Fildor. I just hope it goes away fast. How are things today? A lot of clients?"

"Just enough, just enough," answered the man as he walked away from the window and into the maze-like corridors made up of bookshelves.

The store had big front windows that allowed the outside light to come in, and right now Olivia could see the clouds taking over the once-blue sky. But the inside of the bookshop was always quite dark. The light would get blocked by the mountain of books and shelves, and only a few rays of sunshine would find their way deep into the shop, making it feel secluded, somewhat like a cave where Olivia liked to hide. It was as though the place were too small for that many words. The decoration was simple, or almost inexistent; it was limited to three dark red, suede armchairs that were placed at three different spots around the store. They looked old and worn, just like everything else.

Olivia's days at Lucent Bookshop were pretty much the same. Her job consisted of greeting customers, helping them finding books, giving brief explanations about the titles or suggestions, accepting payments, packing, and finally, handing out the books. It was a job that could easily become boring and uninteresting, making the days into long and dragged hours.

She had found this job unexpectedly. Walking through town by herself one day, she passed this small store and decided to go inside. There, she found Mr. Augusto Fildor, the bookshop owner, and after discussing a bit about Greek civilization and how they contributed to modern society, he offered her a job. "You know books. And I can't work here anymore. My back hurts, my feet hurt … I need to sleep more and carry fewer stories," said the old man, smiling kindly.

Working with books was interesting. But Olivia had spent too much time trying to forget how her life was supposed to be, where she should be, and what she should be doing instead. Unfortunate circumstances had brought her here and made her find a job at this particular bookshop. She distanced herself from all of her plans, including her dream to go to college and study paleontology, something she had longed for since she was a little child. A dream she had built while diving into the greatest adventures with her parents. A dream that was just a dream now. Little by little, she distanced herself from everything she wanted to be or do.

Olivia's parents had died two years ago in a tragic fire. After the accident, Olivia had moved to the City of Leve to live with her grandmother, Mrs. May Halin. About a year ago, the girl started to live, essentially, by herself. Her grandmother wasn't an ordinary old lady. One wouldn't find her telling beautiful stories about the fascinating old days to her granddaughter or encouraging anyone to pursue their dreams. Mrs. Halin always managed to be traveling somewhere around the world, and the travels seemed to be more a way to avoid her granddaughter than a way to explore different places. However, Olivia enjoyed the freedom. She liked to live with her grandmother, but she missed her family too much, and she never felt completely comfortable in that house, surrounded by her grandmother's stuff. When Mrs. Halin was far away, the house got lighter, and life became more enjoyable.

The truth was that the accident scarred Olivia Halin forever, and since then, she felt as if a certain lightness had ceased to exist in everything.

Soon after Olivia arrived at the bookstore, Mr. Fildor left, complaining about his joints and repeating his mantra about his legs and back that hurt so much. She spent the afternoon cleaning some shelves, organizing the self-help books—where someone had made a complete mess—and reading. Since Lucent Bookshop was not a very crowded store, Olivia had plenty of time to read. During this time, all alone and surrounded by mountains of books and thousands of words, her best companions were silence and the universes she created so vividly inside her head. Sometimes, she would get so lost in her wonders that she would actually see new worlds. And she was pretty sure that she had hurt her wrist in one of those alternative worlds. She used to laugh and think that the loneliness was making her slowly mad.

After a whole day of work, the night was dark, and the rain never came. The strange wind ceased as quickly as it had started, leaving hundreds of leaves huddled on the ground in front of the Lucent Bookshop.

"Olie, hello! Can we go?" said a tall, skinny boy with brown hair and brown eyes.

"Not yet…" Olivia said. "There's a customer back there. But I think he'll be done soon. Wait for me just a bit."

The boy nodded and sat with her behind the tall wooden counter. Trevor Meris had been Olivia's best friend for about two years now, but those years seemed like ages. They seemed like a whole life. They had met when Olivia moved to Leve, and they soon built a beautiful friendship that was crucial to Olivia's sanity. Trevor was a key factor in Olivia's recovery from her loss. He stayed by her side, made her laugh and helped her see that life could still be good and full of joy.

Trevor was extremely smart. With him, you wouldn't find much of a gray area. He would always tell the truth, for he was as sincere as they come. And one would probably find this truth full of sarcasm. The boy was also renowned for his laziness, as he very much loved his naps. But he was also very kind, and he quickly became a brother to Olivia. He always went to the Lucent Bookshop after his classes—he was already taking some college classes and excelling at them, of course—and then they would walk home together, since they lived two houses away from each other.

"May I help you with something, sir?" asked Olivia, walking toward the back shelves of the store, carrying her selling smile on her face.

"No, thank you. I've found what I was looking for. I will take this," answered the man, staring deeply into Olivia's eyes.

Olivia looked back at him, studying his face for a moment, and told the man to follow her to the counter. For some reason, his look was one of the scariest things Olivia had ever seen in her life. There was a certain coldness to his stare, his eyes were empty, as if he had no soul. The man was very pale; his hair was a dark blond, very thin and groomed carefully on his head, but none of this made

4

him look any better. He wore an elegant purple suit and had chosen a book about travels to Egypt, with a bony camel on the cover and golden page borders. Olivia gave the man the burgundy bookshop bag, and he shot her a smile, something that looked completely foreign to his face, and left.

Just after the strange man disappeared, Olivia closed the store and left with Trevor. They walked through the same streets as they always did. And even though nothing was different, she felt that something was out of place. A cold shiver ran through her spine every time the not-so-cold breeze touched her skin. On the way home, the leaves on the ground swirled in the wind. And everything seemed a little different. The leaves appeared to be leading the way and also following both of them, slowly forming circles and jumping around in a hypnotic dance.

Olivia barely slept that night. She kept dreaming about that man at the store shape-shifting into a wolf and devouring books all around. She dreamed about the camel on the book's cover desperately running from the big wolf who bought books about Egypt. She dreamed about the light breeze blowing and whispering in her ears with a warm voice, saying: "Be careful. Look where you're going. Be careful."

She woke up after each nightmare and looked around, checking every shadow in her room. Nothing was different.

CHAPTER TWO

TWO MOONS

One more day of work. It was a crisp Saturday, a beautiful autumn day in the beginning of December and once again the leaves were behaving in a peculiar way. As the wind howled, the leaves danced around as if they wanted to show Olivia where to go. They went up and down in the air and drew shapes on the ground. It was as though they were carefully composing a message that Olivia couldn't understand, full of symbols that she was not able to figure out.

Olivia spent the whole day working. She sold just a few books, and she was only able to read a little bit. For most of the time, she was just wondering, writing, drawing and revisiting the shelves in the back of the bookshop in the hopes that she would find some clue about the stranger who bought books about Egypt. The man didn't leave any trace behind, except the impressions that were now haunting Olivia and a receipt of his purchase that didn't say much. She didn't know his name, much less who he was. There was no relevant record of his visit, no vestige.

In a sea of mundane activities, a small mystery like this was an interesting addition to Olivia's calm days. For that reason, she caught herself multiple times creating fantastic conjectures involving the stranger. He could be an evil archaeologist who would go to Egypt to steal treasures hidden inside the pyramids, violating sacred tombs and unleashing a maleficent curse over the world. Or even simpler things, like the fact that he could be a burglar and was planning all the details to steal from Lucent Bookshop. It didn't matter how hard Olivia tried to redirect her thoughts; they always came back to that creepy man, and when she remembered his empty look, a shiver ran down her spine and fear took control of her heart.

Once more, Trevor showed up at the end of the afternoon, and they walked home together. Olivia's heart had been racing all day long as if in a hurry for something to happen, or to prevent something happen; a haunting presentiment washed over her, and she almost told Trevor a thousand times how weird she had been feeling since the day before, since that customer visited the bookshop. But every time she considered doing it, something stopped her. Maybe the realization that she had no reason to have all those sensations and that all of this was just the product of an idle mind.

They were calmly walking and laughing at some anecdotes Trevor was telling, things that happened at his classes and some of his new literary findings. Suddenly, everything went dark. In a flash, the purple light of the setting sun was gone, and all that surrounded them was swallowed by shade. They were abruptly consumed by the earth under their feet, and they couldn't see any sign of light. They were free-falling, of that Olivia was sure. Her hair flew, and she shook her arms aimlessly, looking for something that she could grab onto. Now, all that existed was a knot on her stomach and an overwhelming feeling of desperation.

They fell, and they fell for what felt like long minutes. And their terror was so strong that their screams never came out. They stayed stuck inside their throats, petrified, or like something that just forgot to exist. Olivia and Trevor were so unprepared and surprised that their brains didn't understand the message to scream whenever there was danger. So, they just silently fell, and fell, and fell.

There was no way to avoid the arrival on the ground. They knew it would happen sometime, and they both eventually collapsed clumsily on the floor after what seemed like they were falling for days. Olivia fell on her face and ate a good amount of dirt, or whatever that was. Soon after, Trevor arrived too, as if he was falling from the sky. He landed on his butt and rolled for a bit.

"What the hell? Where did that come from?" raged Trevor, looking from side to side. Looking up, he massaged his butt, which was probably very hurt by the harsh fall.

Olivia shrugged. She looked around, searching for something, she didn't know what. They were in a wasteland, and it was late-night; the sky was overflowing with stars, and two moons shone in the sky.

"Trevor … two moons."

"What, Olie? Was that a hole in the ground? A manhole? What was that? We go through that street every single day and I never saw anything … You know, I'm gonna call someone about that. I could have died or hurt myself. That's it, we must make a complaint.…"

"I think it was a hole, and I don't think it was there before. Trev, there are two moons." Olivia pointed to the sky and looked at Trevor with her eyes wide open in surprise. He finally found her deep gaze, and she repeated, "There are two moons."

They both stared at the sky for a while in complete silence.

"Olie, I can see some lights there. I think it could be a city of some sort … I think we should go there."

The girl nodded. They walked toward the lights, not exchanging a word. Talking at this point seemed impossible and almost unbearable. They couldn't think of anything to say, and the words—and thoughts—were completely shuffled inside their minds. Olivia felt as if a rock had dropped inside her stomach. She wasn't sure if it was only because of the fall or because she was so frightened. She kept thinking about the moment her scream would finally come out, exploding everybody else's eardrums.

They followed a pathway that seemed previously marked by other travelers. Some kind of trail made of dirt showing that this was clearly a very used road. A little bit of grass decorated the ground, some bushes and plants that moved shiftily when Olivia and Trevor passed by them. These plants seemed to feel their presence and shrank, protecting themselves. Olivia looked around at everything with suspicion. All the things appeared to be alive and aware of their presence, the trees, the grass, the rocks. They walked down a hill through some trees and finally saw what appeared to be a small village. If it wasn't for the two moons shining very brightly in the sky, they would probably be lost by now. The bluish moonlight made the path clearer and the walk considerably easier.

It was a small town, and they probably were on its main street. There were a number of stores and some restaurants, and the city lights were lit for no one. The buildings were very similar to each other, some of them made of stone, others of small bricks painted red or very dark green. The street was large and stone paved. All was calm, and the place seemed somewhat abandoned. Maybe that was the reason everything felt so strange and heavy. Olivia and Trevor examined the surroundings, very much afraid of what could show up. Olivia didn't know why, but she was thinking about her nightmares and the vicious wolf she'd seen the night before. She looked around, thinking that at any moment the creature could appear and attack her. Right now, it all seemed real, it all seemed possible, even her wildest wonderings.

"I don't think we're close to home anymore, Trev. We need to find a place where someone can explain to us where we are exactly. And I think we should get out of the streets. Something doesn't feel right here."

"I agree, Olie. That sounds like a good idea."

"I believe it's the only option we have now ..."

They kept walking, and every place seemed to be closed. The city was sleeping. Olivia thought about starting to scream and knock on every door, asking for help, crying, until someone finally decided to assist them. But at the same time, she feared who or what could appear. There were two moons in the sky; who could guarantee that humans would live in this place? Or that they would be friendly?

A silhouette appeared houses away from where they were, approaching fast and decisively. As this person got closer, they could distinguish a tall woman, probably in her seventies. She had a long neck, small brown eyes, and a very pronounced nose. Her eyebrows were thin and well-groomed, having the same brownish tone of her hair. She wore some kind of long, dark-blue dress, and she had a neat and big hair bun at the top of her head. She was beautiful, but her face had a scary expression.

"What are you two thinking? Can you please tell me?" said the woman, getting closer to Olivia and Trevor. Her tone was severe, and her small eyes were filled with concern. "And what are you waiting for? Are you going to be stuck in the middle of the street waiting to be devoured ... or worse? Come on now! Hurry!" She wrapped her arms around them and started pushing Olivia and Trevor, leading them in the direction she came from.

She kept rambling, repeating the same things over and over again: *How could they? What were they thinking? What a reckless thing to do! Who would do something like this, on a day like this?* Olivia and

Trevor only exchanged puzzled looks. They were being pushed around while the woman was still complaining and mumbling.

"Excuse me, ma'am. Even though you seem very kind, we cannot follow you wherever you're going. We would like an explanation first. Where we are going and who are you would be a very good start," Olivia said, stopping abruptly.

"And what would be worse than being devoured would be great to know too … I would strongly appreciate if you would tell me more about that," said Trevor with wide eyes.

The woman looked deeply into Olivia's green eyes as if she were trying to figure something out. As if she were hoping to hear Olivia say that she wasn't being serious. Olivia faced the woman with a defiant look. And with even bigger exasperation, the woman finally said: "Oh, please! For Ourivio's beard! Just follow me and trust. This is not the place for conversations, especially this kind of conversation … and you two should know that. You should know better than this."

For some reason, they obeyed. Olivia and Trevor kept walking with the mysterious, annoyed lady in complete silence, and they felt that somehow it was worth risking it. At least for now. After all, she appeared to be the only living soul in this place. Hence, the only person who could help them.

They walked for little more than ten minutes until they finally reached a beautiful terracotta house. The place had large windows and a small porch. A magnificent garden spilled across the large lawn; however, it was considerably wild. The flowers grew freely everywhere, and branches invaded the porch and created what looked like a small forest. Ivies climbed up the walls, covering the house almost completely. Ferns adorned the roof. It was the right amount of wild.

While the woman approached the door, Olivia and Trevor intentionally stayed behind.

"Olie, do you think it's safe?" Trevor whispered. His curious eyes studied everything around them, including the lady, who they still didn't know anything about.

"What other choice do we have? At least we'll get some answers. She seems like a good person, and she sounded worried about us. Let's just go in and get some answers."

"And then we can go home."

"Yes. And then we'll go home."

The tall lady opened the door, clapping her hands twice.

"Trevor, Olivia, come on in. Hurry." Her tone was now calmer. It was as though being inside was enough of a protection. Olivia and Trevor stepped inside the house and the woman studied the street for a little while, until she finally closed the door behind her.

Her now serene expression made things seem a little better and her face even more trustworthy. A warm feeling of protection filled Olivia and Trevor in the exact moment they entered that house.

It was a beautiful house. Tall ceilings rose above them, classical furniture adorned the area and antiques delicately decorated the amber walls. The place was very neat and organized, but at the same time, there were a lot of things everywhere. The living room was considerably overflowing with details, showing somehow that someone had been living there for a long time. As though all of those things were telling the story of a well-lived life.

Right in the middle of the living room, a big fireplace warmed up the whole room. Over the mantel was a picture of a number of keys, framed by olive branches, flowers, and incomprehensible words, at least to Olivia. At the far right, polished and shining wooden stairs led the way up to the top floor.

The lady went straight to the kitchen, and even in the other room, it was possible to hear her complaining outrageously about something Olivia and Trevor had done, although they had no idea what that would be. While alone in the living room, the two friends planned to question her again about everything. They had to find out where they were, what they could do to go back home, and how this woman knew their names. But everything was so interesting and calm and warm that for a moment they forgot about their current situation and just lost themselves in the small discoveries of that extraordinary living room.

The pictures hanging on the walls were very detailed. They appeared to tell a story, complementing each other in some way. One of them showed what resembled a pine tree with leafless branches and a small flower at the top. Another was a snapshot of the sky, with two stars shining brighter than the others. The drawings were made on a delicate parchment, braided in a way Olivia and Trevor had never seen before. The strong lines were written in black ink, and a number of other figures danced in the margins, designing colorful frames. Blue, green, red, and purple tones highlighted in contrast to the pale parchment. Olivia and

Trevor were under the impression that the lines were subtly moving, making the pictures look more pleasant to the eyes and also very hypnotic.

Placed in a glass dome over the mantel was a silver dagger with a big red stone decorating the guard. The stone shone with a sad glare, one that made one's heart hurt, like in a song about loss, about death. Olivia struggled to take her eyes off of it; the sorrow of the object filled her until she was lost in it.

An unusual scent drifted from the kitchen. The lady entered the living room carrying a mirrored tray with three white cups and a teapot. She rested the tray on the wooden coffee table and sat down in a yellow armchair, looking profoundly to Olivia and Trevor. She looked into their eyes intensely, making it very clear that a thousand thoughts were going through her mind. Her thoughts were so loud that Olivia felt she could almost hear them all.

"Ma'am, would you please tell us your name?" asked Trevor once more, sounding overly polite.

"You don't know my name?" she asked.

"No. We don't. Could you tell us what it is?" repeated Trevor. The fact that she kept avoiding to answer was making him worry more and more.

"You don't remember anything? How you got here? Do you have any recollection of that?" said the woman, still ignoring what Trevor was saying.

"We fell," answered Olivia.

"We fell and now we're here. A huge fall, actually. Now please, could you tell us where we are and your name?" repeated Trevor resolutely.

The woman lost her gaze inside the trembling fire and finally gasped: "Alas."

CHAPTER THREE

ALLANDRIO

"My name is Cordella Terraciem." She sighed. "I'm one of the Guardians of the Portals. And it's most unfortunate that you two don't remember. It's unfortunate and extremely dangerous. I'm afraid I can't answer all your questions right now. I thought we would still have some time, but my worst fear was realized today. This much I can say: you two have been coming to Tartae for a while. In the dark of the night, you leave your world and travel here, always returning to Leve before dawn."

Olivia and Trevor's eyes were wide open in disbelief, but the lady was too serious and paying too much attention to the story she was telling to notice any kind of reaction from them. Olivia sipped her rosy tea for the first time. It tasted like cinnamon, but it was even more warming and calming. The liquid gave her the sensation that something was hugging her heart and making all her fears and anxieties go away. Olivia looked inside the cup and lost herself in there for a while, thinking about how she got to that place and what she could possibly do to get out of there, if she should or should not believe in that complete stranger who was telling them a bunch of weird things. Things that could easily not be true.

"I'm sorry, Ms. Terraciem. But I think you're wrong," said Olivia, putting her teacup back on the coffee table and exchanging a decisive look with Trevor. "We didn't come here on purpose today, and we have never been here before."

Cordella studied Olivia carefully. It was clear that she was analyzing every movement and every single word the girl was saying.

"No, Olivia. We met years ago. I mean, years ago here, in Tartae. Is your wrist paining you?" Cordella looked at Olivia, who was quietly massaging her right wrist.

"I beg your pardon?" asked Olivia with a puzzled expression.

"Your wrist? I have been trying to heal you, but unfortunately, I haven't been completely successful yet."

"How do you know about my wrist? I've been living with this pain for a while, and I have no memory of what happened…" said Olivia. With every passing minute things were making less and less sense. She had no idea how to organize her thoughts in order to ask the right questions, but she tried anyway. "Where are we? How do we leave this place?"

"My dear Olivia … Going back to your world now wouldn't be easy, considering all that's happening. Handling the Portals would be extremely dangerous and terribly audacious. The Portals' energy is altered and turbulent now, with you two arriving this way. However, staying here or going back to your world was always your choice."

"What do you mean by 'handling the Portals?'" asked Trevor. "Can't you just show us the way back home? The way back to Leve?"

"No, Trevor. It's awfully more complex than that," answered Cordella. Her eyes now had a strange look, as though she were drowning more and more into despair. She didn't even seem to make an effort to hide it anymore.

"And what the hell are these Portals?" asked Trevor, raising his voice a little and putting a pinch of comedy into his tone.

"For Ourivio's sake! What a disrespectful way to talk! I wasn't aware that you had forgotten your manners too on this unexpected journey here. Or did you knock your head when you fell?" Cordella got up, grunting once more, and her cheeks were flushed. She went back to the kitchen and was apparently getting ready to sleep, turning off all lights and closing the curtains.

"You shouldn't have done that …" whispered Olivia carefully.

"Done what?"

"Talked about these Portals that way!"

"But I don't know what these Portals are! And she never explains anything! Did you notice that she got up and never answered my question? I even wonder if she was really offended by the language I used or if she was just trying to get away."

14

"I think you played with fire there. Who knows where she can send us using these Portals?" Olivia gave a discreet but mischievous laugh.

"I won't do that anymore. And who the hell is Ourivio?"

"I'm pretty sure you should avoid speaking about this man like that too … He seems to be important around here."

Cordella came back to the room carrying a glass of water. She didn't sit again and seemed more direct now.

"Olivia, do you remember your magic?" she questioned with a hopeful expression, while still standing next to a big lamp gleaming a yellowish light.

"Huh?" Olivia half-smiled. She was certain the woman was trying to prank her. How could nothing make sense?

"This is worse than I thought … You two don't remember anything because you didn't get to Tartae the way you were used to or supposed to. Every time you traveled using Portals it was all rehearsed and measured. You came here protected and were able to fulfill your purpose."

At this moment, Olivia and Trevor started to speak, but Cordella waved her hand, stopping them, and continued. "We don't have time, and we must be cautious. The allandrio tea should be working by now, and you will soon be able to rest. I won't say any more today … There's no time. Your bedroom is ready, as always, and tomorrow morning we will leave."

"Where is our…?" Olivia started to ask but Cordella interrupted her.

"Upstairs, second door on your left," said Cordella, and she added, "I just ask you to trust. We cannot say much more here."

They trusted, but they didn't feel that they would have enough strength to do anything else. Olivia's body was heavy and her muscles completely relaxed. All of her troubles seemed now to be a faraway, blurred reality, something lost in the past. It was clear that the allandrio tea had made her feel this way. She would be scared if she weren't so cozy and if the allandrio allowed her to feel anything besides complete relaxation.

Cordella quickly went to her room, disappearing down a hallway near the stairs. Olivia and Trevor went upstairs slowly, arriving in a broad corridor surrounded by doors made of dark wood that led to the rooms on the second floor. At the end of the hallway, an oval mirror hung over a side table, which was decorated with a vase filled with colossal sunflowers. They opened the second door to their left and found two beds covered with navy quilts full of silver stars. The quilts were quite childish but very beautiful. Over the dresser, Olivia found a black notebook. She opened it and instantly recognized her handwriting, her sketches, some dreams she remembered faintly.

"Trev, I'm starting to think that we've been here before. This notebook is mine, look." She showed him her sketches and her handwriting. Trevor looked into her eyes, and they could feel the same shiver, at the same time.

At the foot of each bed, there was a wooden chest, and they looked like actual tree trunks. They were majestic, carefully adorned with small blue stones and flowery writings. Olivia's name was written on one, and Trevor's on the other.

As they opened them, they found weapons. Inside Trevor's chest was a wooden bow and a number of arrows, all green, adorned with green feathers. His bow had small three-leaf cloves engraved along its length. It was an astonishing work, something otherworldly. In the other chest, Olivia found a long silver sword with small leaves engraved on its grip. The weapon was almost too big to fit into the chest. The scabbard was violet, made out of something that resembled velvet, but much more resistant and solid. The material became hard when protecting the sword, but when empty, it was just a light fabric. Olivia also found small glass bottles filled with multicolored liquids. Some of them were biphasic, some had bubbles flying around, and one had just white smoke. She didn't dare to open any of them.

There were also some carefully folded clothes over the beds and two pairs of sneakers on the floor as if they were waiting to be stored by Olivia and Trevor. Everything was very clean and well-kept. Tons of books with marked pages, maps, and parchments were resting over a desk next to the bedroom window. Olivia and Trevor looked around and felt an urge to read and discover more, but they couldn't. They were now so sleepy that their eyes were closing involuntarily.

After so many discoveries, Olivia and Trevor fell asleep fast and almost without even noticing it. Deep down, they still hoped to wake up in their beds, in the world they so comfortably knew. However, when Olivia thought about that possibility, she didn't feel as happy as she would have thought. There was something interesting about the unknown, a growing feeling of excitement when considering what could happen in that foreign place. It was new, it was adventurous. It was considerably different from the life she had at the peaceful City of Leve.

CHAPTER FOUR

THE FIRST STEPS OF A JOURNEY

Olivia woke up after a restful sleep. She didn't remember having any dreams; nothing good, nothing bad. She only had the feeling of complete relaxation and peace that usually overflows one's body and mind after a good night's sleep. The sleep of the righteous, as some might say.

She opened her eyes and forgot where she was for a second. She ran her hand over her face and sat up in bed, looking around. The big bedroom window was still closed, but the white curtains were letting weak orange sunlight in. It was very early in the morning. Trevor was still fast asleep, and everything seemed to be suspended, on pause. Waiting for something to happen.

Olivia was always quite weird about these things. She always felt—or sensed—that something was about to happen. But she never had a vision or saw clear images, and she didn't dream about the future, read tarot cards or know how to do a palm reading. She could only feel something inexplicable all around, like a discreet alarm that made her shoulders heavy and her heart ache. However, she never knew what it was or when it was going to happen. She could only feel the changes, the heavy weight on her back, the beast eating her stomach. It was like that when her parents passed away. During the entire week before the fire, Olivia had this disturbing and unsettling feeling as her companion.

She felt this way now. And even though the morning was calm and the sunrise beautiful, she was certain that something was there, lurking, waiting for an opportunity to make something evil happen. Olivia thought about her home in Leve, and her heart shrank a little more. What if they were never able to come back? What if the magic of that place was so strong that people would simply forget their existence? All of her thoughts danced inside her mind. She wanted to know everything, ask everything, but truly, she had no idea when her questions would be fully answered or even if the answers would bring her what she needed to hear.

Magic… Cordella had asked about her magic. Olivia knew that spells were a myth. She believed that love, friendship, and hard work could work like magic, but she understood that magic was too powerful to be human. Something that could easily change people, end lives, crush beliefs. Magic was too dangerous to be real.

A delicious scent coming from outside the room woke her from her thoughts. She looked at Trevor, who was still sleeping, breathing soundly and slowly, and walked to the door. As she opened it, the scent became more intense, and her stomach howled at the promise of breakfast. She went down the stairs as if she was being pulled by that aroma until she got to the kitchen, where she found Cordella taking a cake out of the oven.

"Good morning, Olivia! How was your night?" Cordella's eyes were filled with expectation. It was clear that she hoped Olivia would remember everything after a good night's sleep. However, her face fell as she looked at Olivia.

"Good morning, Cordella. I slept well," Olivia answered with a half-hearted smile. "Everything smells great!"

"I improvised a quick breakfast for us. Eat, eat! I've already prepared some of it for us to take on our trip. As I said yesterday, we will be leaving soon. The others were warned already."

"Others?" asked Olivia.

"Yes. The Guardians." Cordella shot a sad look at Olivia. The girl was about to burst with questions, but it never happened. They seemed to dissolve in her mouth, dying when they were just about to pop. The scent of the spices Cordella had used was taking over Olivia's mind, and she started to eat without giving it a lot of thought.

Everything was truly delicious. Banana and cinnamon cake, hot chocolate with small chocolate chips melting slowly and giving a heavenly creaminess to the drink, pastries, loaves of bread, jams … all of it carefully placed on a beautiful table set by Cordella. Nothing seemed improvised.

It didn't take long for Trevor to burst down the stairs, clearly upset and considerably disheveled. He probably thought for a moment that Olivia had left without him, or he simply didn't remember exactly what happened the night before.

"Eat a little, Trevor," said Cordella, leaving the room with her quick pace.

"Do you happen to know where we're going, Olie?" asked Trevor, sitting and serving himself a glass of apple juice. Olivia only shook her head, she was quite embarrassed for not asking about this, or even worse, for not discovering anything.

Trevor looked at her in disbelief. He seemed to be preparing his lecture when she interrupted him.

"I didn't ask anything because I couldn't, okay? I just couldn't. I know that wasn't brave, but I wanted to avoid this whole story for a moment and not ask her all the questions I've been asking myself since we got here. I don't know where we're going yet, but I believe we're going to know soon enough, and we won't need to ask much. I believe she'll soon tell us everything … But I'm not sure we're going to like it. And, in my defense, I also just got here. I just woke up too."

"I'm gonna ask her now. I thought I would wake up at home and this would be a dream or a bad fairy tale where everybody wakes up after the 'adventure' and discovers that it was all just a dream … I need to know at least where we're going. And you should have asked."

Trevor left the kitchen in a bad mood and was soon followed by Olivia. He looked for Cordella and found her on the balcony, staring incessantly at the horizon as if she were waiting for something to happen in the sky.

"Cordella, where are we going?" Trevor asked harshly. Cordella didn't face him; she kept looking straight at the horizon. From time to time, she squinted her eyes.

"We are going to meet the others, and then we will go to the Strage Castle," said Cordella, who didn't seem worried about what the boy could be thinking. Her body language was very rigid, and sometimes she would stretch her neck, which was already very long, to see a little further.

A small dot appeared far away in the sky. Cordella relaxed and turned, looking deeply at Trevor for the first time since he arrived on the balcony.

"We are going to the Strage Castle to destroy the Book of the Portals, and I hope you two can complete this journey with us. It's time to go."

"Strage Castle? Destroy what?" asked Trevor, noticing that the information didn't help him much after all.

"We need to destroy the Book of the Portals," Cordella whispered without paying much attention since she was already getting ready to leave. "Hurry up. It's not safe to talk about this here."

"I don't mean to be rude, but I'm not leaving. Cordella, I have no idea what you're talking about. You've been talking about books and meeting people, and we can barely understand where we are. You can't expect us to follow you around when we don't know anything." Trevor was trying to sound polite and in complete control of it all, but his voice and his wide, desperate eyes gave him away. As he said all of those things, something inside Olivia clicked, and she could see his point more clearly. It was as though she had been numb, maybe because this whole idea seemed more interesting than the life she was living. Or maybe it was something else. Perhaps she was under some kind of spell.

"I thought I had given you enough information yesterday. I'm so sorry, Trevor, but there's no way I can say more than that." Cordella was calm, and her voice was as soft as the morning itself. Olivia felt like she had seen that understanding look before.

"Well, I need more. And I'm sure Olivia needs more too."

"Cordella." Olivia spoke for the first time, walking toward the woman. "Just help us understand a little more. Why can't we know everything now? What could happen?"

Cordella sighed and was quiet for a while, breathing deeply and clearly carefully considering her next step.

"You've always wanted to learn more, and I've always taught you," she whispered very low. "Tartae is now a dangerous place— especially for the pair of you—and things can get deadly quickly. Someone brought you here when they shouldn't have, and that says something. All I can tell you at this moment is that we will be meeting with other people who can help and protect you. And I promise, if you choose to go back to Leve, you will. I know it may seem too much to ask from you, but I need you to trust. Find it in your heart to trust in me."

Cordella finished speaking and walked toward some bags on the balcony's floor. Apparently, all of their stuff was already there, and they should be ready to go. Trevor took one of the bags from Cordella's hand and put a backpack on his back. Olivia grabbed some things too. It wasn't much, and it was very light.

"Are you sure this is everything, Cordella?" asked Olivia.

"These bags seem hardly enough for a journey. But, I have no idea of how much someone should take to rescue a book," said Trevor with a puzzled look on his face.

"Yes. It's all here. One of the perks of having magic," said Cordella with a smirk. It was the first time they'd seen her make a joke.

There was a strange mood hovering over them now. Olivia and Trevor wanted answers and they felt somewhat guilty. It seemed that they were there to help, but apparently, they had forgotten everything they once knew. At this point, they would probably only be in everybody's way. They had done next to nothing until now, but the little they did was wrong: getting there by surprise in the middle of the night in a city that was under alert for some reason they still didn't know. And of course, they couldn't remember a thing.

"Your weapons." Cordella handed the bow and arrow to Trevor and the silver sword to Olivia. As Olivia touched it, a shiver ran down her spine.

Olivia and Trevor looked at their weapons for a moment. They had no courage to look at each other or to make any questions to Cordella anymore. But inside their minds, they were trying to make sense of it all. How many times had they used those weapons before, for what reason did they use them and why did they have them in the first place? Would the answer to these questions scare them? Maybe some things are better left in the dark.

CHAPTER FIVE

THE GUARDIANS

They walked in silence. Olivia, Trevor, and Cordella marched down through what looked like the main street of the village. The same street surrounded by houses, restaurants, and stores where they arrived the night before. The difference now was that Cordella wasn't terrified anymore. Maybe there was no real threat now, no one hunting them during the day; maybe the real danger was only at night. But at the same time, Cordella was measuring her words as if simply saying something wrong could be their doom. Maybe … The enormous number of "maybes" started to suffocate Olivia. The increasing number of unanswered questions was making her stomach turn; it was something physical, it was a fact. Her stomach was probably protesting against the persistent sensation of despair and uncertainty.

The street was still very empty, and all the stores were closed. Only a few people passed by here and there, and Cordella seemed to be hiding from them. She walked quickly, and Olivia and Trevor were doing their best to keep up with her, but they were also looking around and analyzing all that surrounded them.

"Why is this village this way … so quiet? It looks abandoned," said Trevor.

"Victro wasn't always like this, Trevor," answered Cordella. "Victro was once a colorful city, full of life. But when its people felt the changes, they wanted to protect their loved ones, and they started to hide or abandon their homes. Even though no one, except for the Clan, really knows what is happening, people can feel something has changed."

Cordella led them to an old building. It looked like the remains of a restaurant, vacant a long time ago. Its signage was falling apart, and the wooden walls were full of mold and dirt, giving the place such an unappealing aspect that it was hard to believe that the restaurant was still operating. 'Fox's Mouth' was written on the sign, and the letter "x" hung by a thread. Some of the other letters were long gone, leaving only a light shadow there to tell the story.

The small group entered through a door made of glass rectangles blurred by layers and layers of dirt that showed years of noticeable lack of tidiness. Inside, the bar was exactly what one would expect: dark and all made of old wood. Strange music played, out of key and strident. Behind the counter, an old man with long, curly white hair stood with his back to the door, cleaning the glasses on the shelf. Besides him, there was only one other person, sitting at a table. This red-haired man got up as soon as he saw the group enter and proceeded to the back door, holding it open for them.

Olivia and Trevor followed as though they were blindfolded. The group walked for a while through a green field with some trees here and there. They passed by the bar fences and saw some horses and two men dressed in what looked like Tartae's latest fashion: dark pants, loose buttoned shirts, and vests.

"How does it look, Cordella?" asked the red-haired man in an almost inaudible whisper, tilting his head in Cordella's direction. His hair and beard were so intensely red that they looked like fire. He was of average height and a little overweight, carrying most of his weight right in his belly. His light green shirt was covered by a brown vest, adorned with red embellishments that sparkled when exposed to the sun.

"Dreadful. We are in the dark. We might as well only have started today. We need to act," she answered, not flinching away.

Olivia and Trevor looked at each other. They were aware that the strange man and Cordella were talking about them and their current situation, but that conversation could be the prelude of a more elaborate explanation that Olivia and Trevor so needed. So they let it go on, not even dreaming of interrupting Cordella and the red-haired man.

They finally arrived where the rest of the group was waiting. Cordella stopped and took a deep breath.

"Olivia, Trevor, as I said before, we are going to the Strage Castle, and these are our companions. This is Alavro Talbote; he's one of the Guardians of the Portals and Ourivio's Keys." She pointed politely to the men with hair like fire. His small eyes were a deep, bright blue and filled with kindness. He inclined his head in reverence and shook their hands. It was clear that he was trying to make this whole introduction look natural, but his anguish was almost palpable.

"This is Bran Talbote," continued Cordella, introducing them to a tall, handsome young man. His hair was black and fell gracefully on his face; he had equally bright blue eyes. "He is Alavro's son. And this is Kirk Saye, our friend and helper. They are your friends. You can trust them with your life." Kirk was strong and had brownish hair. His eyes were happy and black, and his nose very small and pointy. He wore a big smile on his face, the only one in the group who didn't seem bothered by anything.

"It's very nice to meet you all," said Olivia, smiling, followed by an awkward silence that she soon broke. "Cordella ... Could you tell us more about this Strage Castle?"

"The Strage Castle is located east of Victro, our village, where we are right now. We must leave here quickly and keep you two safe. Here, we are nothing but an easy target. You two need to train, need to get back on your feet and remember what you have already learned. I mean, if you choose to come with us to Strage."

"I understand you two have a lot of questions, but it's impossible to discuss them here," said Alavro, looking kindly at both of them. "We need to keep your arrival a secret, and no one can know you don't remember a thing about Tartae. This is *their* doing. Their plan. And that's why we must make them believe it hasn't happened."

"Wouldn't it be better if you all go on without us? Wouldn't it be better for us to just go back to where we came from now?"

"Maybe, Trevor. And believe us when we say you two have that choice. It won't be easy to take you back now, but we can always try. Nevertheless, your presence here is crucial, and you knew that, which is why you have always chosen to stay, and then to come back. Our lives are made of choices, and as soon as we find a safe place to talk, you will be able to make yours again." Alavro finished his speech with an enigmatic look. A mix of hope and disappointment.

The group started to climb onto their horses. Olivia and Trevor hesitated; it's been a long time since Olivia last been on a horse's back and Trevor had never ridden one before, and those two looked particularly huge. Noticing their hesitation, Bran offered to help.

"Is this horse called Skyscraper, by any chance?" Trevor looked at the brown stallion with disdain. But the animal seemed to know him and was waiting to be petted. Olivia thought to herself that this was what usually happened: Trevor would see his loyal companion after a long time away and pet him a little bit before they were off once again in an adventure of some sort. When Trevor started to climb awkwardly onto the horse, Olivia couldn't hold in a laugh. "Oh, my furry friend … there'll be no treats for you today."

"Do you also need help?" asked Bran, looking at Olivia, who smiled and nodded. "All right, let me help you. It's simple enough, you see."

Bran was spectacularly strong, and Olivia felt like a leaf while being lifted by the boy. Maybe people could have superpowers in this land, or maybe she was just too weak … And even so, she could be going to war carrying a sword any day now. She smiled at the irony.

"Thank you, Bran," said Olivia, still feeling quite uncomfortable on the horse. But the animal was gentle and also appeared to know her well, making her feel more relaxed by the minute. She ran her fingers through the horse's white mane and golden coat, feeling the pureness of the creature. It made her heart warm.

They finally left to the east, riding at an easy pace so Olivia and Trevor could follow.

They rode down a tranquil road. Nothing different or dangerous seemed to prowl around here. The road was nothing more than a road; a place with no surprises. They were surrounded by green fields, grass, and some bushes. From time to time, Olivia felt as if some of the plants were moving and shrinking as they passed by, just like the night before. The plants around that place behaved in a very different way than what she was used to. And even though things seemed to be unexceptional, it was better to be prepared for surprises.

"How is your wrist?" asked Bran, getting closer to her.

"It's okay, but it still hurts. By the way, how do you know about my wrist?" Olivia glanced at him angrily but quickly looked back to her horse, clearly nervous about the experience. The horse was tall and slipping to the sides was a strong possibility.

"I was with you when that happened. We were all together. You can relax; I heard my father say they will tell you everything soon, and I don't think I should get in their way."

"I happen to think otherwise. I think you should tell us what you know now. We're in the dark, we don't know anything, and being very honest, it gets scarier with every passing minute. Look at Trevor!" Trevor was riding just in front of them and complaining all the time. His mumbles were loud and solemnly ignored by Alavro and Cordella, who were just next to him and talked about trivialities such as the seasonal flowers they had in their gardens, and how they needed to be cultivated with special soil that was only found in Slintor, and how they bloomed beautifully at dawn.

Bran smiled and stayed by Olivia's side. Apparently, everyone thought that ignoring them and their questions was the best thing to do. Olivia just hoped that it wouldn't always be like this.

Kirk was galloping much faster than the others; he appeared to be too anxious to keep the easy pace. From time to time, he looked back and slowed down, trying to wait for the rest of the group. However, it was noticeable that he wasn't capable of maintaining that for a long time. At least they were all showing a certain kind of tranquility, and that made Olivia calmer too. She couldn't help but think that they could have gotten another kind of transportation if they were really in a hurry. It could be something other than fast cars, something that was available in a place like Tartae. Maybe a carriage of some sort would be a good option, considering no one would have to slow down because of the two beginners.

Since no one seemed to be willing to give Olivia any answers, she figured this would be a good time just to observe. She had learned through past experiences that when she silently observed people, she could discover a lot. Much more than what scratched the surface, much more than what the words chose to show. People would say things when they didn't mean them. And sometimes Olivia wished that she were a little bit more like that, and a little less transparent. Her eyes would tell everyone everything. Even, and especially, when she just wanted them to stay silent.

Olivia studied the group, noticing the small details. How everybody was always too close to her and Trevor; how every so often they looked up. Bran was always by her side, and a gorgeous white eagle flew over them. The animal was enormous, and some of the feathers adorning its wings and chest were sand-colored, others almost red.

The eagle flew very low sometimes, almost touching Cordella's head. Then it would go farther away and higher. But no one said anything or looked disturbed by the bird.

"Bran, look." Olivia discreetly pointed to the sky. "I think that bird is following us." Bran looked and answered calmly:

"It's Atlas, one of the Guardians."

Olivia had no reason to worry.

CHAPTER SIX

THE WHOLE STORY

The sun was starting to set when Alavro announced that they would stop and settle where they were for the night. It was a place under some trees and considerably far from the main road where they had started their journey hours ago. At some point, they had left the marked trail behind them and followed their own path into the green fields. The group unpacked and set up the tents that Alavro and Bran brought with them. Cordella set the tents by just waving her hands around, like a maestro. Trevor climbed down from his horse with a thousand complaints. He said over and over that this was outrageous, he hadn't signed up for this and that every single bone of his body was hurting. And he had a point. He went inside the first tent he saw, ignoring anything anyone said to him.

Bran had collected some wood for the fire and was now setting it up. This was really the border of a very dense forest, and it felt like a protected and enchanted place. He lit the fire while Olivia observed his attempts, sitting with crossed legs right in front of him, across the fire.

"How is your memory?" he asked. "Is it true that neither of you remembers ever coming here?"

"I don't remember anything. I mean, I remember everything that happened on the other side, in the other world ... I don't know what you'd call it exactly."

"I'm sorry. But I can help you if you want. I don't think I can help you remember, but tomorrow we can train how to fight, and you will be more prepared when the time comes. I don't like the

Strage Castle. If I could choose, I would never go there."

Cordella approached them with an impatient look on her face, she was frowning and twitching her lips and she lit the fire by simply waving her right hand.

"For Ourivio's Keys ... I thought you would know at least this, Olivia ..." she sighed. "Please, follow me."

Olivia got up in a flash and her blood was cold inside her body. She looked at Bran and recognized something in his smile. Complicity, maybe. It felt good to recognize something, even though she didn't remember anything. Even though this was all very contradictory.

Alavro and Trevor were waiting for them, sitting beneath the moons, keeping a certain distance from the others. Trevor still looked very tired, but his expression had clearly changed. There was terror, anxiety, and curiosity in his eyes, in his posture, in his whole face.

The two moons glistened in the sky. Being so far away from the lights of the city, it was possible to see an infinity of stars, of things Olivia and Trevor had never seen before. The sky was clear, and the two gigantic full moons made a day out of the night. If not for the freezing breeze that seemed to precede the horror, the scenery would be perfect.

Olivia thought about some movies she had seen where the war always painted the sky red. Would this be true? Would she see it with her own eyes? A weird feeling in her gut grew again and followed her to the truth, just a few steps ahead.

"We won't keep this any longer. And this is a protected place. The Forest of Lis is big, dense, magical and powerful. Nothing evil ever dares to come near here. It's still a pure place, and evil doesn't like pureness," said Alavro, almost singing. Olivia wanted to go inside that forest and dance around the trees.

"There are Portals between our worlds," Cordella explained. "In the old days, people were able to travel between realms without a problem... frequently. They would travel through the Portal, learn, help one another, and then they would come back, not altering anything. However, as it happens oftentimes, some people started to look with greedy eyes to the possibilities of conquering other worlds. They knew that the Portal could give them incredible power; it could give them the opportunity of prolonging their lives, their wealth, to use magic that was unknown to others. Realizing that, before the chaos was established, Ourivio Brut, an old sage from Tartae, the world we are right now, decided to close the Great Portal by himself. But the Great Portal had a strong and unpredictable magic, and instead of disappearing, it shattered, and the Great Portal was divided into thirteen small fractions of itself. They were scattered everywhere and unprotected, leaving the path between the worlds wide open. The tension between the witches and wizards of Tartae rose. People traveled through the worlds unintentionally, children got lost, and some people lost their minds after seeing so many unexpected things. It was then that Ourivio Brut summoned twelve wizards who had his utmost trust. They were all high priests and priestesses with deep knowledge about the Great Portal. They studied extensively how the small Portals worked, and they tested their abilities a number of times before trying anything. With all that acquired knowledge and dedication, they were successful this time. No explosion happened.

"However, Ourivio still believed that the Portals could be useful. After all, there were diseases to be cured, new technology that could be helpful to the other world. It would be a great loss to seal the Portals forever, not to mention that it would be violating nature, since it created the world with a Portal and possibilities. With that in mind, Ourivio created a Key to each Portal, and he wrote down all that he knew about it in a book: The Book of The Portals. Some people call it The Unveiling Book.

"Ourivio didn't expect that his highly skilled sorcery wouldn't be enough to hold someone's voracious interest. And for a long time, he was right. He lived for years and years keeping everything himself. He hid the Keys in caves and forests in Tartae and the Book was very protected in his house. But what he didn't know was that the silence was hiding trickery: wizards who were deeply intrigued and interested in his knowledge and in reopening the Portals. Miniso Lor, one of the wizards responsible for sealing the Portals, learned about the Book and became extremely disturbed by its existence. After a number of arguments with Ourivio, Miniso was consumed by hate and killed Ourivio in his sleep. Once he completed his cruel deed, he looked everywhere inside Ourivio's house for the Book. He went through all Ourivio's belongings until he finally found The Book of the Portals and decided that from now on, his sole purpose would be to find and dominate all the

Keys. And now you can imagine what happened next... war, Portals, death, evil. It was a time of terror. Until a group decided to find and protect all the Portal Keys. They were all considerably young, and they all had been directly affected by the greed generated by the Portals. They witnessed a time filled with blood and betrayal. They had lost loved ones, friends and family ...

"And even though their success seemed impossible, they were determined, and they had strength. And it looks like the Universe really helps people with good intentions. The group found the Keys after fourteen months of restlessly looking for them. They had studied Ourivio's life and the paths he took during his journeys carefully. And they also followed every single clue they had about the Portal Keys. Weird events and rumors that seemed to talk about the Portals. And that's how they kept tracking the artifacts. After gathering all the Keys, they decided to create the Clan, in which each one of them would be responsible for a Key of the Portal and they would keep them safe, even if they had to do so with their lives. Miniso Lor was also a victim of the greed created around the Portals. He was assassinated before the Guardians could do anything about that. He died with the Book of the Portals wrapped tightly in his arms, and after that, the Book was also protected by the Guardians."

Olivia and Trevor looked attentively at Cordella, who paused to breathe and then continued to tell what was obviously a long story. And even though it was all very interesting and dangerous, Olivia and Trevor were still asking themselves how had they gotten there. How did two teenagers from the City of Leve get to Tartae, and why did it look like they were important somehow to this story?

"The Clan worked out. Everyone involved had pure and honest intentions, and their will to fight for what is right created a powerful magic that helped protect their lives, the Keys and the Book. Time went by, the wars came to an end, the world was getting back to normal, and most of the people who were interested in the Portals ended up being each other's doom. Greed is very destructive.

"The Clan was still using the Portals for good deeds. They traveled to your world and helped to cure diseases, end wars ... And that's how they lived for a long time. For eras, I might as well say. The Law established that all the knowledge about the Portals should go to a direct relative, someone related by blood who would be previously chosen. The successor was kept in secret until he or she could finally become a Guardian. They had to promise loyalty, and plenty of spells were made to guarantee that the chosen one was trustworthy.

"Years had passed, and a lot of people became part of the Clan, and then it was our time. We are the third generation of Guardians," said Cordella. "As in the beginning, there were thirteen of us. Me, my husband Zervio—who passed away—Alavro, and ten more honorable ones. You will hear a lot about them when the time comes.

Olivia and Trevor were under the vivid impression that if they took a loud breath, they could miss a crucial part of the story.

"We had a great deal of responsibility, but our lives were considerably calm. We had our families, and work, and keeping the Portals safe was almost a magical celebration. Mainly because in our time, the Portals were opened very rarely.

"And then Anya and Maldo Arbre were brutally murdered, along with one of their daughters, Vitia, and the pursuit of the Keys started again. But the attacker was not successful. The Arbre family protected the Portal Key with their lives, with tenacity. Alegra, the other daughter of the Arbres, was able to flee their house during the attack. She took some of her father's notes and the Key they were keeping. Since the first news about the attack, we knew the intentions of the person who invaded the Arbres' home and destroyed all that was in his or her way. This person wanted the Keys; this person wanted the power of the Portals.

"Alegra took some time to completely recover from the attack, and her testimony finally brought some mysteries to light. Edmund Lars was revealed to be the one responsible for trying to steal the Key and brutally murdering the family. It all came as a hurtful surprise. Edmund Lars is the son of Alcion Lars, one of the Guardians of the Portals. He used to be a very determined and applied boy. His family was wealthy and well-known in Tartae. A family of powerful wizards. Obviously, he was being considered to take his father's place as a Guardian.

"Apparently, Lars found out about the Keys at a very young age and became a Portal enthusiast. As he grew up, his intentions changed, and his heart began to darken. He was tempted by all the possibilities the Portals represented and grew frustrated with his father and all the other Guardians. He simply couldn't understand why no one fully explored the Portal's immense potential. However, few were the times when he completely demonstrated his deep interest in gaining power. Finally, when Alcion Lars performed the series of proving spells on his son so the young man could become a Guardian, he noticed something quite out of place. Realizing that his father was coming close to figuring out his intentions, Lars decided to put his plans to work and started his hunt for the Arbres. He killed almost everyone on the Arbres family, and then he moved on to his next victims.

"Lars' parents were heartbroken. His father abstained from his position as a Guardian, as he had no strength to control and protect the Key anymore. When the misery fills our hearts, magic can become dark and extremely dangerous.

"When Edmund finally hit his next target, the Gronde family, he got his hands on his first Portal Key. It was time to end his plan. He was still working in the shadows, searching and hunting Guardians only, and threatening his parents with sophisticated magic that none of us knew he had mastered. We knew that soon enough he would stop aiming only for the Clan and the terror would spread. We also knew that he could find people to follow him in his pursuit of the Keys, of power, and he was for too long too close to all that he desired.

"And this is how you two become part of the story.

"In his Book, Ourivio wrote down details about how to open Portals and how to use the Keys. He also wrote about his impressions of protecting the Portals and destroying them permanently. He discovered in his studies—and you must remember that he dedicated a long period of his life to the study of the Portals—that it would be impossible to close the Portals once for all unless the other world consented.

"In your world, your people lost all knowledge about the Portals. As the eras passed, the Portals were forgotten, and so were the Ancient Magic and the Old Mores. Right now, and for quite a long time, all of this has become folklore, lost tales, legends. It all just danced in the wind for a while until it dried and decomposed, like a leaf falling from a tree in the first days of fall.

"After a series of spells and dreams, Ourivio discovered that only the blood of someone who was born in the other world and had lived most of their life there would be capable of sealing the

Portals permanently. Oh, and this person would be determined by the stars. And that's what we decided to do. Seal the Portals forever.

"We took a long time considering this. And finally, we decided that, even though it would be a violation of nature, it would be better to put an end to these countless attacks and wars for power. It would be for the best to close the Portals once and for all.

"We looked to the stars for an answer and they showed you, Olivia." Cordella looked at the girl, who was deeply focused on each word the witch was saying. "At that time you were sixteen years old. The Clan was very resistant. You would inevitably take part in tremendously dangerous events and would be in deathly peril daily.

"When we brought you, something extraordinary and unexpected happened: The Portal brought Trevor too. And then the stars started to show two of the Earth folks.

"However, when we tried to destroy the Portals as soon as you two got here, our plan didn't work as expected. We learned that to gather all the magic and strength necessary to do this deed, all of the involved had to be connected to the Portals. Everyone had to know the Portals' energy and be in synchronicity with it. We told you all we knew about the Portals and all that could happen in both of our worlds, and you two decided to stay. You decided to join forces to destroy the Portals and defeat Edmund Lars.

"We designed a complicated way to bring you two here periodically. You would come during the night when you would be sleeping in your world, and you would always come back before dawn. The spells I had to come up with were complex, especially because no one could notice your absence. You started to prepare to fight, and you learned about our history and the history of the Portals. And in time, we were looking for the lost Key. We have been together in some journeys and battles too, which resulted in a couple of traumas that followed you to your world." Cordella looked at Olivia's hands, took a deep calm breath, and continued, "You have been coming to Tartae for over a year if you measure the time as you do in your world. But here, time runs differently."

Apparently, her story was over, and her expression showed exhaustion. Alavro continued, still keeping the same tone that Cordella used to tell the story: deep and solemn.

"We need you two in order to defeat Edmund Lars. We need

you to seal the Portals once and for all. To destroy them. It's only with your help that we can reach our purpose, but this does not mean that you can't give up and go back to Leve. And if you decide to do so, it doesn't mean that we won't keep moving forward, trying to finalize our plan. You have a choice to make, and I would like to point out that we always have a choice and you won't be held accountable for it. Not in this case. It's your life; you are the ones who best know what to do with it. The best path to take. And we are aware that you did not choose to come here, to fight this fight with us."

"There's no need to answer right now. Sleep on it. Think about it. But we will need an answer no later than tomorrow, I'm afraid. We have no time to waste. In case you want to go back, we will try to send you back. But since you didn't come here as you were supposed to, I can't guarantee anything," Cordella concluded. Her eyes stared deeply at Olivia and Trevor.

"I don't understand one thing," started Olivia, who was quickly interrupted by Trevor:

"I don't understand a number of things…"

"How did we get here if the Clan wasn't involved?" asked Olivia.

"Lars found a way," answered Alavro.

"What?" said Olivia and Trevor in unison.

"How could this happen? Is it this easy?" said Trevor loudly. His eyes were wide and filled with uncertainty.

"It's a collection of everything he learned and heard during his whole life. Edmund Lars is not a common person. He was always very smart and talented and he became a brilliant wizard. He studied a lot and created his own version of the Book of the Portals. He started to test his discoveries and, occasionally, to get impressive results," explained Alavro, clearly disturbed by his own words. "But we are convinced that not everything happened according to his plan."

"And what do you think his plan was?" asked Olivia.

"We can only speculate," Cordella said. "He might have intended that you would lose your memories and, consequently, all your connection to the Portals, giving him more time for his bigger plans. Or he could have been looking for a way to kill you both. And we believe that it was the latter." Cordella's tone was soft, while Olivia and Trevor's eyes grew so wide that they looked like they might explode. "You have to understand that you two protect the Portals more than you can imagine. The sole fact that you exist and feel the need to protect the Portals already creates a powerful shield. Only this already makes it harder for Lars to find the Book or the remaining Portal Keys, or to use the Portals at his will. That's why he made such a colossal effort to bring you two here the way he did. You got here unexpectedly, and anything could have happened on your journey. But note this: you didn't come to him, even though he brought you here. The Portal brought you to us."

"And, being very direct, he is probably gathering a legion of followers. Followers who believe that the Portals are power, and this power should be shared or conquered by those who are capable enough. People have started to witness troll attacks, which haven't happened in years. We have been hearing the name Edmund Lars more often than we would like, and we have reason to believe that he has been collecting admirers." Alavro rose, looking genuinely worried.

Olivia and Trevor's faces had no color whatsoever. It was hard to process all this information, which could easily be the crazy ramblings of two senile people whom they didn't actually know. But at the same time, they were there. They were in a place with two gigantic moons in the sky.

"And how can you send us back if the Clan doesn't have one of the Portal Keys anymore? Is that possible at all?" asked Olivia.

"If there was a way for Edmund Lars to bring you two here with just one Key, then there is a way for us to open the Portals even if we are missing one Key. It may seem hard now, due to all that you have heard, but don't underestimate us. We are here to protect the Portals and to protect you two. And if you decide not to stay in Tartae, we will do our best to send you back to Leve. It will be challenging, but we have faced worse circumstances," answered Cordella, looking deeply into Olivia's eyes.

"How do we know we can trust you?" asked Trevor. "How do we know this is the truth and that's what we should believe?"

"You must feel this in your hearts. We can't force you to follow us, and we only want what's best for you," Cordella answered with a kind voice, but there was also sadness there. Olivia and Trevor were silent for a moment, thinking about all they had just heard.

"So, he has one Portal Key and a book of improvisations, and he was able to bring us here when he wanted?" insisted Trevor with a weird and scared look on his face. The story only seemed to get worse and worse.

"Yes. And we think that he wants the original Book and will try to steal it soon. That's why we are going to reclaim it at the Strage Castle."

"I have one more question," continued Olivia. "If we don't remember anything, how can we destroy the Portals?"

"Olivia, I believe that deep down you didn't forget the Portals. The Portals will still accept you. They will recognize you and all your efforts. But also, that's why you two should use this time to prepare and learn as much as you can."

With that, Cordella ended the conversation. She got up quickly, telling the others she was going to sleep. Alavro stopped for a moment and observed the moons. Trevor walked closer to him, full of questions, but only got two pats on his back from an Alavro who got away faster than a shooting star.

In the end, there were only two teenagers with a thousand questions stuck in their throats. They walked in silence to the tents until Trevor asked the dreaded question:

"So, should we stay?"

"Do you believe them?" asked Olivia, almost whispering.

"Yes, I do. You?"

"I believe them. But even so, I think going home could be our best option. With that said, I don't think we should run away from this. I believe that it's just a matter of time until this Edmund Lars uses the Portals to go to our world too, don't you think?"

"Yes, I do. I don't like to think about this. I'm afraid of what could happen."

"Me too. I think our decision is made."

Olivia said this looking forward, her head spinning. She wished Trevor good night and got inside the tent that she was sharing with Cordella, who was either already sound asleep or just pretending to be.

Olivia tried to sleep but had no success. Her thoughts flew around like wild birds. She kept pondering how nothing she had heard that night made sense or rang any bells. A paralyzing fear, almost as bad as when her parents died, took over her body. Finally, she fell into a very light sleep, disturbed. In a way, she was like a child bearing plastic guns in a war against a cruel and brutally real monster that was ready to strike her at any time.

CHAPTER SEVEN

THE FOREST OF LIS

T he next morning, the sun shone brightly in a cloudless sky. Olivia woke to noises and voices coming from outside her tent: conversations and fire crackling. It looked like Cordella had woken a long time ago, and only Olivia's things remained. Everyone was getting ready to leave for Strage.

The day was scorching, and it was even worse inside her tent. Olivia organized her things and every chore she completed, every piece of clothing she folded was a step further into the unknown. Everybody else was already gathered around the fire eating breakfast when she finally left the tent. She soon found Trevor's eyes and looked there for confirmation. They would stay in Tartae; they would destroy the Portals.

"Good morning, Olivia! I hope you had a good night's sleep," said Alavro.

"I hope you did. We almost lost the day waiting for you!" said Kirk, looking at Olivia with disapproval.

"I'm sorry, but I took a long time to fall asleep, and I think I was trying to compensate for it." Olivia looked at Trevor and continued, "Cordella, Alavro, we need to talk to you."

The energy changed quickly. The air became heavy, as if the expectation were a big elephant standing there, right in the middle of the group.

"Trevor and I talked yesterday, and there's not much to say except that we will be staying in Tartae and we will help you destroy the Portals. We will help as best we can." Olivia said the words in haste while holding Trevor's hand. Alavro and Cordella got up promptly, bearing proud smiles, and proceeded to hug Olivia and Trevor.

"So, what are we waiting for? Let's go!" Kirk was already getting up, and his voice was so filled with excitement that he was almost yelling.

They left the campsite soon after that. According to Bran, the journey to Strage Castle would take them three days, if they had no interruptions along the way. Bran didn't like Strage Castle. This much was clear. His face would twitch visibly when he talked about the place, but he did his best to hide his emotions and Olivia went along with it, pretending not to notice. She was actually pretending even to herself. She had no intention of freaking out before it was completely unavoidable. She would rather just wait and see.

It didn't take long until Alavro broke into a tale. Before Olivia and Trevor asked, he told them about Strage's history, and he did it like a bard. Enunciating and almost singing every word.

Strage Castle was the Book of the Portals' home, and it was once home of Edmund Lars. A beautiful mansion surrounded by well-kept gardens that belonged to Lars' parents. Time had passed, and Lars' parents grew old and went away to travel and live by the ocean, giving Lars enough space to be his true self. And that alone made the place change and adapt itself to its new reality. Strage Castle became a reflection of Edmund Lars' evil intentions, and one could feel it in every room, in each piece of furniture, in all the employees.

Lars was able to bring some of Strage's employees into his madness. They now worked for him, disregarding all ethics. They were the first ones to join him in his pursuit of the Portals, and they only followed the laws created by Lars. The ones who didn't want to take part in this or tried to warn his parents were used as experiments and eventually killed. The way Lars treated everyone who didn't agree with him was reason enough for the Guardians to believe that he would commit the most monstrous atrocities against those who stood in his way. And they could also foresee how some people would easily break.

The castle became a place for experiments and a trap for those who wandered carelessly in its surroundings, and it was this way for some time. Edmund Lars managed to keep it all very secret, to silently kill and discreetly do his hateful acts. Finally, Lars decided to leave Strage and brought with him his most loyal employees. He left behind a place that was only a shadow of what it was before. A faded fragment of what Lars' life used to be and an old house, deteriorating due to the effects of time.

Shortly after the Arbres were attacked, the Guardians went to Strage to look for Lars. When they got there, there was no sign of him. He left behind only an insolent note that talked about power, death, and destiny, and it didn't surprise most of the Guardians.

As a way of honoring Alcion and Maleuca Lars–and because it would probably be the last place where Edmund would look–the Clan decided to hide the Book of the Portals in Strage Castle. They guarded the place with multiple layers of protection spells and made sure that the mansion was always empty.

All of Tartae's newspapers talked about the attacks against the Arbres and the Grondes when they happened. Both of those families were well known in Tartae, so, it was expected that their sad stories would make the front pages. And it's important to say that everyone knew about the history of the Portals, and everyone knew that those families were part of the Clan. But the newspapers reported what they knew, and that was not the whole story. The Clan decided that–at that moment–it would be best not to release all the details about what happened to the Arbres and the Grondes. So the public had no idea that the two families were assassinated by Edmund Lars. After a great deal of consideration, the Clan concluded that if Tartae's people knew all the details, this would be the glory for Edmund Lars. It would do his job of spreading despair, and it would also spread the word about his intentions, which could awaken a group of followers. People would be tempted to help him with his pursuit. Lars was still a silent threat, and the Clan hoped to keep it this way, at least for a while longer.

However, even with the Clan's best efforts, there were already rumors of people joining Greedy Factions, as they were called. People were disappearing, and dark magic manuals detailing how to use the Portals' energy were being distributed in the darkest corners of Tartae's cities.

The energy was heavy all around Tartae. Some people were already considering hiding, some were avoiding the main roads, and some were even protecting themselves with spells around their homes or powerful locks on their doors. People felt something slowly shifting. They could feel the Portals behaving erratically. And even though a lot of them didn't have deep knowledge about the Portals, they knew enough to be scared. There was not one living soul in Tartae that had not grown up listening to disturbing stories about the old times and the bloody wars.

Every little piece of information Olivia and Trevor learned about Tartae was dark and sad. They were now galloping through a path filled with grass and wild yellow flowers. It was a very green plain, with just a few trees and no houses at sight. This was an alternative road, far away from the main one used by Tartae's merchants and travelers in not-so-alarming times.

"Do you study about the Portals at school? Like, everyone at Tartae has to learn about that?" Trevor asked, intrigued by how it would be to learn all of this as part of some kind of lesson. As if it was something ordinary.

"Every person who is born in Tartae studies the history of the Portals at some point in their lives," said Alavro, keeping his tone calm. "Of course, you can hardly say that what people study at school about the First War is what actually happened. In most of the books, you would be able to find stories that are more flourished and less cruel than the reality. In these stories, they kindly ignore the part some important members of society played in the pursuit of power, in an effort to keep their names clean and their family legacy intact. Nevertheless, for those who truly desire to unveil most of the mysteries enveloping the Portals' history, it is possible to find documents and even books lost inside some of Tartae's libraries that have pretty accurate facts and much deeper knowledge on the subject. In those, you can find more details about the first bloody war generated by the Portals. One would only have to dig a little deeper to find the truth."

"So, everybody in Tartae knows who you are? They all know that you're part of the Clan and that you're probably up to something?" continued Trevor.

"Yes and no. That's one of the reasons we are being careful. That's why we're always choosing hidden paths and the roads less traveled. If we can avoid people seeing us, it's best. Having said that, people don't usually pay that much attention to what we're doing, mainly because they know that now, the Clan doesn't do much. As Cordella said before, until a while ago we were just talking and celebrating the Portals. And that's pretty much all that the others have been doing, I must say." Alavro found Cordella's judging gaze.

"It's not kind to talk about the others this way, Alavro," warned Cordella, raising her dark eyebrows.

"Oh, well. I guess some of them are quite old. That's a fact. There's not much else they can do than just talk, and eat, and talk, and eat. And drink tea. Oh, the tea is a must!" He laughed hard, and the others followed him. Apparently, he had spoken the kind of truth that made everybody a little uncomfortable because it was quite harsh but utterly undeniable.

Once again, the group stopped to rest. The sun was now setting, and Alavro seemed to know all of the calculations even without checking his pocket watch. They set the camp on a more protected space, under some old, tall cedar trees with very large trunks.

According to Cordella, this was an isolated place, and they would be staying there for more than one night so they could train some of their forgotten abilities. Kirk was particularly interested in a little more action; all the lull was visibly bothering the boy. He looked bored and restless most of the time. At dinner that day, they only heard Kirk's voice. He would plan their training, talk about war techniques and challenge Bran on whom was the best trainer.

When the first ray of sun shone, Olivia and Trevor were ready to train. The breakfast was heavy so they could have enough strength to bear arms and fight. But some of the food was hard for Olivia to eat. It seemed just unbearable to eat a bowl of yams and mushroom soup so early in the morning. Her picky stomach was used to much lighter fare at this time of the day. Kirk insisted that she eat everything, and after she completed what looked like a test, her stomach was not as upset as she expected.

Kirk and Bran had already prepared everything for the training session: targets, hay dummies, and arrows, and it was all set carefully in a clearing between the tall trees. The training site was improvised with what they could find in the woods.

"Trevor, here is your bow and your arrows," said Kirk, who was extremely excited while handing Trevor his weapons. "Do you remember how to handle it?"

Trevor shook his head, but his body seemed to say otherwise. As Kirk taught him the correct posture and movements, Trevor repeated all of it almost instinctively. His body appeared to know and expect each movement, making everything look natural. Olivia was impressed. It was amazing how easy Trevor made everything look.

"His body remembers, see?" noted Bran, getting closer to her with two swords in his hands. "How are you feeling?"

"I'm not feeling anything yet..." answered Olivia, still observing Trevor's movements. The boy was now learning how to handle the arrows. He took the arrows out of the compartment on his back and put them on the bow while moving around the field.

"And you don't remember anything? Anything at all?"

Olivia looked away from Trevor's training for the first time and stared at Bran. There was a sparkle in his eyes, some sort of expectation, she could tell. But she only shook her head lightly.

"Maybe some time I'll say that I remember just to give you some good news..." Olivia gave him a discreet smile, hoping to keep seeing that light in his eyes. But it faded quickly. He gave her one of the swords he was holding and said:

"Here. She might feel heavy at first, but you will get used to her."

Olivia grabbed the sword with one hand and it was heavy in weight and energy. This thrill went up her arm and throughout her whole body. It wasn't bad; it seemed that the weapon completed her arm in some way, she was eager to start her training.

"Feels good, right?" said Bran smiling.

Olivia only smiled back in response and they began training. Bran taught her techniques and exercises to improve her strength and concentration. He would teach something and then challenge her, pointing out what she could do next, her best and worst moves. He was an incredible teacher. He knew how to give her a certain amount of motivation to keep her going further. He would stress the importance of balance and agility, and he would say that when in a fight, she needed to be in a meditative state, almost. She needed to be all there. All at that moment. Her mind could not be wandering or even thinking about the end of the fight. She needed to be grounded. That's the only way her sword will also be there. The only way to win.

From time to time, Alavro would show up to check on their training. He would watch them from afar with his hands on his waist and would laugh when someone fell over in the dirt. But for the most part, he would stay on the camping site, talking to Cordella. In the few breaks Olivia had, she heard Cordella and Alavro having avid discussions about something, but she could barely understand what they were saying at that distance. Around them, there were numerous maps and papers. Her training was amazing, but Olivia also wanted to be there with them, learning all there was to learn about the Portals, about Tartae.

Her divagations were always soon interrupted by Bran yelling or coming at her. He would say that he was only preparing her for the battlefield, which was full of screams and scares. Olivia would quickly return her attention to the training, forgetting about all the conversations Cordella and Alavro might be having. And all about what she could be learning.

Olivia, Trevor, Bran, and Kirk trained until the night came and a little more. They were completely exhausted at the end but filled with the great sensation one has after finishing a match of a favorite game. They went back to their camp and to the fire Cordella had just lit, longing for a little rest and lots of tasty foods.

"How were our warriors?" asked Alavro, embracing his sweaty son and giving him a broad smile.

"They did a great job. It was impressive, all things considered! I would even say that they didn't forget everything," answered Bran.

"I agree. But I think we can train at night too. Fights can start at any time. We must be prepared, and you two must remember much more than what you remembered today … or learned. What do you think about continuing? We can eat and then go back to the clearing." Kirk stood. Even though Trevor was very excited about everything, he gave Kirk a look full of judgment and disapproval, as someone would look to a frantic madman who wants to lure them into the same madness he was in.

"Don't even dream about it! If you want to torture me and crush all my bones before even going into battle, please, let me know now! Today, I'll be staying here, resting. I won't be training anymore! A-N-Y-M-O-R-E! The only training I'll have now is on how to sleep soundly," said Trevor.

"You must get ready for supper. There's no point in training all day long and draining all your strength away." As soon as Cordella finished her sentence, everybody went to get ready.

Olivia rushed through everything. She wanted to have a moment alone with Cordella to talk and try to discover more about their quest and Edmund Lars. Cordella had been quiet, and that was bothering Olivia. If at first the lady was energetic and annoyed all the time, now she seemed too contemplative and silent. She was always avoiding starting conversations with Olivia, always trying to be left alone or with Alavro.

Olivia left her tent like a rocket and found Cordella alone, standing with her hands on her waist and admiring the two moons.

"Hello, Cordella!" said Olivia, trying to hide her anxiety. So far, everything was going according to the plan. There was no sign of anyone else.

"Hello, Olivia. Beautiful night, huh?" Cordella was still staring at the sky. It was indeed a beautiful night, and the two moons were always a crowd pleaser. They were sublime in the sky, big, shiny and glorious. And they were, until now, the biggest difference between the two worlds. The two moons were the constant reminders that Olivia and Trevor were not home.

"Cordella, do you have one of those books about the Portals here with you? I'd like to know more."

With her eyes still fixed on the horizon, Cordella answered, "I have just one, but I think it might be useful for you. But I warn you, it's not light reading. It's sad and bloody. You won't find anything about Lars in there either."

"You can tell me more about him, can't you?" Olivia said expectantly, but Cordella's tone was soft.

"Yes. We knew Edmund Lars since he was a little boy, and no, he had not shown inclinations to evil deeds of any sorts at a young age. He did have a strong interest in the Portals. But then again, a lot of people do. We loved him, and maybe we were all quite blind to his monstrosity. After what happened, all the deaths he was responsible for, some of the Guardians said that they were always suspicious. I loved Edmund as a son. I wasn't suspicious."

"Do you blame yourself for that?" As soon as Olivia said it, she thought she might have gone too far.

"Yes. I blame myself every day. And if some days I was suspicious of Edmund, I felt guilty about it too. Until it happened, I wouldn't believe he could be capable of such atrocities. When I arrived at Strage after the attack, I was expecting and hoping with all my heart to find another explanation that would not involve Edmund. I'm sorry, Olivia, but I'm afraid my emotions regarding this subject are a bit clouded. I don't know if I was simply trying to ignore my internal voices about what Lars might be planning or if those voices didn't even exist."

"And what about Lars' parents? Did someone suspect them?"

"Alcion and Maleuca isolated themselves. They apologized to the other Guardians and left all that they had behind. We don't know exactly where they went or where they are now. The last time I heard about them, they were traveling through the Mountains of Lotre, probably seeking peace. They feel responsible for what happened more than anyone else. And they probably go through everything that happened and through all that they lived as a family trying to find a reason or a sign to all of this. Edmund is now someone else. But I still want to look into his eyes once more. Let's not talk about suspicion, Olivia. It can be as harmful as greed. Trust is better for our hearts."

"Did you see Lars after what happened?"

"Some of the Guardians saw him. But I didn't. Lars ran away to perfect everything that he considers necessary to achieve his goals. I had other things to worry about ... I needed to train you two, find ways to protect us all and those sorts of things."

"What about Alegra? What happened to her?" Cordella looked at Olivia and sat on a big rock nearby.

"She is a strong woman. But I don't dare to say that she is well. She managed to protect her sister from Lars when he first attacked her family, and she was already running away with her when he struck again. This time, Alegra didn't have time to do anything. Trevor knew Alegra very well ... It's really a pity that you two don't remember."

"You said that maybe there was a way to send us back to our world. Isn't there a way to make us remember?" Noises came from the tents. Any time now, the rest of the group would join them, and the conversation would be over. Olivia was firing questions quickly, barely having time to think.

"There's no spell that I know of. But we are looking for a way ..."

At this moment, Alavro and Bran left their tent, followed by Kirk and lastly by Trevor.

Olivia was still hoping to ask some more questions, but her mind was filled with brand new information, and the rest of the group quickly joined them. The opportunity to have some time alone with Cordella slipped through Olivia's hands. Cordella took a deep breath and walked toward the group. Her face was full of sorrow, and she wasn't trying to hide it.

Olivia felt guilty. Her questions were the reason for Cordella's sad eyes. She had made Cordella revisit some catastrophic events of her life. But what else could Olivia do? And what other means could she use to prepare herself for what was to come?

As Olivia followed Cordella back to the group, she was thinking of everything she learned about Tartae until now and the part she played in all of this. It seemed to her that she was poking an anthill. The more she poked, the more ants would emerge. The more questions she asked, the more questions would arise, the more unsettling things she would discover. But she had to know. As Cordella would say, they had no time to waste anymore. They needed to learn how to fight, and they needed to learn about the Portals. Olivia told them that she would do her best, and that's what she was doing. It was only sad that sometimes it cost the smile of someone she was growing to love.

CHAPTER EIGHT

TARTAE'S MAGIC

They had a relaxing dinner filled with laughter. It was light and almost worriless, going very well with the night, which was fresh and fairly bright. Apparently, Cordella was already feeling better with all the merriment. Kirk and Bran told Cordella and Alavro all about the training session they had earlier that day and also remembered things from their past adventures, quests and journeys full of adrenaline and excitement, which seemed to bring up everyone's spirits. Alavro took advantage of that and started to tell some of his own adventures. He had a special rhythm when telling stories, which made everything turn into a song. The words he chose carefully, composing enchanting rhymes, and they would fit perfectly in his sentences, making everyone who was listening get deeply involved, as if they were being carried into a dream that wasn't theirs.

Cordella and Alavro had some interesting stories as well. Their adventures began at a very young age, and they had been through a lot trying to learn and cast protection spells on their journeys. One time, Alavro accidentally made a gigantic stone wall appear around them. By that time, they were still apprentices, and it took them no less than a week to make it disappear. "You must admit, it was a powerful protection!" joked Alavro, a big smile lighting up his round face. Apparently, Alavro, Cordella, and Zervio, Cordella's husband who passed away many moons ago, used to be great friends when they were young.

Kirk and Bran were simulating a vigorous fight to the beat of Alavro's clapping–who was already a bit drunk with the wine–when

Trevor got closer to Olivia while she was getting more soup from the pewter cauldron hanging over the fire.

"It's been forever since we've talked, Olie. How are you doing?" Trevor practically whispered. He didn't want anyone to hear or interrupt them. They needed some time for themselves, which was difficult these days with all the riding and now the training.

"I'm doing well. You?"

Trevor nodded and continued, "Did you find out anything else? I saw you talking with Cordella earlier. That's why I took so long to leave my tent. I didn't want to get in your way."

"Yes, we talked for a bit. But we didn't discuss anything very important. She promised to lend me a book about the history of the Portals, the only book she brought with her. I think it's gonna be enough for now. But as you can imagine, there's nothing there about Lars …"

"And did you find out anything else about him?" asked Trevor. His face was glowing with expectation.

"They all knew Lars since he was a child, and I don't think anyone ever suspected him. Cordella seemed to love him very much. I could tell that it wasn't an easy subject for her. She told me that he was passionate about the Portals since a very young age, but I guess anybody could feel that way. It's an interesting thing to study. We can blame him for a lot of things, but not for that."

"Yes, I guess. But in this case, that means that he has been studying the Portals for a long time. He knows a lot about it, so he can do a lot of damage … I believe," said Trevor with a somber look on his face. Olivia found it interesting that even though she knew Trevor so well, there were some sides of him that she had never seen before. This sad and worried look was a great example. "And has anyone seen Lars after what happened?"

"He disappeared, and almost no one saw him after the attacks. And on a lighter note, you used to be very good friends with Alegra!"

Trevor seemed a little surprised and he chuckled softly, letting a glimpse of sadness show in his eyes, "There's no use in having friends when you don't remember a thing … Do you know if there's a way to …?"

"To remember? They haven't discovered one yet. But it seems that they're trying."

Olivia and Trevor looked at each other and, even though they had never discussed it, they both kept thinking about a solution.

Maybe they could find one themselves. But how? Unlike Edmund Lars, they had just found out about this reality. Portals, magic, Tartae ... it was all new for them.

"I heard something," Trevor said, breaking the silence. "We'll make a stop before Strage. We'll see a Guardian. I heard Alavro talking to Bran. I think they need to ask this person for help with something."

"Did you hear a name?"

"No. But I wonder why they didn't tell us. Enough with the secrets already!"

"They surely have a reason, Trev. It's not possible that they're still hiding stuff from us. Don't you think?" Olivia looked at Trevor, hoping for confirmation. She needed to trust the Guardians at least.

"I hope so."

Olivia and Trevor sat there watching the rest of the group for a while, but they soon got up and went to sleep. They were feeling more and more tired as a result of that hard training day. Until they all went to their tents, no one had mentioned anything about making a stop, and that was making Olivia and Trevor pretty uneasy.

Before going to bed, Cordella gave the book to Olivia. She started to read it at once, cozying up under the light of the candle next to her bed. She read some pages but couldn't fight the sleepiness for long and quickly and inevitably fell asleep.

Olivia woke the next day and took some time to finally get up. She kept thinking about all that she had discovered until now. Edmund Lars was around, free, and he had a plan. He had a book— it wasn't the real one, but still, this was considerably dangerous—and he had determination, eagerness, and some followers. And to make matters worse, he had managed to successfully bring her and Trevor to Tartae.

It was very frustrating not to have any recollection of their past experiences in Tartae. She had no idea how she hurt her wrist or anything that she had gone through before this time. Olivia couldn't help but think that if she remembered it all, it would be easier to feel calmer about the battles ahead ...

Suddenly, the possibility of Lars discovering the Clan's plan fell over Olivia like a giant rock. Fear rose in the back of her throat. What if he was expecting them? How come no one was counting on that? Why were they so confident?

Olivia got up in a flash and went to find Cordella. The witch was sitting alone outside the tent. Olivia screamed Cordella's name as soon as she saw her.

"For Ourivio's Keys! What happened?" Cordella answered, walking in Olivia's direction.

"I'm sorry, Cordella. Were you meditating?" Olivia never waited for an answer, she just kept talking. "Are you sure Lars doesn't know we plan on destroying the Portals now? How can you be so sure and so calm?"

"Calm down, Olivia. Take a breath. We are only sure of the part we play in this story. And we are confident about our goals. What exists beyond that is just going to confuse our minds. We are ready, and this must ease you."

"Ready?" Olivia could only think about how the Clan had missed Lars' attacks before. But could she bring this up without offending Cordella and all her life's work?

"We are here, aren't we? We are getting ready for this the best way we can. There's nothing to worry about besides that," said Cordella calmly. And she was so calm that it was hard to see in her that same scared lady they met when they arrived in Tartae. It was possible that she was only trying to make Olivia feel better, because there was probably nothing else to do beyond what they were already doing.

"But ... but he managed to bring us. He can open Portals. He might know that we're here with you and that our plans had changed. He might know that we're on the move. He must be expecting that!"

"Yes, he did manage to bring you and Trevor. But he doesn't know what happened after he opened that Portal. He doesn't know if you two died or got lost or even if you came here stronger than ever. Not even all the Guardians know that you're here. We're in hiding. This is all a secret." Cordella sounded confident, and she looked deeply into Olivia's eyes. "No good will come from getting anxious. He's smart, but for all we know, he has no idea if his plan worked."

At this time, Trevor, Bran, and Kirk left one of the tents. They were talking about some of the movements they had practiced the day before. Alavro came right behind them with a peaceful and quite funny expression on his face.

"Good," Cordella said, looking at everyone. "We are going to make a stop on our way to Strage. We will be seeing one of the Guardians, Freya Fosterim. Be ready for that."

Trevor and Olivia exchanged looks.

"And why are we going there, may I ask?" inquired Trevor, trying to sound careless, as if he were asking something trivial.

"Time will tell. There, you will be able to rest more and get ready for Strage," said Cordella.

The group headed to their training space in the woods. Bran and Kirk attacked Trevor, teaching him how to defend himself when outnumbered. Olivia observed the fight from afar, waiting for her turn when Cordella got closer to her.

"Olivia, come with me, please."

She got up and followed Cordella to a more distant space, where the trees were thick and numerous and the sunlight scarcer.

"You need to remember Tartae's magic," said Cordella. "I know it's still in there, inside you somewhere. Reconnecting can take a while, but I think today is a good day to start." She paused, gave Olivia a brief and kind smile, and continued. "First of all, you must know that our magic comes from nature and from our hearts. From all that is around us. Together, nature and our hearts can work as one and do the most wondrous things. You must forget all of your preconceptions and believe that you can do what you imagine. Our preconceptions will weaken the magic, but you will need reason to control your mind and your intentions. You will understand that balance is an important part of magic. Here in Tartae, there is magic in all the things. All nature that surrounds us is magic, and we are part of nature." Cordella looked around and showed Olivia the trees, the leaves that were subtly moving in the wind. The forest was singing. "In order to work with the elements, you first have to connect with nature. You must show your respect for Her; you must honor Her. You must never manipulate the elements disrespectfully or carelessly. This will make the energy change into something that we can never predict."

Olivia looked at Cordella with attention, trying to grasp each word the witch said and keep them forever locked inside her mind, her skin, her whole self. She thought that it would be much simpler if it were like a cake recipe: "get a wand, wave it the right way and say *abracadabra* three times. If you desire, you can add a bat eye."

"Let's try something. First, let's empty our minds with a meditation exercise. It's very simple; worry not," Cordella suggested, sitting on the ground. "Now, try to concentrate on your breathing, filling your body with energy and breathing out all the negativity. Connect with the earth and feel its energy spreading through your body."

At first, the meditation was very hard. Olivia's mind couldn't stop thinking. Images of Lucent Bookshop, of the man who wanted books about Egypt kept appearing; a Portal opening between the books, her parents vanishing into the darkness. The meditation was not working, and her heart shrunk and hurt.

Cordella got closer to Olivia, holding her hand.

"Olivia, let go. Look inside and be still. There's a world inside of you, and for you to think clearly, this world needs to be peaceful."

Olivia tried to make all her thoughts disappear as if they were being carried away like clouds in the wind. She concentrated on her breathing, slowing it down and paying attention to the sound it made, like ocean waves coming and going. She was slightly better. When Olivia was finally breathing calmly, Cordella said, "Let's try a spell. Something simple. Let's work with the fire element and build a fire right here." Cordella pointed to a spot right across from Olivia, covered in fresh green grass, with no dry leaves or sticks. However, Olivia thought she shouldn't point out the bad conditions for a fire, and she just went for it.

One word now could spoil everything. This moment was like a prayer. It was silent and full of concentration. The smell of the grass had gotten stronger, and there was no wind blowing the trees anymore. All was quiet.

Olivia looked at the ground and visualized the fire burning. She did it with all the strength she had, squinting and twitching her face, and nothing happened. She tried for a while, but time passed and her concentration faded. She began to think that Cordella was wrong and she would never be able to do this.

"Our magic comes from inside, Olivia. Don't think, do. You need to connect with the elements. Find them inside you. They are waiting for you," interrupted Cordella.

Olivia closed her eyes again and felt the earth beneath her, touching her feet and exhaling a strong scent of pure nature. She thought about the sun and its warmth, and then something burned inside her chest. A sensation completely new that scared and inspired her at the same time. She opened her eyes and a faint flame was floating just above the ground. It trembled a little and burned timidly, but it was undeniably there.

"Bravissima!" complimented Cordella.

It was a small accomplishment, but Olivia was about to start jumping around. It felt like something so extremely important. A couple hours ago she would never have imagined being able to do something even slightly like this.

"It came from my heart," Olivia said in amazement. "I felt the earth and then the sun, and then I just knew."

"Yes, my dear! I know the feeling. I'm very happy for you!" said Cordella with the most beautiful smile on her face. "This is a start. We will keep practicing, especially protection spells, because you might need it. The next one I'm teaching you is the shield spell. To achieve complete protection, you must--"

"Cordella, what about my family? How is my grandma doing while I'm here?" Olivia interrupted Cordella. The meditation made her think, and this could be the proper moment to ask questions. She was alone with Cordella, and that was rare.

"Our time here in Tartae runs differently from your time. That's why you were always able to come while you were supposed to be sleeping in your world and it had no major effect on your routine. If you spend some days here in Tartae, it will only be one night in your world. You don't have to worry about your grandma. She is safe."

"But what happens when we aren't there? Can't they tell?"

"Yes. You won't be there. However, I've woven an illusion spell, and since you two are only absent for a few hours, it has always worked. We hope to solve everything fast enough this time. You two will be back before anyone gets worried. Now, let's carry on."

Cordella resumed the training quickly. She was able to concentrate and focus on the spells with no visible effort, probably due to years of training and to the fact that magic was a part of her life. She explained to Olivia how to protect herself from spells on the battlefield.

"Stand up tall. Your posture must represent your strength and courage. You can make a circle with your hands or just focus on this image. Now, manipulate the air around you and build a circle of protection surrounding you. Olivia, throw a fireball at me."

Olivia struggled, but after a number of frustrated tries–in which she was able to throw a sparkle–a small fireball flew in Cordella's direction, and Cordella protected herself. The fireball disintegrated, and Cordella was unharmed.

"Now it's your turn. Protect yourself," said Cordella, looking at Olivia.

Cordella barely gave Olivia time to prepare and threw a robust, flaming red fireball the size of cantaloupe in Olivia's direction, which scared the soul out of her. The ball became red dust when it touched Olivia's body.

"Defend yourself!" yelled Cordella, who kept throwing even bigger fireballs. Olivia's clothes were all stained with red tint by now. Finally, after multiple attempts, Olivia was able to defend herself. She managed to forget Cordella's voice and the noise of the fireballs. She imagined a protection coming from her heart, and she saw the air and her body becoming one. The fireballs were not getting to her anymore. But it didn't last. Her spells were clearly too weak and unstable.

"It's enough for today. You did a wonderful job, but you need to focus. You need to believe more and connect with what surrounds you. I advise you to keep on practicing and meditating … I know it might seem hard at first." Cordella sat on the ground again. "Come on, let's meditate a bit more. This way we calm our minds and strengthen our bodies."

Olivia sat next to Cordella and closed her eyes. The earth beneath her vibrated. Everything that surrounded her had awakened.

***

It was already night, and the group was done with their training and was back to the campsite. Bran, Trevor, and Kirk were exhausted. In fact, it was only when Olivia saw Trevor's face all flushed and his sweat messing up his hair that she noticed how tired she was. The only difference was that her tiredness was not so physical or so transparent.

Alavro had made dinner, and as soon as they all cleaned up, they had some pumpkin soup with freshly harvested rosemary. Exhaustion had taken over the group, and there was no conversation or laughter today. It was all very quiet, and every single conversation started and died very quickly.

"We will leave our camp early in the morning tomorrow. Be ready," said Alavro calmly.

Bran looked away from his bowl of soup and glanced at his father, who only nodded. The Strage Castle was closer.

There wasn't much discussion about anything. Everyone who had any sort of information about their destiny got away very quickly, leaving Olivia and Trevor with their soup bowls in their hands and questions jumping on their tongues. It didn't matter that this lack of explanations happened quite frequently; they never got used to it.

"How was your day today, Olie? Did you train with Cordella?"

"It was interesting. She tried to make me remember some spells ... but I must say that I wasn't very successful. I managed to make some things happen, but it was clear that it wasn't enough to defend myself or anything of that sort."

"What did you do?" asked Trevor, laughing from what was about to come.

Olivia raised her hand a little and made a small flame appear on her right palm.

"Something like this. However, I've no idea how a spark might help me with anything ..."

"A spark can start a fire, Olie! You need to be more positive. Look at what you just did! When could you possibly have imagined doing something like this? At least when we were in our world, I mean."

"I know. It's just that I'm mentally exhausted. Cordella asked me to meditate, but that was the hardest part. And before I forget, she explained to me a little about how time works differently in our worlds. Apparently, one night in Leve is equivalent to some days here. But she never told me how many."

"So, it's possible that my dad doesn't know that I'm not there. I was already imagining a thousand police cars in front of my house and my dad going completely bald."

"I don't think we have a reason to worry yet." Olivia understood her friend's despair. Trevor and his dad were very close, and after Trevor's mother passed away, Mr. Meris became considerably overprotective. Olivia couldn't help but feel sad that her grandma would probably take days to notice her absence.

Mrs. Halin was on a long cruise once more, and she rarely called to find out if her granddaughter was doing well.

Cordella was already sleeping when Olivia got inside the tent. As she sat on her bed, Olivia saw the book about Tartae and thought about how reckless she was for not taking some time to dissect it. She blew the candle out and fell asleep instantly.

CHAPTER NINE

THE FLOWERS' MANOR

Alavro woke the others by singing loudly and banging pots and pans while getting ready to leave. It was very early in the morning, and a faint mist covered the surroundings. When Olivia left her tent, Cordella was already outside talking to Trevor. Everything was quickly set to leave. The group had breakfast and soon started their journey to Freya Fosterin's house.

"Easy, Skyscraper." Trevor was trying to reason with his horse, who wanted to run beyond his grasp.

"His name is not Skyscraper, Trevor. It's Lito …" said Bran, clearly not approving of the way Trevor was talking to his horse. "That's why he doesn't listen to you."

"It used to be Lito. Now that my judgment is not impaired, I'm gonna call him Skyscraper. He's just too tall! He'll get used to it soon enough, won't you, Skyscraper?" Trevor was already getting attached to the horse. He finished his sentence by petting Lito's head, and the horse seemed to calm down for the first time since they left their camping site.

Bran shook his head in disapproval.

"And what about mine, Bran? What's its name?" Olivia asked quickly, meaning to make the unnecessary tension go away.

"Her name is Myrrh."

"Hi, Myrrh! What a beautiful name." Olivia petted her mare's head and looked back at Bran, who gave her a smile. He looked at her with so much contentment that it was hard to believe it was just because she didn't want to change her horse's name.

"Freya Fosterim is a Guardian too, right?" Olivia took

advantage of the slow pace they were galloping to try to ask some questions. Trevor quickly noticed what she was doing and focused on the conversation, instantly getting closer to Olivia's mare.

"Yes, she's one of the Guardians of the Portals. But she is quite peculiar and tends to have an odd opinion about a lot of things," answered Cordella.

"What do you mean?" asked Trevor.

"Freya wants to protect the world, but she also wants her own protection. Since the beginning, when she was considered to become part of the Clan, she was very honest about that and made sure to make her intentions clear. She would protect the Key with her life because she believes in the balance of nature over all things. Nevertheless, she would not take sides on wars or confrontations of any sorts. She would never compromise her kin."

"And ... why are we going there?" asked Trevor.

"Obviously, we're going there because we don't have another choice. Freya has a unique power and she's extremely strong. A natural power. We must seek her help, especially for you two. Maybe she is the only one who can reverse what was made." Cordella looked at Trevor and Olivia. They couldn't figure out her expression. It wasn't clear if it was hopeful or if she knew that it was already a lost battle. "Let's go faster. I want to get to the fields before nightfall."

Everyone followed her lead. Olivia and Trevor were still a bit afraid of falling off their horses and had some trouble keeping the same pace as the others. They were always a little behind, and Bran would slow down to keep close, always protecting them.

The road was still very similar to what they had seen before, and even though it was well delineated, it was clear that travelers didn't use it very often. When the sun was setting, Cordella took a right turn, entering a forest, but she didn't slow down, even when facing the completely different conditions.

The forest was filled with tall trees and moss covering all things one's eye could see. Even the thick trunks of the trees were enveloped in other plants and the roots were jumping out of the ground. Deep into the woods, the birds were chirping loudly, and the temperature was lower. It was possible to hear water running at a distance. They were surely close to a waterfall.

After a while, Cordella led the group out of the woods, soon arriving in an open field covered in grass and dotted with trees here and there. It was already night. Their journey was only possible because of the bright light of the two moons that painted the whole forest blue. They galloped for a little bit more until Cordella finally signaled to stop.

"We won't be setting camp today. We will only stay here for a while, and we will leave as soon as the sun wakes," said Cordella, interrupting Kirk, who was already taking one of the tents out of his bag.

They slept under a large old oak tree and used their bags as pillows. The night went by fast, and before Olivia knew it, the faint rays of sunshine were waking them.

They kept going until the sun was strong and the sky completely blue. It took them around six hours, stopping briefly only for water and food, to finally arrive at the Flowers' Manor, home of Freya Fosterim.

The Flowers' Manor was grand, very noticeable even from afar. A long path led the visitors to its doors, surrounded by robust trees on both sides. The tree branches were covered in pink flowers, and immediately after the horses stepped onto the pathway made of small colored gemstones, all the flowers from all the trees, fell on the ground, leaving the trees' brown branches completely naked. The vivid grass was now covered in pink petals, creating a carpet of flowers. As the group walked down the pathway, the petals went up and down slowly, creating what resembled the shapes of women's bodies. These figures kept following the group along the way, observing each one of them, whispering incomprehensible words, studying every step they took.

The whole group was silent. It was an undeniably beautiful image, but quite horrifying as well. Something about this whole situation was unsettling, and that meticulous observation was deeply disturbing. Olivia and Trevor held strongly to their horses while the petal women got extremely close to their faces, analyzing their eyes, reading their expressions. After each movement these petal creatures made, Olivia thought that this entire scene could have been very enchanting if there were any space for appreciation when it all was so strange.

After some time, all the petal women started to walk side by side with them, not hovering anymore. They only lingered for a bit on Kirk, but he didn't seem to mind it at all.

"I think I already have a date for dinner!" he joked.

Little by little, the intriguing creatures went away, going back to the trees. Only two of them stayed, leading the group to the house. When they got to the manor's door, the petal creatures took a bow and disappeared. The trees were slowly being covered with flowers again.

The horses stayed outside the mansion, resting under some trees and having food and fresh water. When the group got nearer to the door, it opened, and a short young man wearing a long green robe with golden embroidery welcomed them. His hair was shaved almost completely, with only a thin brown braid starting on the top of his head and going all the way down to his feet. The man had a discreet, welcoming smile as he opened the door and let everybody in.

The entrance hall was all white. Almost blindingly white. Its floors were made of marble, and the decoration was very minimal. Adorning the room were only three crystal chandeliers hanging on the tall ceilings and walls that were also painted white. A little further, there was the main hall, which also had a very simple decoration. The ceiling was high and some chairs were placed in front of a big fireplace adorned with gray stones and located right in the middle of an all-glass wall, allowing the room to have a marvelous view of the garden.

"Good morning," said the short woman standing by the fireplace.

"Good morning, Freya," answered Cordella, using the same empty tone.

Freya turned to the group and looked directly at Olivia and Trevor. The woman was very pale, with big, expressive hazel eyes that were even brighter due to her long, dark eyelashes and thick eyebrows. Her hair was short and pixie-like. She also wore a long robe, resembling a toga, with some layers in blush pink and others in red. She was barefoot.

Olivia stared right back at her. Freya Fosterim resembled a fantastic being; her voice was deep and soft at the same time. And Olivia felt that she heard it before. There was nothing human about Freya's appearance; the woman looked like a creature of some sort.

"I hope you had a good trip. I'm Freya Fosterim. Welcome to the Flowers' Manor." She got closer to Olivia and Trevor, shaking their hands politely.

"So, you understand what happened?" asked Alavro.

"Yes, Alavro. I also know why you are here. However, I'm afraid I won't be of any help …" Freya walked slowly back to the fireplace.

Cordella interrupted. "You can't help, or you don't want to, Freya?"

Freya kept staring at the fire. Cordella was firm and urgent, but she was using the same tone as Freya, without noticeable alterations. The energy was weird. Olivia couldn't tell if it was tense or simply normal. Freya's house had a peculiar effect on her, one that she wasn't able to describe. It was something between amazement and an urgency to leave.

Freya turned quickly to the group again and, still looking at Cordella, she said, "Maino, make sure that our guests have a good place to sleep and dinner. I believe you are in need of rest and good food."

The same young man who opened the manor's door left the room, arriving minutes later and inviting the group to their rooms. Cordella didn't move. While the rest of the group walked away, she stood there, staring at Freya.

Olivia did her best to hear what was happening and began to walk away very slowly, constantly looking back. Alavro, who noticed Olivia's maneuvers, slowed down and put his arms over her shoulders.

"What do you think about this marvelous marble, Olivia? Don't you think these columns are the most perfect?"

Olivia nodded and frowned. Trevor looked at them and laughed at the far from subtle attempt Alavro was making to keep Olivia away from Cordella and Freya. He went on and on about all the kinds of marble available in Tartae and how people used them for decoration.

"Is there any difference in your world?" he asked, waking Olivia up from her wonderings.

"Er … I'm not sure …" answered Olivia with uncertainty in her voice. She had no idea what Alavro had been talking about for the last few minutes. Her mind was obviously elsewhere.

They went to their bedrooms after going up the very cold marble stairs. Olivia took a quick shower and changed her clothes, putting on some clean jeans and a green sweatshirt. She was tempted to crawl into the bed, which seemed particularly comfortable, maybe because she had been sleeping in not-so-perfect conditions for the last few days. But she resisted and went downstairs to look for Freya and Cordella. She should try to hear any conversation they were having.

Olivia walked silently and reached the main hall, which was already empty. She got closer to the fireplace and felt the warmth of the fire on her skin. She looked through the glass and stared at the garden. The trees were completely full of flowers again. There was no wind, and it all looked very peaceful.

"You've always admired the Nefilas." Freya broke the silence.

"They are very beautiful, indeed. And amazing. But a bit strange," answered Olivia, who was a little startled by Freya's presence. She hadn't heard steps approaching, and the woman appeared suddenly in the room.

"Yes. I guess they are a bit strange. But who isn't?" said Freya, her gaze lost in the flowers over the garden. Olivia only looked at her, not really sure of how to talk to Freya. "What do you remember about your travel here to Tartae?" asked the woman, her eyes now almost perforating Olivia's.

"We were walking and then we fell. There was only darkness for a while until we meet the ground."

"Was that all?"

"Yes, that was it. Should it be more?" asked Olivia. Freya didn't say anything in return, and her face didn't change, not even a little bit, after Olivia's answer. With her, there always seemed to be something between the lines. Something that she was holding back to her own gain. Olivia had this irritating feeling that Freya was only trying to get what she needed from Olivia and from this conversation. None of these questions were intended to help her memory. These tricky ways were making Olivia considerably annoyed. She wanted to make the woman talk and be honest, but that seemed to be something far from Freya's ways.

"I need some time alone with you and Trevor. I can't measure the damages without having a moment with you both."

"That is simple enough. He'll probably be coming down soon; we can start right now." Olivia wanted to get over with it, to talk to Freya and know her verdict.

"I tried to warn you," said Freya. "I tried to communicate multiple times when you were still in your world."

"Was that you? The leaves?" Olivia was surprised, and Freya nodded.

"For some reason that I don't know enough about or because of things you wouldn't want to hear about your people, certain things don't matter as much in your world, such as the power of nature or someone's dreams. This all could have been avoided. You two could still be safe in your world and come back here with your memories untouched. But you never paid attention to your path. Not the way you should."

"You knew what was going to happen?" Olivia couldn't believe it. It wasn't possible that Freya, one of the mighty Guardians, knew what was about to happen and didn't do anything more than just send a message through some leaves.

"I didn't know exactly what was going to happen, but there was a black cloud hovering over the memories I had of you and Trevor. I knew something was about to happen. I knew you could get lost."

"Why didn't you do anything?"

"I warned you, Olivia."

"In a way no one could understand."

"It's not my fault that you don't pay attention to such things in your world. It's not my doing that you lost your connection to nature. I tried to warn you." Her tone was still the same. Calm and cold.

"I think I owe you a thank you, then. It's all in the past now. There's no use to imagine what could have happened if we had understood your message. No one wants to revert this more than Trevor and I. We are the most affected in all of this. Lars probably thinks we are still trained warriors when we don't know how to fight. We don't even have a connection to the Portals anymore."

Olivia was firm in her answer. She wasn't happy to see someone saying bluntly that everything could have been avoided. It was not her fault or Trevor's that they didn't 'read the signs.' You should never blame the victim, and that's what they were. They were victims of Lars, of Ourivio, of the Portals …

Kirk and Bran came loudly downstairs. Soon after, Maino showed up and invited everyone to the dining room, where they all sat and waited for the rest of the group.

The dinner was weird. They barely talked, and every single conversation someone started died quicker than a solar eclipse. After they were finished, Freya asked Trevor and Olivia to follow her. And with a nod to Cordella, as if she were asking for permission, she got up. They walked to another, much smaller room. There was a round bright red rug in the middle of the room, and in the corners, trees were painted on the walls. The room seemed to try to recreate a forest, but just like everything else in Freya's house, it was quite cold and unsettling.

"Olivia, Trevor, I need you to relax," said Freya, sitting on the floor.

"I firmly doubt that is possible. May I sit?" Trevor looked disturbed by this whole situation. He was thinking about what kind of test Freya would be making and if it would be something he would like to be a part of.

Freya nodded, and Olivia and Trevor sat down.

"I just need you two to be calm. I want to feel your energy. That is the only way I can learn about our possibilities."

Both of them tried to keep their nerves under control. Minutes went by without a word. Freya had her eyes closed, and she swung her body lightly from time to time. At some point, she got up and walked around Olivia and Trevor. Round and round, multiple times, until they got a little dizzy. Olivia and Trevor looked at each other without knowing exactly what to do or how to behave.

Freya sat down again and opened her eyes.

"There's nothing I can do." She said it bluntly and got up.

Olivia and Trevor were paralyzed for a moment, still recovering from the strange trance they were in. The solemn atmosphere was abruptly broken by words they didn't want to hear. How were they supposed to do anything if they were going to stay like this? With no memory whatsoever? With no recollection of what they had learned?

Freya was now walking in the direction of the wide wooden door when Olivia yelled, "WHAT DO YOU MEAN? How can you come to that conclusion like that?"

"I think you should give it another try, Freya. I'm much calmer now that I know you'll only shake your body and walk around us." Trevor was extremely serious.

"What is done is done," said Freya, looking at both of them and opening the door. She seemed to not care at all about what they were feeling. "You two got lost on the way." She left the room.

Olivia and Trevor followed Freya, arguing strongly with her.

"How can you give up so easily? Don't you understand that we are exposed to things that we don't know? Don't you see that like this, we are an easy target? Our chances are next to none like this … WE-NEED-TO-REMEMBER!" Olivia was doing her best to convince Freya and using all the arguments she could think of.

Freya walked a little ahead of Olivia, not even looking in the girl's direction.

As they got closer to the main hall, the voices grew louder and more annoyed, and Cordella, Alavro, and Bran came out to see what was happening.

"For crying out loud! What happened?" asked Cordella.

"Freya says she can't do anything," answered Olivia. Freya looked deeply at Cordella, who continued:

"You two need to calm down now! Freya, may I have a minute with you, please?"

Cordella and Freya left the room, and Alavro patted Olivia's and Trevor's backs.

"Calm down … Being upset will not help a thing." Alavro sounded very paternal. His voice had no alteration whatsoever; it sounded calm and kind, as though nothing completely crushing was happening. It almost seemed that they were not doomed.

"How can you say something like that, Alavro? She shook her body a little bit and then she proceeded to say that there was no way! She didn't even care to give us a decent explanation! We need to know why there's no way! I need to know if I agree with that!" Trevor paced from one side to the other, not hiding his anger.

"This is Freya, and it's not going to be you two who are going to change her ways." Alavro was firm. "Now, you two better calm down already. I will fetch some allandrio tea for you."

Alavro left the room, looking for Maino. Soon after, Olivia said, "I'm not feeling very well. Trev, please … help me get to my room."

"I can help you, Olie." Bran promptly stood up, but Olivia quickly said:

"Thank you, Bran. But stay here and wait for your father … let him know we went to our rooms." Olivia squeezed Trevor's arm discreetly, hinting that he should let her lead him.

They walked together slowly until they got to the stairs.

"Trev, we need to hear what Cordella and Freya are discussing." Trevor agreed, and they both marched silently in the same direction the witches had headed minutes before.

They got to a small room that served as the pathway to some kind of greenhouse, where Cordella and Freya were talking. Olivia and Trevor hid between some of the furniture, under a side table that was big enough for both of them and next to an armchair that created a sort of nook. With almost no lights coming into this windowless room, they were able to successfully hide in the shadows. In the room, they could hear Cordella and Freya perfectly, and apparently, the heated mood of the conversation made them both forget about the possibility of being heard by the others.

"Cordella, there's nothing else I could say."

"The way we stand now, Freya, if you choose not to doing anything, you are against us. I understand that you, in your deep knowledge, must know what is to come. That you, in your incredible sensibility, must feel that everything is about to change." Cordella's voice was sad and hopeless. Olivia believed that she had lost hope in Freya, in her capability to commit to the quest.

Olivia and Trevor looked at each other.

"I have always protected the Key. I did my best to bring their memories back."

"Although they say otherwise."

"They got lost, Cordella."

"The Clan was never about giving up. It's the life of two children at stake."

"I have always kept my word. But I was never willing to go to the field. Never. And I trust that my reasons can still be preserved."

"At least something will be preserved, then. Lucky you, Freya. I'm sorry I came here to disturb your quiet manor with our visit. I am also sorry for the precious time that I lost." Cordella stayed there for some time, probably still hoping that Freya would have a change of heart.

"Cordella!" exclaimed Freya, stopping Cordella from leaving the room. "They won't remember. It's a lost cause."

Cordella turned to Freya and said firmly, "Don't you dare abstain and say it's a lost cause."

The witch left the room fast and decisively. Olivia and Trevor were paralyzed, as if being very still would make them invisible. Freya left the greenhouse through the garden, not using the small room as her pathway back to the house. Olivia and Trevor moved out of their hiding spot carefully, checking back on Freya the whole time, trying to avoid any surprises in case she decided to come back from her walk in the garden.

They sneaked back to their rooms in complete silence, and

before Olivia entered her bedroom, Trevor asked, "So, what did you think?"

Olivia's eyes were lost. She had no idea how to answer Trevor or how to digest everything that had happened in the last hour. She stared at the hallway wall for some time, as though it could help her figure something out.

"Why do you think Freya doesn't want to be a part of it?" said Olivia after a while. "I think she is scared of something."

"It doesn't matter what it is. I think she is a coward, Olie. The world is ending, and she is here, in this mansion ... just watching everything fall apart. I must tell you, I have been very scared. But I'm here and I will fight ..."

"She also knew that something would happen to us. She told me that she tried to warn us while we were still in Leve."

"What do you mean? When did she say that?" Trevor's eyes were as big as the two moons in Tartae's sky.

"We talked for a short while before everyone came down for dinner. She told me that she tried to warn us and that she had done her part."

"But we didn't get any message ..."

"Apparently, the fact that we didn't get any of her subtle messages is all our fault. She said that our people forgot how to seek meaning in the important things in life, and she cannot take responsibility for that." Trevor rolled his eyes. "But I must be honest with you, Trev. When we were still in Leve, I noticed some things were out of place. About two days before we fell into the Portal, I noticed that the leaves were behaving peculiarly. Maybe I should have talked about that with you, maybe I should have had paid more attention. But at the time, I just thought that I was going mad or seeing things that were not there."

"Don't blame yourself, Olie. How would you, in your right mind, think that the leaves were writing you a message? She should have put more effort into it."

Olivia sighed. She felt part of the blame. She could have been more careful, she could have taken better care of her friend.

"I think we should go to bed before someone sees us," said Olivia, looking around. Just the thought of seeing Freya's face made her stomach turn.

Trevor agreed and left to his room, walking slowly through the dark hallway. Olivia took a deep breath and went inside her room, closing the door slowly behind her.

That night, Olivia dreamed of a man acting suspiciously, a forest drying up completely and turning to dust. As she woke from each nightmare, she thought that maybe the allandrio tea should become part of her bedtime routine.

CHAPTER TEN

THE STRAGE CASTLE

A t the first ray of sunlight, Cordella woke up and called all the others. Maino was still setting up the breakfast table when Cordella told him that the group wouldn't be staying any longer. The tension was almost palpable, and Cordella's face was one big frown.

The group gathered by the entrance door, waiting for the hostess to say their goodbyes. Walking down the hall slowly, Freya finally appeared, wearing a long white robe adorned with green and golden embroidery. The fabric was light as a breeze, and it shifted graciously with each step she took.

"I was hoping you would stay for a farewell breakfast," she said, getting closer to the group.

"We have a long way ahead of us, Freya. And a great deal to do. You know better than anyone else that we can't afford losing any kind of time." Cordella's voice was dry and urgent. "Nevertheless, we appreciate your hospitality and your time. And I still hope to see you soon … doing what's right."

Freya nodded and smiled. Everyone said their farewells and went out the door.

Outside, the horses were waiting for them, and the weather was rather odd. The enormous amount of clouds in the sky and the cold wind that was gusting incessantly made the fresh morning look like late afternoon. And every time the wind blew, something crawled inside Olivia's body. And she wasn't the only one noticing the heavy energy. The first thing Cordella and Freya did as they left the house was study the sky and exchange a scared look. Something was definitely out of place.

Everyone climbed onto their horses and waved goodbye once more. The Flowers' Manor was left behind, and even from afar, Olivia could still see Freya next to the door. Observing.

Freya's behavior was completely indecipherable to Olivia. She tried to warn Olivia, communicating through worlds. She seemed worried, and she was still there, observing them from a distance. Her eyes locked on the group. She stood there looking at Olivia as if she was about to say something or do something. However, her actions had been nothing but disappointment during the last day. Freya didn't seem to put a lot of effort into helping Olivia and Trevor, and she didn't even seem to care that much.

But now there she was. And even though the Flowers' Manor was getting more and more distant, far enough that not even a scream would be heard, there was still a connection between their hearts. And it was a disconcerting feeling.

"And off we go to Strage," sighed Bran, interrupting Olivia's thoughts and easing the odd sensation she had in her heart.

It wasn't a long journey from the Flowers' Manor to Strage Castle, if they managed to keep a fast pace. Cordella explained as soon as they journeyed away from Freya's home. If everything went according to plan, they would arrive at Strage Castle the next morning. Cordella wanted to get there as quickly as possible, and for that reason, they didn't plan a lot of stops. The pace was now the fastest they had galloped.

There was something different about the group now. It was possible to feel that some hope was lost. They didn't talk much and barely looked at each other. And once more, Olivia and Trevor had an unsettling feeling that they had done something wrong. They kept thinking and thinking about what they could possibly do to recover their memory. And they were both trying. They kept searching for a spark that could unlock their memories. More often than not, they felt that Tartae was asking too much of them, but at the same time, they were certain that they could help somehow. As if they were bound to be there.

Olivia was deepening in her thoughts and about to drown in them. All of the questions and the pressure she was inflicting on herself, all the things that were said the day before were starting to choke her. She needed to come out for air. So, she decided to break the reigning silence.

"Hey, Bran. Tell me something about us. Something that you think I can remember. A good memory or a bad one. You pick." She tried to smile and make the question sound light and breezy. More than it truly was. She figured this could be a good way to remember something. Maybe a good enough or bad enough memory would unlock what was inside her mind, and all of their problems–or at least a part of them–would be solved.

But Bran was completely startled by her question. His eyes were wide and about to pop out as he looked from her to the others. Kirk made a weird sound with his throat and finally broke the awkward silence:

"Let me help my friend here! If you don't mind, I have a tale for you."

"I don't mind at all. Amuse me!" challenged Olivia, looking away from Bran and doing her best to keep a lighter tone. Trevor was now closer to the rest of the group, and everyone was galloping quite slowly, allowing the conversation to happen.

"We were in a fight when you hurt your wrist. We were looking for the lost Key, and you were hit by a troll; you fell off your horse and broke your wrist. It was a harsh fall, and you had an exposed fracture. That's why you're still in so much pain. The wound was so bad that Cordella wasn't sure if you would be able to get through the Portal, back to your world. When it happened, your scream was so loud that the world seemed to stop for a while, and then you fainted."

"I was truly expecting something good, but okay. Thank you! I'll keep trying to remember this delightful moment!" Olivia said sarcastically while Kirk laughed.

"I heard you asking about your wrist multiple times. Don't act like you didn't want to know!" laughed Kirk. "And the stories about good and nice things are boring. They don't have battles and blood."

"And you are a huge fan of blood, aren't ya?" Bran spoke for the first time since Olivia's question.

"Yes, I am. I've always been a great fan of BLOOOOOOD!" yelled Kirk, almost singing, as if he were in an opera.

"What about me? Any bad tales to tell?" Trevor asked, smiling.

"Hmm ... Let me see ... Oh! I have a good one. The first time you encountered a mermaid, you fell so madly in love that Olivia had to cast a spell on you so that you could go back to your senses! And she was as ugly as a mutant rat who woke up on the wrong side of the moon. But then again, love is blind!" Kirk laughed out loud with Bran.

"I'd really like to remember that ..." laughed Olivia.

"You're so lucky that I don't remember anything about you ..." Trevor had a mischievous look and seemed slightly annoyed.

It was clear that they were all friends and that they had been through a lot together. It was a pity that Olivia and Trevor could not remember any of it. At least now they could grasp onto those memories, and try to recreate them and then, who knew ... maybe spark the real memory that they hoped was deep inside. It was a good plan for now.

Cordella and Alavro traveled side by side most of the time, not exchanging a single word. They looked worried and lost in their thoughts. Olivia could only wonder about what they might be thinking. And since that last day at Freya's house, the two Guardians were much more serious.

The scenery didn't change much along the way. There were green fields, trees, and flowers followed by more green fields, more trees, and more flowers. From time to time, one could feel raindrops falling here and there. Only enough to justify the clouded skies. To Olivia, the weather seemed to reflect the way things were: constantly gray with occasional tears.

It was easy to get lost in thought while galloping, especially when she wasn't talking to anyone and had an uncertain future lying ahead of her. That combination was marvelous to make one's mind wonder. And Olivia would find herself just like that pretty much the whole time: wondering. Thinking about things she didn't know, things she could see, things she should remember.

They stopped for some food and made a small fire under a tree, just enough to keep them warm and prepare something to eat. They couldn't lose a lot of time, so everything was very simple today. They ate and slept without setting up the tents.

As soon as the day was born, they woke to birds singing loudly. The mood was still odd and quite alarming. They got ready very fast and left the campsite in no time. Strage Castle was getting nearer, and Olivia had goosebumps just thinking about that. She didn't know what to expect, and deep down in her heart, she wasn't sure she wanted to know. Maybe being surprised was better than arriving there filled with fear.

After around three hours galloping, the scenery started to change. They took a turn on a road that seemed abandoned, much denser than the path they had been following until now. There were trees surrounding them and a putrid odor all around, impregnating the air and making everyone a bit nauseous.

"Let's go faster!" Cordella yelled, looking back and then leading the group.

As they kept going, a big rocky construction appeared between the trees and the mist that was now rising before their eyes. And alone, on the top of a slight hill, was Strage Castle.

The energy was strong in this place. They got closer to the house, and Olivia shivered. She felt some voices talking inside her head. She felt the voices, she didn't hear them. It was as though a spell that was cast to the wind ages ago was now inside her, stretching, howling, looking for a way out. A sharp pain rose between her eyebrows. Nothing of this was pleasant, nothing seemed right.

They were now very close to the main door of Strage, but still at a certain distance. Cordella stopped the group and got down from her horse, looking at the castle. She analyzed the place for a moment, took a deep breath, and put her hands in the air, closing her eyes in prayer. The energy lifted. Cordella removed the protection spell that was enveloping the place and got back on her horse.

After a short while galloping, they were at Strage's majestic wooden doors.

"Olivia, Trevor, you come with us. Bran and Kirk, you stay outside. We shouldn't be long." Cordella said the words while studying the whole group. Bran and Kirk only nodded and took their weapons. The rest of them entered Strage.

CHAPTER ELEVEN

THE BOOK OF THE PORTALS

Olivia and Trevor slowly entered Strage Castle, walking carefully and studying everything they set their eyes on. But there wasn't much to see. The place was abandoned, and there were not a lot of furniture or decorations to tell the story they so eagerly wanted to hear. It was a series of empty room after empty room, spiderwebs and dust covering all that was left.

Olivia couldn't help but keep touching her head. Cordella looked at the girl and said kindly, "You're trying to fight the magic in this place. And there is a lot of magic around here. We have put up multiple protection spells to guard the castle, and the Book bears a great deal of energy too, good and bad. The Book carries the intentions people had with the Portals. You are feeling your third eye; it's trying to block all this magic. You will soon get used to it. But for now, try to let it go."

"Thank you. I can definitely feel something in here. I think I can *feel* the magic," Olivia said calmly.

"The Book is hidden in the basement. We will be there in an instant, and then we will leave this place quickly."

They walked a little further through those empty halls until they got to a wall covered in a sophisticated yet dated wallpaper. Its flowers and colors were now fading due to time and bad conditions. Cordella whispered some words that Olivia couldn't understand, and a doorknob appeared. She opened the door and went downstairs, followed by Alavro, Olivia and Trevor. The basement was even creepier, colder and darker than the rest of the house. There was no warmth in this Book, Olivia thought.

Cordella and Alavro walked to a bronze chest. They opened it at once, and there it was, the Book of the Portals.

Olivia thought that something amazing would happen when they finally saw the Book. Something like fireworks or angels singing. But she didn't hear or feel anything. There was nothing. Just this big thick book with brown leather covers lying there, inanimate.

"I figured something would happen now." Her expression was full of disappointment, and she didn't take her eyes off the Book.

"My thoughts exactly, Olie. I'm afraid to say that I was expecting more," added Trevor.

Cordella and Alavro were still standing next to the chest. The witch took a white cloth from her bag and got ready to wrap the Book of the Portals in it. The two Guardians exchanged words, more like whispers, nearly inaudible sounds to Olivia and Trevor, but they seemed deeply focused on what they were doing.

"May I see the Book?" asked Olivia, reaching for it. She wanted to touch the Book, and the words jumped out of her mouth like she wasn't able to stop them.

"Yes, my dear. This could be a good sign; the Book wants to speak to you!" Alavro had hope in his eyes and handed the Book to her.

Olivia took it carefully while Trevor got closer to take a better look at the Book of the Portals himself. Something felt weird. Olivia couldn't remember all that had happened in Tartae, but she had this feeling that she would remember this sensation somehow, some way. She was almost sure that she would recognize the sensation of touching so much history, so much magic. She would feel this. This proximity to the Portals. But there was just this emptiness.

Suddenly, Olivia's hands started to burn like she was holding a very hot pan with her bare hands. And then there was no doubt.

"This isn't the Book," she whispered. There was no color left in her face. Her eyes were wide and filled with horror.

"What are you saying, Olivia?" asked Alavro, getting closer to her, his voice shaking. Cordella looked from the book to Olivia, from Olivia to the book, trying to understand what was happening.

"THIS IS NOT THE BOOK! THIS IS NOT THE BOOK!" Trevor screamed desperately, and when he tried to touch the book, he couldn't. His face was pure despair. "OLIE, LET GO! IT'S

BURNING US! IT'S BURNING YOU! LET GO NOW!"

"I CAN'T!" screamed Olivia, trying to get rid of the book, which seemed to be glued to her hands.

Trevor kept trying to help, but it was impossible for him to touch the thing. It was as though the book was in flames. He felt its warmth even without touching it. Cordella and Alavro were confused and paralyzed. It took them some time to fully comprehend what was happening and finally help Olivia. The girl screamed in pain while Cordella tried some spells to free her from the book. But nothing seemed to change, and nothing seemed to work.

They were all desperate, and none of them knew exactly what to do. Olivia's screams echoed in the almost empty room, only making the feeling of desperation grow and cloud their minds even more.

After a while, the book disintegrated, and fell away from Olivia's hands slowly. Its pages transformed into ashes and fell onto the floor. Olivia finally stopped screaming, but her expression was still completely panicked. Her hands were red and covered in blisters. Cordella drew nearer and studied the mess the book had made on Olivia. The witch placed her right hand over Olivia's hands and started to move them slowly, drawing circles in the air, and after a while she said:

"This won't heal you completely, but you will feel better. This mess was made by magic, so magic ought to cure it. Follow my lead and hear my thoughts. Think about cure." Cordella looked deeply into Olivia's eyes.

"Okay." Tears ran down Olivia's face. She made a strong effort not to think about the pain or about Lars.

Cordella kept going for a few minutes until they heard noises coming from outside the house. The witch abruptly stopped and exchanged an enigmatic look with Alavro, who quickly said that they should leave at once. Cordella wrapped Olivia's hand with the same cloth she was going to wrap the book with, and Olivia felt a bit better. The blisters on her hands were completely gone, but her hands were still red and inflamed, and the veins in her arms were now bright red. They were visible through her skin, gleaming.

The group headed back upstairs, and Trevor threw his arm around Olivia to help her. As they got nearer to the hallway, the noises grew louder and clearer. Something was happening outside.

They all ran toward the front door.

"Stay here, Olie. We'll see what's happening," said Trevor, who had an expression on his face that Olivia had never seen before. His voice was comforting and confident. He seemed to have everything under control.

Olivia just nodded, as she figured there was not much to discuss. There wasn't enough time for weighing options or much to say on her behalf. She was wounded, and it didn't seem that what was happening outside was something good. As they opened the door, it became clear. The sounds of the battle became louder, there was people screaming and weapons clanging.

Olivia waited inside. For how long, she had no idea. The time seemed to go on slowly, and the sensation of being confined while her friends were going through hell was like torture. Her friends were there, fighting a fight that was also hers, and this realization kept growing inside her until she couldn't bear it anymore. She kept pacing from side to side in the dusty, dark room. She walked faster and faster as if she were running from something inside herself. Finally, she got her sword and felt a piercing pain in her hand, but that didn't stop her. Olivia proceeded to the door and opened it without any trace of hesitation.

"Not so fast, Olivia," said the man standing just outside the door.

Olivia stepped back and searched the man's face. He wore a dark purple suit; his hair was carefully groomed. She recognized him instantly.

"So ... You remember me. I'm flattered! Let me introduce myself properly. I am Baltazar Fletce, and it's a delight to officially meet you. I have been watching you, and I feel that we already have this history ... A boring history, I must say. Does everybody in that place you live lead such a boring life? Or was that just you and your little friend? You could have had more action. It would have made it more entertaining for me." The man paused, waiting for Olivia's reaction. But she just stared at him with a serious look. "I hope you have enjoyed the surprise we prepared! I can see you are actually on fire!" Baltazar laughed while looking at Olivia's arms, which were still completely red and burned. Once again, the smile looked foreign on his face. As if he were stretching muscles that were stunted long ago.

"What do you want?" Olivia finally spoke. Her voice was firm and dry. "It seems that you've got what you wanted. Let us leave. Or at least let them leave."

"You are right, Olivia. They don't need you ... However, I don't either, and I don't care. And, talking about our surprises, I hope you liked your trip to Tartae, because, my darling ... it was the last one."

Baltazar waved his hand and threw one of the small wooden side tables in the room in Olivia's direction. The impact pushed Olivia back, and she fell on the other side of the room. Her sword dropped to the floor. She had not the slightest idea how to use magic in a real fight. Baltazar was getting ready to attack again, walking toward Olivia. She quickly stood and did the only thing she was capable of remembering: a small fireball with her hands.

The man chuckled softly and looked extremely happy with how well all of this was going. He would be able to kill Olivia, and he would be exalted by Edmund Lars. Before Olivia managed to finish her flame, Baltazar moved his hands in the air, and the spiderwebs that were spread all over the room started to crawl in his direction, climbing up to his hands and forming what seemed to be a miniature shield. He then gave a light push with his hand, throwing the tangled spider webs at Olivia, who was able to dodge. Another flame formed on Olivia's right palm, but this time she put all her strength into that spell, which made the fire grow, and grow, and grow, until she finally threw the fireball at Baltazar.

Some parts of his purple suit were on fire, which gave Olivia enough time to reach for her sword and strike him in the stomach.

"Stupid girl. This isn't enough." He seemed annoyed by it, and his eyes were now all red.

"It should be!" said Olivia, blowing one more fireball into Baltazar's wound. It was the first thing that really seemed to hurt him. He felt pain and was left completely stunned. Not sure how long Baltazar would take to recover his focus, Olivia took the chance to run and flew from the room, finally joining the others in battle.

Bran, Trevor, Alavro, Cordella, and Kirk were fighting with creatures Olivia had never seen before. They were tall and dark green, and their necks were slightly bent forward. They looked like bears without the fur, with broad noses, big black eyes and mouths full of gigantic teeth. They used axes and swords as weapons, and they had no mercy during the fight. The group was clearly at a disadvantage. There were about fifteen creatures against the five of them and Olivia knew that Baltazar would be coming for her soon.

One of the creatures walked toward Olivia, and they started to fight. For some reason that she didn't know, her hands were not paining her as much as she thought they would. Their swords clashed loudly and violently against each other until Olivia saw a blade coming through the creature's chest that fell down with wide empty eyes. Behind the creature, a tall centaur was standing and said with a low voice, "Don't put your guard down."

A group of centaurs came out of the woods, and joined the battle, making the situation easier on the Guardians. The centaurs were tall and fearless.

The battle went by bloodily. Luckily the adrenaline was so high, and the fear was now so encouraging, that Olivia didn't have the time to notice the blood building up in her hair, the bodies lying on the floor and all those screams. The battle was a blur. She could barely see her friends, only the creatures who burst toward her, screaming and growling. The battlefield was even more horrifying than what she had imagined.

The sword noises echoed in her ears. At this moment, Bran got closer and yelled:

"Let's make them dance!" he said and smiled, and they started to fight together instinctively.

The green creatures got closer to them, and Olivia and Bran attacked with coordinated movements, always protecting each other's backs. They were so synchronized that Olivia felt, for a split second, like they had done it before. They knew each other's movements, and they complemented each other's attacks.

Suddenly, there was a painful scream and Olivia looked back. It was the first time she had focused her gaze during the whole battle. Bran was hit by a burly, gigantic creature that was preparing its ax for the final strike. Olivia wielded her sword and jumped on the creature with all her strength, landing with her feet on the creature's large chest. She carved the weapon into the creature's neck and let the blade deepen as its body fell onto the ground.

The fall gave fear enough time to take over Olivia's heart again. She ran to Bran, who was breathing erratically until he completely lost consciousness. He was covered in blood and dirt, which made it impossible to know how deep the wound was. Olivia looked around, but no one had noticed what had happened yet.

She dragged Bran's body to the trees, taking him away from the battlefield. As she saw some centaurs getting closer to them, she yelled, "HELP! PLEASE! WE NEED HELP!"

The centaurs didn't ask a thing. One of them took Bran in his arms, and the other asked Olivia to join them.

"We will take you to a safe place. Don't be scared. We are friends of your people, and we are here to protect the Portals as well."

Olivia hesitated for a moment. None of the options she had sounded like good ones. She couldn't leave her friends fighting those creatures alone, but also, how could she abandon Bran now? The young man's face was quickly losing all its color. They needed to move fast, that much was clear.

"Come on, we must go!" said one of the centaurs, grabbing Olivia's hand. She looked at him and mounted on his back, not too sure yet if that was the best option.

They galloped away among the trees until the field became a dense forest. Olivia kept looking back, thinking a million things and at the same time, nothing at all. She was nauseated thinking of what could have happened to Bran, imagining that this unsettling feeling of loneliness and fear could stay with her forever.

CHAPTER TWELVE

THE SON OF THE FOREST

The centaurs were galloping extremely fast. They were much faster than any horses Olivia had ever seen—and she had known a lot of them during her adventures with her parents—and for that reason, Olivia held tightly to the centaur's back, doing her best not to fall. The wind was blowing her hair and the ground trembled with the centaurs' heavy steps. They went on faster than an arrow for more than an hour, going deeper and deeper into the woods until they started to slow the pace a little. As soon as they slowed down, a third centaur joined them.

"It's over. The others are coming."

"All of them? Or ... or did someone stay behind?" Olivia asked, fearing the answer more than anything.

"No one was left behind," answered the centaur firmly.

Olivia was relieved and the centaurs appeared to share the same feeling. For the first time, she really looked around and paid attention to what surrounded her. She seemed to be at the heart of an old forest. She was surrounded by numerous large, ancient trees all covered in moss, ferns, and wildflowers. Life spread through everything: the rocks, the grounds, the tree trunks. Everywhere Olivia looked was green, colorful and covered with dew.

"We will take him to the healer. He needs to go quickly," one of the centaurs said, interrupting Olivia's thoughts. Clearly, they had arrived at their destination and Olivia dismounted the centaur. "You should come too. You are bleeding."

"This is nothing. Thank you, but I'll wait for my friends. I'm feeling well; there's no rush."

"By the way, forgive my manners. I had no time due to the circumstances ... My name is Orion, and this is Firlo. And you are in the Laliamo Forest, where the King Belenos lives." The centaurs took a bow. They were tall and majestic. They had low voices and always spoke in calm and courteous tones, like true gentlemen. Firlo and Orion were both strong and handsome. Their hair was as black as a raven and adorned with braids and plants.

"I'm Olivia Halin. Thank you again for bringing us here. I hope I can return the favor one day," said Olivia, smiling discreetly but honestly. The centaurs left and took Bran with them, leaving Olivia alone to wait for the others.

She spent some time just looking at where she was, analyzing every tree and every leaf. And then, she started to look in the same direction she came from, waiting to see her friends' faces again, with no blood, with no screams echoing. She tried with all her strength not to think the worst.

There were so many unanswered questions. What were those green creatures? What exactly happened inside Strage Castle? What would they do now? A thousand thoughts went through Olivia's mind, followed by a thousand premature conclusions. And no one knew about Baltazar Fletce yet, and she had no idea where he had gone. Olivia had waited for him to come for her in the battle, but that had never happened. There was no sign of the man after she left that foul house. She found it hard to believe that she had scared him away. So, there was another reason for him to give up killing her, and that wouldn't be good.

Of one thing she was certain: Tartae's universe was more present in her world than the Clan knew about, and she could feel it, even though she still had no memory of it. Olivia now understood why she felt so uneasy about Baltazar when he paid her a visit at the Lucent Bookshop. Even then she had felt that something was wrong, although she couldn't have known exactly what. And she had so many disturbing dreams ... She knew. Deep down in her heart, she knew.

Olivia heard some steps coming closer and looked back. A man approached her bearing a peaceful smile on his impressive face.

"Welcome, Olivia. It's a pleasure to have you here in the Laliamo Forest. I'm Belenos," he said, getting closer to her slowly. His tone was solemn, and his energy was so pure that he seemed to be part of the forest, part of Olivia. Everything appeared to be united. His voice echoed inside her.

"Thank you for having us, and for helping us," said Olivia, feeling a bit intimidated by Belenos' presence, which was so overwhelming. The man was extremely tall, muscular and handsome. His blondish hair fell down to his shoulders in natural waves that shone while reflecting the discreet light in the forest. His face was delicate, his eyes as blue as the skies, framed by thick brown eyebrows. His beauty was so perfect and delicate, and at the same time so masculine that he looked like a force of nature.

Belenos stopped next to Olivia and looked in the same direction as she did. They waited in silence, staring at the path ahead of them with their hearts full of hope and anxiety. The sound of horses was getting louder and then it was possible to see all the centaurs coming back with Trevor, Alavro, Cordella, and Kirk riding their horses.

Olivia ran to Trevor, and they hugged. They both felt a weight leaving their shoulders, a pressure leaving their hearts. As they let go, they looked at each other and smiled, not saying a word. They analyzed each other's face: tired eyes, all covered in mud, blood, terror, and relief.

"Where is Bran?" asked Alavro, jumping off his horse. His face was pale in despair, his voice trembling.

"Firlo will take you to him, my friend," answered Belenos, waving to Firlo, who waited next to the mansion's door. Alavro followed him, walking fast, almost running.

"Belenos, thank you for having us. We will be eternally grateful." Cordella walked toward the man, holding his hand in a friendly gesture once she got closer.

"There's no need to thank me, Cordella. I'm glad to be of help."

"We were taken by surprise in Strage, and we were outnumbered. I don't know what would have become of us if it weren't for the centaurs." Cordella shook her head. Her face was dirty, carrying signs of the battle, and her robe was a little torn. "The Book of the Portals was not there. Lars got to it before us, and we put ourselves at risk for no reason at all. We did exactly what he wanted."

Belenos was clearly not expecting this news. There was a subtle twitch in his eyes, and for a second, he lost all color in his face.

"Not everything went according to his plan," he finally said. "You are all here, and you are all alive." They exchanged an amiable look, and Cordella took a deep breath.

"Trevor, Kirk, this is Belenos from Laliamo. King of the Laliamo Forest. I believe you two have met already, Olivia," Cordella said, looking from Olivia to Belenos.

"Nice to meet you, Kirk, Trevor." Belenos shook Trevor's hand, looking deeply into his eyes, as if he was looking into the boy's soul. Even Olivia felt a shiver going through her spine just by witnessing that. There was something very enchanting about Belenos, and something quite familiar too. "Please, follow me. Here in my home you will be safe."

They all walked toward the manor's doors. The place was like a big majestic tree of some sort, ancient and full of life. Its structure was all made of wood and rocks, resembling the wide trunk of a tree, but with windows made of delicate and colorful glass here and there. Moss and ivy crawled over the walls, and flowers adorned everywhere on the exterior. They grew wildly all around alongside bird's nests, beehives, rabbit holes. It was like all life was there, and all life was created there.

They walked through the blue wooden doors and entered a common room that was as amazing as the house's facade. Flowers and herbs hung from the ceiling, and petals were spread across the floor. On the left, there were stairs to the second floor. Belenos kept walking along the rooms until they left the house and arrived at a more modest cabin outside. There, were three women and a man wearing colorful robes and waiting for them.

"These are Agatha, Frico, Jasmo, and Olea. They are healers; Cordella is acquainted. You couldn't be in better hands." Belenos introduced them and soon left the cabin.

The group stayed there while the healers did their job. Olivia got new bandages on her hands and Olea–a wise woman around her sixties with black eyes full of wisdom–repeated the same movements Cordella had done before on Olivia's hands until finally curing her. Olivia was dismissed soon after that, and Orion guided her to where she would be staying for the following nights.

Olivia took a shower in the most interesting bathroom she had ever set her eyes on. The water fell like a waterfall, and it was all made of rocks, with quartz that made everything sparkle with the slightest touch of light. After the shower, she got dressed and went downstairs, finding Cordella in the common room with the rest of the group. They were all discussing something when Olivia sat down, trying to keep up with the conversation.

"Lars' plans are far more advanced than we thought. We can't go on alone, Cordella. We need a better strategy. It's time to find our allies and be prepared for the worst. We were lucky at Strage." Alavro had an urgent tone, but he was still calm and restrained. His face was pale and his expression rigid. Olivia figured that Bran's situation must not have changed.

"Lars has a plan and allies," continued Kirk.

"And Lars has the Book of the Portals," said Olivia. Everyone turned to her. Apparently, Kirk still didn't know that, and his eyes automatically filled with terror. For an instant, they all dove into their own thoughts, and there was only silence.

"What were those allies?" Trevor asked, breaking the weird silence that was weighing on them.

"Trolls. Greedy and aggressive creatures. I'm not surprised that they chose to fight for Lars," answered Kirk. "They love meat from other worlds. They would have the time of their lives if they could feast over the thirteen Portals."

"I think you should start telling us about these vicious creatures before we have to fight them. It's just not possible that there isn't some kind of book that explains about them all. Olie and I can't keep putting ourselves out there without any knowledge whatsoever. We don't remember anything, and we have to live with this feeling of constant fear and surprise. This is not fair ... It could be only fear. And by the way, what a stupid idea to hide the most important book in the world inside the house that once belonged to the person who cannot find the book! That was a ridiculous idea!" Trevor stopped speaking abruptly, maybe because everyone was staring at him and he quickly figured that–probably–the person who had this most unfortunate idea could very well be in that room.

"I invite you all to spend some time here in the Forest with me. You need to recover, think about what went wrong and design a strategy so the Portals can be protected again. Trevor, I have a library here in my home and a number of books that can help you learn more about Tartae, and also, the centaurs are exceptional storytellers. They will be pleased to share their knowledge with you and Olivia. And I'm also available, in case you need or want my help," said Belenos.

Trevor only nodded and whispered to Olivia, "Now we just need to learn who this Belenos guy is ..."

Olivia gave Trevor a half smile and burst out in an uncertain voice:

"There's one more thing. One thing that makes Trevor's point even more important. I couldn't stay inside the castle for long. I decided to join you in the battle and help somehow. But when I opened the door, there was a man there, Baltazar Fletce ... He didn't let me leave, and we fought. He fought more than me, because he was very skilled in magic and I could barely defend myself. I was able to run in a moment of luck." Cordella and Trevor looked at Olivia with despair in their eyes. "We can't wait for long, and I don't think we have the lead here. Lars knows Trevor and I are in Tartae, and he probably knows that we are not what we used to be, because Baltazar asked me what I thought about our surprise journey. I'm not saying that Lars knows we have forgotten everything, but he sure knows that something is not the same as before. And if he didn't, he knows now. I could barely stay alive during that fight. If we used to be skilled warriors or if I used to be a skilled witch, he noticed that it's not the case anymore. They're not in the dark now. It's clear that we need a different strategy. In my opinion, we should stay here and learn what we can, while we gather allies to go after Lars. With each mistake we make, we get further away from destroying the Portals."

Something changed in Belenos' face when Olivia finished her sentence. His look was of sadness. She couldn't help but wonder if they could really trust the man, and at the moment, she wasn't in a very trustful place.

Cordella got up and said, "It's settled. We will stay here for a while, and we will establish our next move soon enough. For now, let's just get back on our feet emotionally and physically. That's the only way we will be ready for what's to come." As soon as Cordella concluded, everyone got up. When she left the room, Olivia took hold of Trevor's hand and pulled him along, following Cordella.

"Cordella, about Baltazar ... Do you know who this man is?"

"I'm afraid not, Olivia. But it seems to me that all of our fears are coming true. This man is clearly an admirer, a follower. Lars is gathering them, and we must beware."

"Something else happened. That was not the first time I saw

him. A couple of days before we arrived here, he went to the bookstore where I work in the City of Leve. Trevor was there too. At that time, he didn't do anything suspicious, he barely said a word. But this made me think that Lars is more present and knows more about our world than the Guardians know of."

Cordella stared at Olivia. It was possible to see that the witch was considering what to do with this new information. Olivia could almost hear Cordella's mind working, trying to connect the dots and find sense in all of it.

"What exactly happened during that visit, Olivia?" asked Cordella.

"It's like I said, nothing very important happened. He entered the bookshop a little before it was time to close. Walked to the back and stayed there for a good ten minutes. When it was time to close the store, I went to him and asked if he needed something, if he needed help. He got a book, paid and left. Nothing out of the ordinary happened, but I was left with an unsettling feeling, and I swear I heard something like a bang as soon as I got nearer to the corridor he was in."

Cordella took some time considering that information. Olivia and Trevor were silent, observing her and anxious for her next words.

"You are right, Olivia. We can't underestimate Lars, and we need to prepare ourselves for the worst-case scenario. We must be ready. Clearly, we won't be able to close the Portals and send you two home as quickly and easily as we thought. But we will do it. I believe in this, and so should you," said Cordella, looking into their eyes with a confident expression.

"And can we trust Belenos? Something changed in his expression when I talked about the Portals," asked Olivia.

"And who exactly is Belenos? Because I don't even know that," said Trevor ironically.

"Yes, I would trust Belenos with my life. And we are all alive thanks to him. The centaurs are creatures of the forest, and they live here freely. Belenos was the one who asked them to go to our aide. This place is magical; I'm sure you can feel it. Belenos was born on the first day of May, and he grew up here, in the deeps of the woods. No one knows about his parents. Some say they have never existed and that Belenos was born and raised by the forest herself. He grew up and started to keep the forest, protecting it from anyone with less than good intentions. And, since I have known him, he had been a great ally to the Guardians, as you can see." Cordella subtly interrupted Olivia as the girl opened her mouth to ask a question. "Now, I will go to my room and rest. I'm sure you two have a lot to talk about and would like to be left alone."

Cordella left them, and Olivia and Trevor walked toward a window.

"Was that all that happened at the bookshop, Olie?" asked Trevor, stopping by the window and looking at her. He appeared to be worried and intrigued.

"Yes, that is all. Do you remember him?"

"Vaguely. But I feel something weird when I think about this."

"I had a dream about him that night. He changed into a wolf or werewolf. Do you think that could be possible ... that they can be real here?"

"I've no idea! But I wouldn't be surprised... all of these strange things."

"I know. But I find it fascinating, I must admit." Olivia looked through the window. Outside, the night was dark, and the trees shook lightly in the wind.

"And what do you think about this Belenos guy?"

"Also fascinating."

"Aren't you saying that just because of his looks?"

"No, Trev. I feel safe here, as if something that is beyond our knowledge protects this place."

"Then maybe this would be a better place to hide the Book of the Portals," joked Trevor, and they laughed.

Olivia and Trevor went to their rooms. They were tired and looking forward to finally resting in a place they actually felt comfortable in. Trevor wouldn't say anything, as he didn't want to give in, but even he was feeling more protected and at home in Belenos' house. As if they could finally relax for a while, without worrying so much. This last day was the most challenging they'd had in Tartae, and it seemed like a prelude for what was to come.

Olivia fell asleep quickly, sleeping peacefully through the whole night. The first thought to cross her mind when she woke the next morning was that the Laliamo Forest seemed to have some kind of effect on her. Something good, because she didn't remember sleeping so well since her parents died. Olivia got dressed and went downstairs. No one was gathered to have breakfast yet. It was either too early in the morning or they were all still concerned with their own things. As she walked towards the dining room window, she noticed that the sun was still with that morning glow, fresh and light, coloring the forest in different tones from the night before. That moment seemed frozen in time or running at the right pace. There was no hurry, no slowness.

Olivia decided to explore the Laliamo Forest. She went to the kitchen to fetch some bread and left through the kitchen door, which was already wide open. The kitchen was spacious, full of windows, a large table, and wooden chairs, spices hanging on the ceiling and fancy pottery pots and bowls all around. All was rustic and elegant, a duality that seemed to be in everything Belenos touched or represented.

Olivia took a deep breath once she left the house. The smells that came from the forest were hypnotic, a blend of earth, plants, and water. She heard the sound of running water coming from afar and decided to follow it. After walking for a while, she found a river with clear waters, dotted with some small rocks that made the water dance delicately as it bypassed the obstacles. She sat on the river's edge, washed her face in the cold water and closed her eyes, filled with only one thought: She needed to see Bran.

CHAPTER THIRTEEN

THOSE LOST MEMORIES

B ran was alone when Olivia entered the room. She stepped inside moving slowly and making an effort to be silent. The air inside was fresh as a spring morning and the windows were all open, making the curtains dance gracefully to the easy breeze. The sunlight was shining on Bran's face while he was still unconscious. However, his face was already gaining some color, little by little. That morbid pallor was slowly going away and making room for the Bran Olivia knew.

Olivia stood next to Bran's bed for a while, just staring at him. He was breathing steadily, and she wished that he would open his eyes, look at her. She sat down on a chair that was strategically placed near the bed, probably where Alavro was spending most of his time these days. After a while, immersed in that silence and tranquility, Olivia fell asleep without even noticing it. She lost all notion of time or of where she was.

"Olie?" whispered Bran. His voice was weak and low, like the voice of someone who had slept for too long and didn't quite know where they woke up. Olivia was still sleeping soundly; her head was resting on Bran's bed, her hands over Bran's arm. "Olie?"

Olivia lifted her head and, still feeling quite lost, looked at Bran. But it took her some time to believe what she was seeing.

"Bran! You're awake!" exclaimed Olivia with a big smile on her face.

"Did you sleep here? With me?"

"How are you feeling? Are you feeling any pain?" Olivia didn't answer. For some reason, she was mortified of sleeping there the way she did.

"Olie, did you sleep here with me?"

"I didn't spend the night, if that's what you're thinking. I just woke up too early and I'm tired … You know, the battle and all. I fell asleep. That's all," said Olivia timidly, rushing through the words. She quickly continued, "I need to call your father. He's going to be so happy!"

Olivia got up and turned to the door, but Bran stopped her, grabbing her gently by the hand. In that same moment, a shiver ran down her spine, and her arms went a little numb. It was as if Bran's slightest touch made everything spin out of control. Olivia turned her head to him, looking into his eyes.

"You don't remember anything? Anything at all?" Bran had hope in his voice and a certain despair in his eyes. The expectations were so high that Olivia felt them hovering over her, weighing on her shoulders, stealing her breath. "You need to remember something. You must remember us," continued Bran, staring deeply into Olivia's eyes.

"Bran …" said Olivia, weakly. "I … I don't remember anything. I'm sorry. But you can always help me."

They gazed deeply into each other's eyes as if they were locked together. Bran's eyes were like the ocean, a mix of different tones of blue, deep and calm. Time seemed to be frozen, all things on hold, waiting for something to happen. Their hands were glued together, and Olivia could feel his warmth as she got closer to him. And in a stampede, the door was opened, letting Cordella, Alavro, and Trevor into the room. The sudden noise took Bran and Olivia out of their trance, and she quickly let go of his hand, jumping back like a wild kangaroo.

"For Ourivio! Bran, you're awake!" Alavro ran toward the bed with his arms wide open, ready to give his son a hug. "And you have color on your face! This is a sign of health, isn't it, Cordella?! You will be out of this bed in no time, my son. In no time! I can tell!"

Cordella agreed and got closer to the bed. With all that frenzy, they had forgotten Olivia was there, and she took the cue to discreetly leave the room until she met Trevor's gaze. He had a suspicious look on his face and quite a mischievous smile, as though he was trying not to burst out laughing. Olivia's face burned, flushed. Trevor followed her into the hallway and, as soon as they were out of Cordella and Alavro's reach, he asked:

"What was happening in there, Olie?"

"Er … I'm not sure, actually. I think I was supposed to remember something. Something about Bran. I don't think we were just friends, Trev."

"You don't think? All of this drama to tell me you don't think you two were just friends? This much was quite clear for all of us …"

"What? What are you talking about?

"Oh, come on, Olie. It's quite obvious that something happened or was about to happen between you two. The way you look at each other, the way he talks to you and even the way he acts when you're around. Have you noticed how he is when he's training me? He's not at all as sweet as when you're around. This is the 'Olie effect', as we like to call it."

"We?"

"Yes, me and Kirk. We joke about this quite often … But that was all that happened? You two were in there finding out that maybe something might have happened one day in the past?"

"Pretty much … He woke up and asked me if I had actually forgotten everything. He seemed upset, quite sad actually."

"I get him. This is something you really don't want a girl to forget, especially your girlfriend," said Trevor, meeting Olivia's disapproving look. Olivia's face was now completely bright red again. "Okay, okay. I'm sorry. I was only expecting something juicier. Put yourself in my place. Your eyes were really wide when we got into the room. And your jump … ah, your jump was remarkable."

They both laughed and walked to the library. She couldn't say much on their way downstairs, her mind kept going from thought to thought. At least something was starting to make sense. And as for now, this was enough. Something about her forgotten past was unveiled, even if not completely. Something pure, something that she truly would never like to have forgotten.

In Belenos' mansion, things started to change, finally. As Bran's condition improved, the energy got lighter, even though this meant getting closer to a dangerous future.

Olivia and Trevor began to visit the library every day and for long hours. The collection of books Belenos had was fantastic, and it wasn't limited to books about the history of Tartae; it included manuscripts written by important people in Tartae's history, epic poems about Tartae's sages and forests, practical guides about working with the elements, performing magic and enchantments. There were also a number of diaries that belonged to previous Guardians of the Portals. It was thrilling to touch those pages that were telling about spells, potions, but also the daily life of the Guardian. Nonetheless, it was possible to sense the Portals influencing their everyday life, even the most mundane things they did.

Most of the time, Olivia and Trevor studied alone. The centaurs were indeed skilled storytellers, but almost never available. They also had the tendency to use a very pompous speech and flourish the facts, which wasn't useful at this particular time. Olivia and Trevor eventually found help. A young witch called Emma Svender sat with them and explained details about a lot that happened in Tartae. She knew a great deal about the history of the Portals, history of magic, healing herbs and how to magically work with the water. Olivia was under the impression that Emma had read all the books in Belenos' library, not only because she was very smart, but also because she was practically a walking catalog. If Olivia or Trevor mentioned something or asked about anything, Emma knew exactly what book to look for and where to look for it in that immense, and sometimes a bit disorganized, library.

Emma was young, almost too young to carry so much wisdom. She had short red hair that resembled the fading sun during the sunset hours and shiny hazel eyes. And, even knowing so many tragic and sad aspects of Tartae's history, she had a happiness that was contagious. Olivia and Trevor were always waiting for her to come along and join them in their studies; she was like a fresh breeze amidst the complexity of all the things they felt the need—or the pressure—to learn. Emma was also a walking reminder of Olivia's family. Her light heart, the red hair and her love for life. It was like having a sister around, or a close cousin. It was nice.

By now, Olivia and Trevor had learned some of Tartae's history. They were feeling more confident about the part they were playing in this quest and beginning to feel like part of that world. They quickly learned that Tartae was a marvelous place that unfortunately had to deal with a world of problems because of the greediness some people had. They also learned that where there was magic, there was good and bad magic. And it was impossible to control its existence. Magic was energy, and all forms of energy had variations. No one was completely good or bad, no magic was completely pure or evil. One must find the balance.

The days went by, and everything seemed fairly normal. It was almost impossible to notice that something evil was waiting around, prowling. When Kirk was completely recovered from his battle wounds and Olivia's hands were all better, the training sessions started again. Olivia and Trevor divided their time between books and training, this time more demanding and exhausting. Olivia didn't have any more trouble sleeping at this point. Once the day was done, she felt like she was sleeping even before she would lie in her bed. Her tiredness was physical, mental and tangible.

She was now visiting Bran every day, but she never found him alone again. There was always someone with him. Sometimes it was Alavro, others Belenos. He was recovering fast, as fast as possible with a wound like that.

CHAPTER FOURTEEN

A PLACE IN THE FOREST

It was the eighth time Olivia tried to read the same paragraph of *The Art of Manipulating the Elements: A Guide to Be Successful and Respectful*, by *Gillian Gorks*. She was imprisoned by those words, not because they were exciting and were carrying her away into some adventure, but because she felt stupid and incapable of completely understand their meaning.

> *To successfully manipulate the water element, you need to consider three important factors: the predominant color of the water, wind conditions and the state of energy. By 'color of the water' one understands the overall perception of the waters you plan to use. The most common are: green, light blue and dark green. However, it's possible to find interesting variations such as red and black.*

"Argh. This is the ninth time I read this, and I simply can't understand it. I can't move on. I'm stuck, I'm stuck in this book!" complained Olivia to Trevor, resting her head on the book and banging it multiple times on its yellowish pages.

"You need to take a break. Rest for a bit," Trevor said without looking away from what he was reading. Apparently, the boy wasn't having the same issue as Olivia and didn't want to lose his focus.

Olivia tried to read the paragraph one more time and had no success. "I've had enough …" said Olivia, finally closing the book with frustration. "I'm gonna eat something. Do you want anything?"

Trevor only shook his head, making it clear that Olivia was disturbing his studies with all her complaints and questions. She quickly got the hint and walked to the kitchen. Belenos' house seemed empty, the sound of her own steps was echoing in the corridors. Once she got into the kitchen, the sunlight coming into the room was so warm and inviting that it immediately took Olivia's mind off of it all. She lost herself looking through the window for a moment. A walk in the woods would probably be the best thing to do now, a way to change her energy and recover her long-lost concentration.

She left the house, meaning to find the river she had visited some days earlier. Once again, she followed the water sounds, but for some reason, she couldn't find the stream. She kept walking through some oak trees, passing by elderflowers and dandelions, hearing the tinkles of the water from afar, but it never seemed to get closer. Even though she didn't know exactly how long she had walked the other day, she had this uneasy feeling that she wasn't getting to the right place. Or that she wasn't getting to any place whatsoever. She kept walking and walking, and nothing around her seemed to change. It was almost like she wasn't moving at all.

"Don't listen to what is outside you. Listen to what is in you." Olivia recognized the hoarse voice instantly and found Emma resting her body against a tree, looking at Olivia with interested eyes. "Yes, I know. That kind of stuff used to annoy me too. In addition to getting lost in the woods, what people say to help doesn't make much sense. But pay attention. It makes all the sense!"

"Er ... Emma, what are you talking about?"

"You must trust what's inside you. That's the only way you will find the right path, the strength, what you need to get where you want. You're too tired, Olie. You need to relax."

"I regret to say that you're becoming one of those people who used to annoy you. Nothing you're saying is making much sense now, Emma ..."

Emma wrapped one arm around Olivia, and they started to walk together, Emma leading the way.

"The Laliamo Forest is immense. And it stretches far from where the common eye can see. And frankly, we were waiting for the day you would make it here."

"Here where?"

"In Lirianthis."

Olivia looked away from Emma and they were now in what looked like a small village. But it was much more impressive than any other village she had ever been in before or even imagined. The place was so fantastic that Olivia couldn't talk for a moment. She kept looking around, completely astonished by what surrounded her.

There were blackthorn trees and gigantic oaks enveloped in moss all around, and attached to the big oaks were delicate wooden structures that reminded Olivia of treehouses. Among the trees, little windows here and there shone brightly every time the sun reflected on the glass.

It seemed that the houses were spread across the forest floor, the trees and the stones in a wild disorganization that only made sense because it was there. And nothing else would be more perfect there. Some houses were completely covered by plants, others were painted in terracotta, brown or green. The breeze was blowing softly, and the place smelled like sandalwood and myrrh. All the constructions had a peculiar design, following the shape of the trees and there were stairs all around, going up into the trees, in front of the houses, in between the stones. And even though it seemed quite wild and maybe unorganized, it was all done meticulously. Every door was sculpted carefully, every banister had a different and beautiful shape. Every wall was painted with such care that it all looked perfect.

"Emma, what is this place?" asked Olivia, still in shock at what she was seeing. Her eyes moved from side to side, trying to discover every little detail.

"This is where I live, Olie! It's Lirianthis. It's beautiful, don't you think?"

Olivia nodded. Saying that this place was "beautiful" was an understatement, far away from the ideal adjectives to correctly describe Lirianthis.

"I think you will like to meet Diana. Let's go to her house and then we can go to mine, if you're not in a hurry to get back."

"No hurry at all!"

Olivia could barely think about what was bothering her before she got there. She barely remembered the library at Belenos' house and the books she'd thought about reading today. It was interesting how a place so different from what she was used to, so far away from Leve, could make her feel so much at home. And that was how she felt at each place she went in Tartae. And sometimes, when she was being brutally honest with herself, she would admit that going back didn't seem to be the right option. At least for her.

Olivia and Emma walked a little more through the pathway between the trees, and Emma would point and explain some things to Olivia. But the truth was that Emma didn't seem to have any idea of how this village was different from the places Olivia was used to.

"There. That's where I live. That window right above the red flowers, can you see it? I planted them there!" said Emma, sounding very proud of herself. She had a big smile on her face, and her eyes were glowing. "It wasn't easy, I must tell you. I had to use techniques to rightfully manipulate water and earth that I never thought I would need. But everything worked out, and they bloom from spring until autumn. Now I have an easy way to spot my house from afar, at least during a portion of the year. And see that clearing over there? That's where we like to throw our seasonal celebrations. I hope you can join us one day." Emma pointed to a place a little further, over some blackthorn trees.

"What is that like?"

"We gather to celebrate the seasons and how nature changes and adapts. We also commemorate the phases of the moons. You have only one moon in your world, right?"

"Yes. Two moons, twice the magic, I guess."

"Yes! I guess so. All the celebrations are beautiful. They have a lot of food, music, and dancing. Life around here is calm and peaceful. But lately, we've been feeling the energy changing. It's because of the Portals, as you might have figured already."

Olivia's heart sank as Emma finished her sentence. To think about those dark energies invading Lirianthis was hurtful, as was remembering what was waiting for her outside this safe place.

"Have you ever seen a Portal?" asked Olivia, trying to shake those thoughts out of her head.

"No. Never. We don't use them as often anymore, you see. Even the Guardians are afraid."

"That's reassuring, very good to know," said Olivia sarcastically. This realization made her blood freeze.

"That's the truth, Olie." Emma had a lost look on her face, as though this was painful for her to say but at the same time, she couldn't bear to lie. "We're here."

In front of them, there was a large cabin with a charming front porch decorated with wooden rocking chairs and warm throws made of yarn. Although the place was rather rustic, it also seemed fancy and sophisticated. Everything had a place, and every place seemed to have been thoughtfully considered.

Emma knocked on the red wooden door, and soon after, a woman appeared. Her black curly hair fell down through her burgundy gown until it reached her waist. The woman gave a happy smile when she saw Olivia and Emma.

"Finally! Welcome to Lirianthis, Olivia. Come on in! When I heard you were in the woods I got anxious to meet you and to see the day you would finally arrive in Lirianthis. Emma is always talking about you, but you know, we can't bring anyone here without having the permission of the Laliamo Forest."

"Hmm ... Actually, I don't know. I don't know much, sorry. Apparently, I forgot everything that could be useful to me."

"There's no need to apologize. Would you like some tea? I have some cake too." Diana got up before Olivia could say anything, and minutes later she was back with a tray full of small round cakes, which she put on the wooden coffee table in front of them. Her face was beautiful and happy as if she had no cares in the world.

On the inside, her house was grand and artsy. A great number of paintings hung on the walls and also sat on the floor, leaning against the wooden walls. Her couch was bright blue and full of cushions, and the windows were extremely large, making all the light that was shining outside come into the living room.

"Can you tell me more about Lirianthis, please? I'm completely fascinated. I've never seen a place so beautiful and different." Olivia wanted to know more. She wanted to buy a house and live there forever. Everywhere she looked had a thousand things: through the windows, she could see ferns growing freely on the other trees and hundreds of colorful flowers growing anywhere they could.

"Thank you! We are glad you like it. Lirianthis is so beautiful because it reflects the intentions and the energy of those who live here. And of course, because we are in the heart of the Laliamo Forest," said Diana. "Here we live to celebrate the cycles of nature and learn about magic. Some may think that our routine is quite boring, but the truth is that a great part of what happens anywhere in Tartae is born here."

"What do you mean?" asked Olivia.

"We dedicate our time and our lives to the study and practice of magic. It's here where we find a cure for certain diseases. In case of any revolution, for example, a lot of the 'weapons' will come from here. We are always experimenting, and we also teach those who want to learn about the ways of nature. But of course, we only teach those who wish to learn and whom the Laliamo Forest allows in here," explained Diana, who was subtly interrupted by Emma.

"Cordella lived here, for example. Some moons ago (or a lot), to learn more about magic and energy," she whispered, smiling. "But not everyone decides to live here forever. This is just a place to learn and grow for some."

"What about you two?"

"I was born here," answered Emma. "My parents lived in Lirianthis until they decided to move; they wanted to live by the ocean. Diana came when she was a child."

"Yes, I came here when I was four. I got lost in the forest and ended up here."

"You got lost? And your parents didn't come to look for you?" asked Olivia.

"Yes, they did. But they soon found out what happened. Don't worry, Olivia. They're well and happy with the path I took," said the woman, smiling pleasantly. Olivia couldn't help but find it odd that a four-year-old child would get lost in a forest and simply decide to live there forever. However, she preferred not to point out the weirdness of that story and decided to follow another track.

"You said that you study and experiment with magic. Could you help me and Trevor get our memories back? Isn't there a potion or a spell that we can use to recover our past experiences?" Olivia was hopeful as she said the words.

"As we said before, magic is a force of nature. And we can only do what the forest allows. Lirianthis is the way you see it today because what we do here only generates good vibrations. This is not true for your actual condition. The black magic, full of hate and anger that brought you and Trevor to Tartae, doesn't allow us to intercede more than we are already." Diana explained it all calmly; she knew it wouldn't be easy for Olivia to understand certain details. Olivia had lived most of her life in another world and then forgot all about the experiences with magic she had had in the past years.

"Didn't you say that you create weapons? Things made for battles or revolutions in Tartae? Doesn't that involve some kind of dark magic? Bad intentions?" challenged Olivia.

"Yes, you are right. But this negativity is nothing close to what Edmund Lars does. Magic always has two sides. And I'm sure that some of the people who live here with us feel tempted by dark magic and its possibilities, but we all made a choice and decided to follow the path of light. We are all building for the good. And our main goal is to achieve only good things." Diana tried to explain clearly.

"Nature is full of nuances and complexity, Olie. And we tried to help," continued Emma under Diana's vigilant gaze. "As soon as you and Trevor arrived, Cordella sent us a message, and we started to look for alternatives. Nothing worked, and some ancient trees started to perish. If we lose our strength, Tartae will lose it too. If Lirianthis gets lost, maybe we won't be able to win this battle."

Once again, the weight of the world fell heavy on Olivia's shoulders. Every time she thought she had found a little hope, it was a disappointment. However, she was becoming quite used to that answer. She couldn't help but think about how Lars was competent and lucky. How could everything work out so well for him?

The silence reigned for a while in the room. Olivia had her gaze locked on the table in front of her, and her thoughts flew wildly all around.

"Oh, for Ourivio! The sun is almost setting!" Emma broke the silence, jumping up at once. "I still want to show you my home, and we have a festival tonight. Why don't you stay for the celebration? Oh, you will love it!"

Olivia looked at Diana as if she were asking for permission. The woman nodded. Olivia thanked her for the round cakes, and they soon left Diana's house. Emma pulled Olivia by the hand while they went up and down the wooden stairs that were everywhere in Lirianthis. Emma described all the food and drinks they had at these festivals, and she was talking so fast that Olivia barely had time to think or process anything that she was saying. Emma's excitement reminded Olivia of a child, and it was good to see. It made Olivia think about a time that was simpler and lighter. A time when the smallest things used to excite her, and she would pull her dad and mom around their house, telling them her plans for the craziest adventures she could think of.

They arrived at Emma's house after climbing a lot of steps. If it wasn't for all the training Olivia had been having with Kirk and Bran, she would probably be fainting by now, and she would have needed to stop multiple times to catch her breath.

"Yes, I know. We're all in very good shape here in Lirianthis. A lot of stairs ... Some might say that this is the downside of Lirianthis. I think that the downside is that we don't have elephants. Every description I read about the animals that you have in your world makes me want to see an elephant. They seem amazing! Are they amazing, Olie?"

"Yes, I guess they are, Emma," said Olie, smiling.

"Oh, I want to see an elephant one day. We don't have them in Tartae, you know?" sighed Emma, opening the door. They had finally arrived at her place.

The inside of Emma's house was just like herself. Unpretentious and joyful, full of books scattered all around and papers filled with notes. The walls were colorful, and there were vases with flowers and pictures of dried leaves hanging on the walls.

"What's the celebration for, Emma?" asked Olivia while she observed the pictures. The dried leaves were accompanied by their names. Some of them were pretty common in Olivia's world, like grape leaf, basil leaf, and marjoram, but others were unique to Tartae, like allandrio leaf or belion leaf.

"It's the start of the summer. Here, we have the same seasons you have in your world. The two moons have no influence on that, only the sun. It's interesting, don't you think?"

Olivia nodded.

"Emma, don't you think I'd better come back? What if they're worried? I don't want to start any wars before it's completely necessary."

"Cordella knows you're here, and Belenos too. You can relax." Emma said this while going through a bunch of papers and books. Olivia wondered how Cordella and Belenos could know where she was, but before she could ask, she was interrupted by Emma, who apparently had found what she was looking for. "Here it is, Olie. I think you will like this. It's a collection of poems inspired by Lirianthis. They were written by a number of wizards and witches who visited us or lived with us at some point."

Olivia grabbed the book, and on the dark green cover adorned with delicate leaves, she read:

Poetry in Lirianthis
Inspired by and to Lirianthis. May the magic always exist and bring enchantment.
Compiled by Almei Grano and Jisofer Tret

The night fell, and Olivia saw the fire being lit under the dark sky, which made Lirianthis look even more intriguing. Little by little, people gathered around the robust fire for the party. There were small points of lights everywhere, and later Olivia discovered that they were fireflies who would actively participate in these celebrations.

All the healers Olivia had met at Belenos house were there for the celebration, and Belenos himself arrived at the forest clearing just after Olivia and Emma. He wore a blue cape that made his eyes even bluer, and he gave a subtle smile in their direction as he arrived.

The mood was light and happy all around. As Emma had said, the food was great and bountiful. There were nuts, bread, honey cakes and berries cakes, fresh fruits, juice and a lot of wine. Olivia ate, drank and even danced a little bit with Emma, but she was exhausted. She felt as though she had walked a thousand miles today, and maybe she had, aside from also having climbed so many steps. As the night went on, Olivia's eyes were getting heavier, and the sleepiness was almost impossible to avoid any longer.

"Emma, I don't wanna be rude. The party is amazing, but I have to go. I need to get some sleep."

"Of course! I will take you to Belenos' home." At this moment, Belenos got closer to them.

"I'm going home as well. I can walk with her, Emma."

Olivia said goodbye to Emma with a hug, thanking her for the wonderful day. The tiredness was really getting the best of her, and Olivia wondered if there was a way to fly home. Maybe a broom. Like in the fairy tales she read in her world.

"You can relax, Olivia. The walk home won't be long," said Belenos, putting an end to Olivia's divagations. He seemed to be reading her thoughts, and that bothered Olivia for a moment. She didn't know if that was a real possibility, but she really didn't want anyone prowling inside her mind.

"Thanks for walking with me. I really wouldn't know how to walk back by myself. The Laliamo Forest seems to change; things look like they're in movement."

"You're welcome," said Belenos kindly.

"Have we met before? I mean, on my previous travels to Tartae?" asked Olivia. There was something about Belenos that she found familiar, but she wasn't sure what it was.

"We saw each other once, but we were never introduced. The times didn't allow that."

"I see," said Olivia, and before she could go on, Belenos asked:

"How are you and Trevor doing? I can imagine that this might be hard. Getting used to so many peculiar things and not remembering what you have done before. What you have learned. Not even with what you committed yourselves ..."

"We're getting by. We're better than we were when we arrived. Maybe it would seem obvious, but I didn't think it would get not even a little better so soon. One thing that makes me handle all of this better is knowing that we've decided to do the right thing. Of that much I'm sure. We'll destroy the Portals, go back home, and everything will be back to normal. And maybe we won't even remember any of this." Olivia's heart ache. She looked at Belenos and there it was; that same twitch in his eyes.

"And you really think this is the right thing to do? Olivia, I don't know if you're familiar with my story. I grew up in the forest. I was raised by her. Here is my home, and she is my mother. And for me, nature is perfect. Everything that is made, is made for a reason. Every action has a consequence, and everything is changing constantly. And that's why I don't believe that we should destroy the Portals."

Olivia looked at Belenos, astounded. A million thoughts crossed her mind, and for a moment she was afraid of Belenos. If he didn't want to destroy the Portals, and if she was there for that reason, this would be the perfect moment for a bloody murder in the middle of the forest. She kept studying his face in the hopes that she could discover his next step. Fear grew inside her.

"I understand the Clan's intentions, Olivia. And I won't interfere. I have said what I think to Cordella and, just like you, I want what's best for all the worlds." Belenos said it all in a very serene way. Olivia slowly calmed down. She started to understand his intentions and how he felt about interfering like that, so harshly, on something that nature had created. "I just don't believe that we should destroy the Portals forever. That's all."

"When you say that you won't interfere … Will you still help us?"

"I'm helping the way I can."

"But are you going after Edmund Lars with us?"

"I haven't decided yet. And it's not only because we have different opinions about the Portals. I just don't know if I can leave the Laliamo Forest alone in a time like this."

"Belenos, we need your help. We already have enough people leaving us behind, deciding to abstain from a crucial position. And we're now in a position that not taking a stand means letting evil win. We're at a disadvantage. And if you don't mind me saying so, the Laliamo Forest will be well on her own. She was always well, she is powerful, and she has raised you. I don't think you need to worry."

They were now at the gardens outside Belenos' house. He seemed to be weighing what Olivia had just said, or at least he was pretending to do so. Olivia couldn't imagine how she had the guts to say so much, considering how intimidated she was by Belenos' presence.

"Have a good night, Olivia. There's no limit to the world that exists inside you. Be aware of that." He disappeared in the shadows of his house.

There was nobody around in Belenos' house when Olivia walked inside. Everyone seemed to be sleeping, and silence reigned in all the rooms, creating the perfect setting for the conversation Olivia just had to repeat multiple times in her head. Olivia kept thinking that she should have pushed more, but she hoped it was enough and that her words would have the expected result on the wizard. Now she should just wait and see.

CHAPTER FIFTEEN

A VISIT IN THE NIGHT

"But why can't you take me there? I wanna see this place. Are the witches pretty?"

"Trevor! Are you really asking me *this* after everything I told you? 'Are the witches pretty'? For crying out loud …" Olivia had just told Trevor about what she had seen in Lirianthis. Including what she discussed with Belenos on their way back to his house. However, even though a number of very important and interesting things had happened, Trevor was far more intrigued by the possibility of a place full of Emmas in Lirianthis. "Unfortunately, I can't take you. *The Forest must take you,*" said Olivia, inflating her voice.

"If there's something I won't miss when I leave this place, it's these weird rules they come up with."

Olivia couldn't help but agree with him.

Alavro and Cordella had traveled the previous afternoon to find the other Guardians and discuss the current situation with them. And one could tell that things started to slowly change. The energy around the house was shifting, and fear was discreetly growing inside Olivia, like a plant in the end of winter waiting for spring. As for Belenos, he was barely seen around the house. Early in the morning, the wizard would vanish into the forest, and no one would see him coming back. According to Emma, Belenos needed the forest. He would always seek all that he needed and all he wanted to learn there, and that was probably what he had been doing these last days.

It was time to train again, and Kirk was waiting for Olivia and Trevor outside in the woods. The day was warm, and as soon as the training started, Olivia could feel the sweat on her face. Kirk was a tougher trainer than Bran; every time she would stop to take a breath, he would attack her again. The result was a collection of bruises all over her body. But in a way, she was happy with the hard training. The last time she encountered Baltazar Fletce was enough to show how unprepared she was for a real fight, magical or not.

They trained for hours until Kirk found in his heart that eating was a necessity and it would be better to take a break. And of course, this only happened after Trevor and Olivia complained a whole lot. Just after they were back to training, they heard some noises coming from the woods. It was Bran, walking with Orion's help. As soon as they saw their friend, they all stopped what they were doing and cheered, clapping happily.

"So, you think it's okay to lower your guard with the faintest distraction? Keep going! I will fight side by side with you. You must get used to my company." Bran sat down on a big rock at the edge of the forest clearing. There was color in his face, and he looked healthy, very different from when Olivia had found him on the battlefield. A memory she would like to erase from her mind.

"My good friend! When can you join us?" Kirk got closer to Bran, smiling, and hugged him carefully.

"He's still in need of rest, but we believe that he will be able to train in a week or two," the centaur answered cheerfully, and his relaxed look really made them believe in what he was saying.

"I'm happy just being here. I couldn't stand that bedroom anymore ... that bed. I was in desperate need of fresh air."

"It's good to have you back, Bran. We've been waiting for this day! And also, the training is easier when you're around ... I get breaks to eat when you're here," said Trevor, also hugging Bran.

Olivia was still looking from afar as if she were expecting that her turn to greet the boy would never come. As soon as Trevor stepped back, Bran looked at her, and she felt as though she were being punched in the stomach. The awkward situation seemed to go on for hours, and she was just there, standing ... not knowing exactly what to do. Finally, she managed to drag her heavy self from that spot and got closer to Bran, giving him a light hug. "Welcome back, Bran," she said. The smell of his hair made her body go numb. For a moment, it was as though she was melting like ice cream on a very hot summer day. Being close to him made her wish they were alone once again. But at the same time, so much had happened since the last time they talked just the two of them that she didn't know anymore what had actually happened and what was a product of her creative imagination.

Olivia, Trevor, and Kirk resumed training and kept going until the night was dark. Bran kept questioning Kirk's rough methods. However, in the end he admitted that it achieved respectful results. Orion just laughed and shared that the centaurs were known to be strong and train too hard. For him, the training they did was awfully light for the battlefield and wouldn't get them anywhere. When centaurs trained, he said, they would only rest when someone had blacked out. Only then it would be considered a successful training day. Trevor was ecstatic and thankful not to be a centaur.

The group walked back to Belenos' house together. It was amazing to see Bran walking and to notice how much his condition had improved. According to Orion, the healers thought that his recovery was impressive. His wound was deep, but his health was strong.

From that day on, Bran was always there, watching the training sessions, even though he wasn't able to join Kirk, Olivia, and Trevor yet. And he helped any way he could, giving ideas of situations they could encounter and analyzing how they were doing from a distance: if they could improve their balance, their peripheral awareness, their endurance. In addition, Emma started to help Olivia with her magical training since Cordella was away. Olivia and Trevor could perceive how they were getting better at all of this. They were becoming faster, skilled and more prepared for the surprises that could happen on the battlefield.

The magical training was Olivia's favorite. She was already able to protect herself from rays of fire and lock her opponents inside water bubbles. Which could seem easy for the untrained eye, but it required an incredible amount of mind control while she successfully manipulated the energy of the water and air. Her abilities with fire were already astonishing. She could create it, expand it and contain it, avoiding attacks and keeping the fire from spreading.

Olivia's biggest obsession was manipulating the flowers that surrounded her. She enjoyed making them climb over Emma's legs during their training sessions. Sometimes, she would do the same with Kirk, making the flowers get to his hand quickly and keeping him from using his sword. Which annoyed him deeply. "Don't mix up the training, Olivia! No magic here!" he would protest impatiently, trying to get away from the daisies that were covering his body.

Olivia and Trevor spent their days studying and training, which made them go by fairly fast. Cordella and Alavro were away for more than a week, but they kept sending messages constantly. However, none of their messages would tell details about what they were doing or which Guardians had decided to join them.

In the sunset of a Thursday, Cordella arrived, galloping quickly, and soon after, Alavro arrived too. It looked like they had coordinated their arrival, which was followed by a small reunion in the main hall of Belenos' home. On the occasion, Cordella and Alavro started to discuss all the things they had discovered during their travels. All of the Guardians were now ready to join them at Belenos house; however, a considerable number of Guardians weren't prepared to fight anymore, or to use and protect themselves from strong spells, leaving the group with a little less hope. Alavro thought about getting other allies, but he decided it was too early for that. At this moment, getting more people involved could mean bringing all of Lars' plans to light and maybe cause despair all around Tartae.

"And we must prepare," advised Alavro. "I don't know about you, Cordella. But I've heard extremely disturbing things in my travels. Trees turning into ashes with no fire, wizards being kidnapped and questioned about what they know about the Portals, books being stolen, and homes invaded."

"Yes, Alavro. I heard rumors too, and I could see some things with my own eyes. Lars is prowling, and the energy all around is beginning to get colder and eviler. We must keep going and act soon. We must discover where Lars is hidden and if he has the Key and the Book of the Portals with him. We need to face him once for all."

"Is there any clue about his whereabouts?" Olivia asked, already a bit afraid of the answer. If they had clues, that would mean leaving Belenos' house and their newfound routine behind. If they didn't, that would mean that they would be once again running against time.

"No clue as of yet. The last time he was seen was many moons ago, and the spells we have cast to find him didn't reveal a lot. He knows how to protect himself very well, I would say," explained Cordella.

"All of the Guardians are now invested in discovering where Lars is. We will communicate once every two days to see if someone has any news. Meanwhile, we will stay here, and you can keep on with your training, and Bran can keep recovering," said Alavro, looking to his son. His eyes were still filled with concern.

"But don't you think it would be dangerous to send messages to the other Guardians? Can't Lars intercept them and find out our plans?" challenged Olivia. Her experience at Strage Castle was still too fresh in her mind to not think the worst. She wanted to make sure to avoid any situation where Edmund Lars could be one step ahead of them.

"We will use the medallion messengers," said Cordella, as if it was clear to everybody what she was saying.

"There's something different every time ... When you think you know all there is to know, something like this happens," complained Trevor, snorting. "What are those? Could someone please tell us?"

"I'm sorry. I always forget that you two don't remember," answered Cordella, seeming a little disturbed. Her face looked quite tired, and her eyes wandered away. "They are special medallions that we make. It's a way to communicate that is impervious to magic, and only the intended receiver can read it. So, there's no danger."

Alavro and Cordella excused themselves and left the room to rest soon after that. Olivia and Trevor went to the library to look for more details about these medallion messengers and how they worked. They had a couple of hours free before dinner, and they expected to spend it all learning as much as they could about these artifacts. Trevor whined the whole time they were researching at the library; he couldn't understand how after all this time they still forgot to mention or explain certain things. "How can they forget that we forgot?" he would say repeatedly. And Olivia understood his point.

The medallion messengers were an ancient communication method used in Tartae, mainly by its witches, wizards, and sages. Those who wanted to exchange messages in total secret would forge a medallion. In order for those objects to work properly, everyone involved would put their hands on the medallion, saying together: "Bring this message only to me, send this message only to the one; may this message be delivered as it is, otherwise this medallion will explode in the sun." After that, the medallion needed to be bathed in the water of Lirianthis. That was how they guaranteed that only wizards, witches, and people who were welcome in Lirianthis would use this method.

The hours went by rapidly, and Belenos finally called them to dinner. Apparently, there was a small party happening.

Belenos figured that after the long journey Cordella and Alavro had made and Bran's impressive recovery, a celebration was in order. Deep down, Olivia knew that this was much more a farewell of some sort. From now on, they would be one step away from the most dangerous moment of their lives.

The table was beautifully set. There was bread, lentils, savory pies, roasted potatoes and a number of other delicious dishes. Alavro, Bran, and Kirk were already at the table when Belenos arrived bringing Olivia and Trevor. It was nice to have a moment like this together, and it was comforting to see everyone gathered around the table and well. The healers had just authorized Bran to train again, and Olivia's hands were completely healed and showed no signs of the damage made by the fake book of the Portals. Things were getting back on track, and soon they would be ready to move on.

Olivia completely forgot that something scary and horrible was about to happen because she was so caught in the lightness of the moment that everything else just faded away. The warm summer breeze danced inside the room, bringing the smell of wildflowers and, immersed in this peaceful mood, everyone let themselves be carried away into the illusion that everything was under control.

They were all being entertained by Alavro's stories and anecdotes. He once more sounded like a bard while reciting his adventurous tales. And even though a lot of it was based on true stories, some of it was too flourished and fantastic to be true, even by Tartae's standards. Like when he noticed that a small dewdrop had been resting on one of his roses for weeks. And it was getting bigger, and bigger. Never bursting.

"I noticed that this drop was growing and growing. Beautiful and robust. Strong and sparkly. And I had never seen something quite like that before. The drop of dew was getting bigger than the rose itself, and one day, I couldn't help but touch it. When I did it, the bubble finally burst, and from inside the dewdrop came the most magnificent rainbow. A rainbow in my own garden!" He finished the story with a huge smile on his face. "You can ask Bran! He was there!"

Bran was just nodding along. Kirk carried on telling one of his stories, which were usually funny but sometimes discreetly censored by Cordella for being too bloody and, according to the witch, unnecessarily disturbing.

As they were too involved in the stories, the group didn't notice how late it was. The night was getting old outside. In the middle of one the many toasts Alavro made, a noise came from the gardens. All went silent, and the doors to the main room burst open. Belenos got up as fast as a lightning bolt, and Cordella was already ready to attack, and through the doors of the dining room came a strong young woman. Even though she wasn't tall or scary looking, she seemed extremely threatening. Her hair was as black as the night outside, and her equally black eyes had a fire within. She walked resolutely, and her expression was a mix of anger and disbelief.

"I can't believe in what I'm seeing!" said the woman with disdain in her eyes. Her face twitched while she looked around the room. As she studied everyone at the table, she clenched her mouth, as if she were trying to restrain herself.

"Alegra!" exclaimed Cordella. "How did you ...?"

"I can't believe you're all here partying while the world is ending outside! We don't have time for *this*," interrupted Alegra. Her tone was getting even more urgent and disappointed.

"There is no party happening here. You can calm down now ..." said Trevor, drinking a little bit of his juice. Alegra just looked back at him with contempt.

"I know where Lars is," said Alegra, changing her expression a bit and looking deeply into Cordella's eyes.

CHAPTER SIXTEEN

THE FIRST STEPS OF A MISSION

I t felt as though the temperature in the room had dropped instantly. They all had their eyes locked on Alegra, who stood in front of the table, slightly out of breath.

"Why are you here? Why are you having a feast? I was hoping to find you all looking for Lars, or at least some answer to my messages," she continued.

"We didn't know where you were, Alegra. No one knew your whereabouts. I looked for you when I was talking to the other Guardians, and there was no sign whatsoever." Cordella used a serene tone, but she was talking considerably fast. It looked as though she wanted to calm down the girl, but Olivia wasn't sure if she was successful at all.

"You didn't know where I was?" Alegra was clearly shocked. "Trevor knew!"

"Me?" Trevor frowned and looked very surprised. He almost spit the juice he had just taken a sip of.

"Yes, you! And don't play dumb. Why didn't you answer my messages?" asked Alegra, looking at Trevor. Her voice had acquired a high-pitched tone.

"I didn't know anything, and I didn't get any messages! What are you talking about?"

Alegra's eyes were still full of disbelief and annoyance. She studied Trevor carefully, looking at his face for a long time.

"Alegra …" interfered Belenos. "They don't have any recollection about what happened in Tartae."

"What?" Alegra's eyes grew wide. Her face changed little by little, giving place to different and sadder expressions. "Trevor, what happened?"

"Lars brought them here this time, and they lost all their memories about Tartae on the way. That's why we are all here ... We are starting over and getting ready," answered Belenos. Alegra was still looking at Olivia and Trevor as if they were two aliens in the room. She looked scared, but also, she looked as though she were waiting for someone to say that she had gotten it all wrong.

"But ... if Trevor and Olivia can't remember, how can we destroy the Portals? Is there still a way?"

"We are taking care of it, Alegra. We believe there's still a way," said Cordella. "Alegra, about Lars ..."

"He's been hiding in some ruins, close to the Tria Plains. That's where I found him. There are some trolls there, and I believe they are protecting Lars. I also saw some people coming and going, so he's not alone."

"Can you tell us if he's building an army?" Kirk spoke for the first time.

"Apparently not. I didn't see a lot of people going there. It was all very discreet, and it all seemed calm enough. But I can't guarantee you that it's still that way. Things may have changed while I was looking for you."

"You should have called me to come with you, Alegra," said Kirk.

"I wasn't alone. Atlas was there with me. And I wasn't planning on facing Lars or anything of that sort, but we couldn't lose more time. I decided to go."

"How long does it take to get there?" asked Alavro.

"Eight days," said Alegra. "If we are fast and don't make a lot of stops. It's located west of the Tria Plains."

"We must get ready," said Cordella resolutely. Her tone was firm and confident.

At this point, it was clear that the dinner was finished. Belenos insisted that Alegra eat something, and finally, after a lot of convincing, the girl sat at the table. People were barely talking now, and they all seemed to be immersed in their own thoughts. Olivia and Trevor could only think about going after Edmund Lars, and they were afraid that if they took too long getting ready, he could move and have more time to put his plans into action, and then who knew what would happen. At the same time, they were reluctant. They didn't know if they were prepared enough. Lars' knowledge about the Portals didn't seem as rudimentary as they first believed, and it kept surprising not only Olivia and Trevor, but also, and more importantly, the other members of the Clan.

Only a few words were exchanged during the rest of the dinner. Oftentimes, Olivia would catch Alegra's gaze staring at her and Trevor. She was clearly having trouble believing that they had lost their memory. It was all written on her face that she was finding that reality too impossible and horrifying to be true. She looked confused and kept staring, making Olivia fairly uncomfortable.

Little by little, people started to leave the table. Cordella was first, and said that she would design a strategy as soon as she woke the next day. Alegra was going to share a bedroom with Olivia, and Belenos left the table saying that he would prepare everything for Alegra's stay. Alegra seemed quite bothered by it and tried to convince him that she didn't need anything. In the end, only Olivia, Trevor, and Bran were left in the room.

"Are you guys okay?" asked Bran, his voice was soft.

"Yes, I just wanted to give her some time. Alegra must want to be alone for a while, so I don't wanna go back to my room yet," answered Olivia.

"Trevor, do you remember getting any messages?" asked Bran.

"No. Do you think she might be lying?"

"No. Alegra is not like that, and this whole thing really sounded like you two. I don't find it weird. You are not used to how we do things around here, and you probably just didn't notice her messages."

They headed out of Belenos' mansion and walked in the forest for a little bit. The cool night was like an instant relief to their worries. Olivia felt as if a monster was now living inside her due to the intense twists and turns happening in her stomach right now. She was scared and nervous. Alegra's arrival brought with it the awareness that their future held something terrifying and dangerous and, as in every future, it was unavoidable. It didn't matter how many beautiful places they visited, or how many interesting people they knew; they were there to fulfill a destiny that was also a burden. At least Olivia found tranquility in her friends, which helped her accept the peril in front of her and made her feel safer, at least for now.

***

When Olivia woke the next morning, Alegra had already left the room. And on the night before, she was already fast asleep when Olivia got to the bedroom. In a way, Olivia preferred it like that, because she didn't know how to talk to the girl, and right now, she needed to handle her own feelings and doubts.

As she looked out the window, she saw Alegra and Trevor talking outside and the conversation didn't seem tense at all. They seemed to be having fun together. Olivia went downstairs and noticed that the house was quite empty again. She soon found out that Cordella, Alavro, and Belenos were not there anymore.

"My dad wasn't in the bedroom when I woke up. I believe that they left even before the sun had risen," said Bran, who was having his breakfast at the kitchen table.

"Any idea where they went?" asked Olivia, and Bran only shook his head. "I think we should get ready to train."

"It's refreshing to see that you didn't change, Olivia!" exclaimed Alegra, entering the room with Trevor and trying too hard to make her voice sound more relaxed than it actually was. "Always eager to train! We must start now. Where is Kirk?"

"I think that he's already in the forest training by himself," said Bran, getting up and grabbing a leather backpack filled with weapons and gadgets for the fight. Apparently, Olivia and Trevor were the only ones who didn't completely prepare for the morning training. They both went back to their rooms and fetched their weapons quickly. Something told Olivia that this wouldn't be an easy day.

Bran, Kirk, and Alegra had an interesting dynamic as teachers. One could easily see that they had worked as a group before and that they had been through a lot together. More often than not, Olivia and Trevor only felt like they were in their way, interrupting what would be great fun for the three warriors.

After dedicating a lot of training to balance, attack, and defense, Olivia was exhausted. Her hair was now glued to her forehead, and mud was spread over her whole body. She was also coming to the conclusion that clearly Alegra's life experience had made her far from patient and built a hard and defensive personality. Which Olivia completely understood, but this also made the training almost impossible. In other words, it only made Olivia's life more difficult.

They trained for long hours. Until the sun started to burn the top of their heads. It was probably midday, because their stomachs were howling in hunger and their arms didn't respond to commands anymore. They were completely weak and had no energy left whatsoever. Bran was always the voice of reason at those times. He was the one to point out that they needed to take a break, have some water or food. And it wasn't different this time.

The walk back to Belenos' house was challenging. It had never seemed so long. Olivia's entire body was aching, and that made her want to lie down and sleep there, in the middle of the forest. Trevor was talking to Alegra the whole time, and Olivia couldn't help but wonder what on earth were they talking about. How did they have so much to discuss? After all, Alegra had just shown up, and Trevor didn't remember anything that had happened before.

They found a big steamy pot of soup brewing on the stove. They ate quickly as if the food was going to evaporate, as if they had no time to waste. Kirk was pouring some more soup for himself when Cordella entered the kitchen.

"We are waiting for you in the library. Please, come as soon as you are finished." She said it calmly and left, leaving the group too nauseated to continue eating.

The windows in the library were all closed, and this was the first time Olivia had seen the room that way. The smell of books was strong and reminded Olivia of the smell in Lucent Bookshop. The smell of another life. Candles and fireflies illuminated the dark library, and everything added mystery, making everyone walk into the room slowly as if they were scared of something. Alavro, Belenos, Cordella, and Orion were already in the library when the others came in.

"Sit down. You look tired," said Belenos, pointing to the comfortable red armchairs, which were usually very inviting. They all sat without giving it too much thought. The fire crackled in the fireplace, and the library was hot and airless.

"We can't wait anymore," said Cordella. "Our plans to this point have failed, and we can't let Lars advance any more. Especially because we don't know what his next move will be. Alegra is right; we need to attack now."

"When are the others coming?" asked Kirk.

"We don't believe that we should involve anyone else at this moment," Cordella said. Kirk tried to say something, but Cordella continued firmly. "As Alegra told us, Lars doesn't have an army to defend him. There's no need to make this into a war or to involve anyone else."

"But we don't know how many are with him! We need more people. We need all the Guardians at least!" protested Kirk.

"We don't need to put anyone else in danger, Kirk," said Olivia, before Kirk could keep protesting. The Clan knew how dangerous this mission was, but they were willing to sacrifice themselves in order to endanger as few people as possible. "What will we do now?"

"We will leave tomorrow before daybreak. We must be fast, and we hope that Alegra can help us get there," Cordella said. Alegra nodded, and Cordella continued. "During our travel, you can't communicate with anyone else outside of our group, using any method. Take as little as you can. When we get there, we will divide into two groups, and you should prepare for the worst. Our main goal is to recover the missing Key and the Book of the Portals. And of course, destroying the Portals when we have a chance."

They all had scared and intense looks in their eyes. This would really be the end of Ourivio Brut's legacy.

"What about Lars? What are we going to do with him?" asked Trevor.

"You don't need to worry about that. There are parts of this mission that are too heavy for your young and hopeful hearts," answered Alavro, speaking for the first time. Even though he had his usual tone, he seemed gloomier and more worried than normal. He sat on a wooden chair, rubbing his hands against each other constantly, like a nervous twitch.

"Now it's time to prepare and get everything in order for our journey. Belenos, we are very grateful for all that you did. I hope that we can soon meet under better circumstances." Cordella gave Belenos a maternal look.

"I'm coming with you," said the man, causing surprising looks from Cordella and Alavro. "I don't believe that the destruction of the Portals is the best solution, but the wise words of a witch made me change my heart. You can count on me." Belenos gazed at Olivia, who had a discreet smile on her face. Cordella and Alavro seemed happier with the news, and soon after that, they ended the meeting. Bran was the first to leave the room, and he did it like a rocket, without looking at anyone. Trevor wrapped his arm around Olivia's shoulders and, bearing his mocking smile, he said sarcastically, "We're going to have so much fun!"

Olivia smiled back and a knot formed in her throat. Her heart shrank when she thought about all the possibilities presented by the unknown.

CHAPTER SEVENTEEN

THE MURMURING WINDS

T he rest of the day went by in a blur. Maybe because of all the things they did in so little time, or because of the anxiety they were all feeling right now. There was a rush, something in the air. Olivia was nauseated the whole time and, in her head, a million questions rose while she got ready to leave. And there was the scariest question of them all, the one that kept repeating over and over: what if they didn't make it?

They packed some of their belongings, only the things they would really need. They wouldn't bring any tents on this trip; they would sleep under the trees in order to avoid losing any time and drawing any sort of attention. Everything was crucial right now. Every small detail mattered, they could easily mean the difference between the success and the failure of the mission. Being alive or dead.

Olivia caught herself thinking about what her life was like just a few weeks ago. Her monotonous daily activities at the Lucent Bookshop; her lazy nights watching TV and dreaming of a world of adventures much different from the one she was in right now. Simpler adventures. Not at all this dangerous or filled with this amount of responsibility. She got her sword, which didn't seem to weight as much as it had in the beginning, and she looked at it for a while. Now, the weapon felt like an extension of herself, of her arm, which was slightly sore due to all the training she had been doing. Another life. Other circumstances. She put the sword inside the purple scabbard and closed her bag. She was ready.

"Hey, Olie. Are you ready?" asked Trevor, coming into the room.

"Yes, I guess so. Unless you mean something other than my bags."

"At least we're almost going home. I like to think that way. It makes me less nervous."

"It's a good way to think indeed," answered Olivia, putting her bag on the floor and sitting on the bed.

"I've been spending a lot of time with Alegra since she arrived, and I found out some things about my past here. It was a little reassuring. I felt more at home."

"Anything helps, right? Especially if you take where we're going now into account ..."

"Exactly. Alegra and I used to be good friends. I can tell from all that I know now. I wanted to know more about that message she sent, why she only sent it to me, and what was she saying. Why did I agree to her going on a suicidal mission to find out where Lars was hiding. She used one of those medallion messengers. Look." Trevor took a small brown medallion out of his pocket and showed it to Olivia. The thing was rustic, and it looked quite rough. Its surface was smooth, with only a few uneven parts here and there. Olivia took the medallion and studied it, raising her eyebrows. "It doesn't look very good, I know. This was in my stuff, but I had no idea what it was and what was it for." Trevor paused briefly and continued. "And I must say that I'm very happy that Atlas joined her at some point in the mission. It's good to know that she wasn't alone, since I couldn't be there with her."

Olivia only nodded.

"And did you find out the answer to your questions?"

"I guess I was bolder before I lost my memories. It looks like she had this idea and I thought it was a good one. That way, we could go after Lars as soon as we got back to Tartae, and we wouldn't lose more time. We decided that attacking Lars first was a better idea than trying to find the Key, or the Book, or any of the other more cautious things the Clan is always planning."

"They want to protect us, Trevor. I think that deep down, they didn't even want us here."

"I see. And I agree with you. But with all that precaution, we ended up staying in Tartae for much longer than we should have." Trevor seemed anxious. His voice was tremulous. "But I don't know, Olie. I started asking all these questions to have a better understanding of what I did in the past, and now I can't stay away from her." Trevor looked away. He seemed confused, and Olivia chuckled.

"I think you're in love!"

"No, Olivia. I'm not. She's older than I am, and she is so …"

"Beautiful? Intense? Smart? Look, Trevor, you didn't come here for a piece of advice, but I'll give it to you anyway. Being brutally honest, we don't even know if we'll be alive next week. And that's not just something I'm saying to encourage you. It's a fact. If you feel like she might feel the same, and I think she does, go for it. And go for it now!"

"Maybe you should follow your own advice, Olie."

"But I'm not in love with Alegra, and if I was, I don't think I'd have a shot. She has never looked at me the same way she looks at you!" said Olivia sarcastically.

"You know what I'm talking about …"

Olivia laughed and set about arranging some books she had in her room. Not long after, Alavro showed up in the doorway and told them that it was time to sleep. The sun had just set, but the next day would start really early.

When Alegra finally arrived in their room, Trevor was still there, and they exchanged a couple of words until Trevor said goodbye and gave Alegra the most awkward hug Olivia had ever witnessed in her life. Olivia tried her best not to laugh and wished her friend a good night.

"He is amazing, isn't he?" Olivia broke the silence.

"Yes, he is. I can only imagine what this experience is like for you two. You would think you had enough trauma the first time … and now you have to repeat it," said Alegra, clearly sad.

"At least we don't remember the first time. This helps. But if you ask me what the lesson in all of this is, I'd say it's to seize the opportunities. Enjoy life. That's very important," said Olivia, finding Alegra's puzzled gaze.

Time went by, and they both fell asleep without much conversation after that. Olivia dreamed of a plain being enveloped by a dense and dark mist. Baltazar Fletce, followed by a number of camels and a giant black wolf, devouring all that existed.

***

Olivia was awakened by Alegra's heavy steps around the room. Olivia's eyes were so heavy and her sleepiness so powerful that she had a hard time understanding what was happening. When she finally sat up in her bed, Alegra was already completely alert and ready to go.

"Let's go, Olivia. It's time," warned Alegra, grabbing her bag and leaving the room at once.

Olivia got ready quickly and went downstairs like a hurricane. There wasn't a sign of the sun in the sky. The night was dark, and the stars shone brightly. Most of the group was already outside, prepping their horses. Olivia didn't feel as bad as she usually would for waking up so late, because Trevor was even later. He was clearly annoyed about waking up before the sun and got to the garden with his eyes still partly closed.

"It's good to know that some things never change!" exclaimed Kirk, who was already very excited about the journey, and probably all the fights and blood that he was about to encounter.

"Don't even think about it, Kirk …" challenged Trevor. He was now petting his horse, who apparently was the only one he didn't consider his enemy this morning.

Emma and Diana approached the group, coming slowly out of the shadows in the Laliamo Forest. Diana was going to take care of Belenos' home, and she promised to keep everybody informed about the forest. Apparently, she was the only exception to Cordella's 'no communication' rule. She was also the person appointed by Cordella to warn the rest of the Guardians in case something happened to them.

Emma got closer to Olivia and Trevor, her eyes bearing an expression that Olivia had never seen before. It was a mix of melancholy and hope.

"We will help as we can in Lirianthis. And I hope I don't see you again!" said Emma, clearly trying to hide her concern. "I was honored to share with you all that I learned!"

"And it was a pleasure to learn from you," said Olivia, exchanging a meaningful look with Emma.

"Here. So you can remember me and our home." Emma handed Olivia a small quartz, carefully cut. It was round and resembled the sky during a dark night. The rock was a very dark shade of purple and had small shiny dots that sparkled like stars, and other spots that reminded Olivia of nebulae. It was as though

Emma had given her a piece of the sky.

"Thank you, Emma! It's beautiful." Olivia's voice trembled. The idea of never seeing Emma again made her feel sad and sort of lost. They hugged tightly until Cordella interrupted.

"It's time. We must go now!" Cordella announced and climbed onto her horse. The rest of the group followed her, galloping fast through the woods. Slowly, the group got once more into their peculiar formation, and they kept it for pretty much the whole day: Cordella, Alegra, Belenos and Orion in the front, Kirk, Alavro, and Bran in the back, and Olivia and Trevor riding in the middle.

As they moved away from Belenos' house, something in the air shifted slowly. It felt as though something was protecting that place, and as they got further away, this protection faded, and Lars' influence could be felt. Stronger. Even in the air. They still hadn't seen anything that resembled what Alavro and Cordella saw. Nothing as strange, nothing as horrifying. But it was possible to sense that that comforting peace of Belenos' home and Lirianthis was gradually vanishing.

The day was dawning, and they started to hear the animals in the Laliamo Forest waking up. Birds chirping, squirrels jumping over the branches, bunnies leaving their burrows. The sky was painted with the colors of the aurora, and at this point, they were already considerably far from the forest that they knew, taking hidden paths into the woods. Right now, Olivia only had one thought: she couldn't be distracted for one minute. If she got lost, she wouldn't have the faintest idea where she was or where to go.

The group galloped north fast and didn't make any stops. Cordella guided them deep into the Laliamo Forest through a path that was faintly marked on the forest floor, showing that it wasn't used frequently. They would take wild turns, following a labyrinthine path that made no sense to Olivia and Trevor and the tracks left by the horses were quickly erased, completely covered by leaves, moss, and flowers. It was as if no one had been there for a while. Galloping through these woods was interesting and would give Olivia a lot to learn and think about if she weren't passing by everything as fast as an arrow.

There was no conversation during this journey. The fast pace wouldn't allow it. Once in a while, Olivia and Trevor exchanged curious looks when the group took an unexpected turn, and both of them, who were still beginners in this whole riding horses thing, would almost fall off.

They didn't stop at all until the sun peaked in the sky. Which led Olivia to believe that it was midday, and her stomach growled as loud as thunder in a storm. Cordella started to slow down for the first time and waved her hand, telling the rest to stop.

"Let's eat something, rest for a bit and keep going," said the witch, studying the place while looking all around. Everyone jumped off their horses and stretched. Apparently, this wasn't only demanding for the beginners. Everyone looked fairly tired and famished. "Please, no fire. Don't do anything that might draw unwanted attention," said Cordella with a severe look.

They stopped under an immense oak tree. Its trunk was thick and old, and its roots were tall, popping out of the ground and creating a cozy place to rest. There was nothing human in sight. There were only the colors of the forest and nature that grew wildly in this place. They all sat down close together and ate some nuts and pieces of honey bread that they had brought from Belenos' house. Which was one of the best things Olivia had ever tasted in her life.

"We are keeping a good pace. If we keep on like this, we will be at the Tria Plains when we expected," said Orion, looking to the horizon and ready to resume the journey. Olivia remembered reading somewhere that the centaurs were strong, and their recovery time was considerably faster than the average human. Long journeys were easy for them, as it would require little of their physical capacity. These forest beings could easily achieve high speeds when galloping, much faster than a horse. Olivia wondered if Orion was bored and running much slower than he normally would just to keep up with the rest of the group.

"I believe we can go even faster. Olivia and Trevor are more used to the horses now. They can handle it, I'm sure." Kirk looked expectantly at Olivia and Trevor and was quickly joined by Alegra. Olivia and Trevor were too ashamed to say that they were having trouble keeping up with the group as it was and that they were afraid of falling. There was too much at stake now, and no room for complaints or concerns of this sort.

"If we push to our limits now, we will be exhausted when we arrive in the Tria Plains. We won't have energy, we won't be able to fight. This is not your everyday journey, Kirk. This is different," said Bran, who was already getting ready to leave, standing up and grabbing his things.

"Bran is right," said Alavro. "We need to save our strength, because we don't know what's waiting for us. Only the Gods of Fate know that now."

"And if we are being very positive, we need to remember that we're only seven and a half days away from our doom!" said Trevor ironically, and Alegra gave a laugh that was almost too exaggerated for the joke or even for her style.

Trevor was being sarcastic, but Olivia thought that this half day went by too fast. Which was good, but also scared her at the same time. It meant that they were half a day closer to facing Edmund Lars. Half a day closer to the biggest challenge of her life. Half a day closer to something that she didn't know if she was ready for.

The group left again. The break was fast, nothing more than fifteen minutes, and they were back to galloping fast through the thick forest. The food jumped all around inside Olivia's stomach. She had no time to rest, and galloping just after eating was quite unpleasant.

As they advanced, the scenery didn't change much. They were traveling in between a great number of trees, and the sun could barely be felt due to the denseness of the forest. The roots of the ancient trees came out of the earth, making the path ahead of them seem impossible to cross. However, as they moved closer to the obstacles, their path was completely cleared, making way for the whole group to pass. Olivia asked herself what that spell was and when she could learn it. This enchantment was the only reason they were able to move through the woods so fast.

The afternoon went by quickly, and the night brought with it a cold wind that made the journey scarier. The noises made by the wind sounded like voices whispering plans, making warnings that no one else seemed to hear or understand. Olivia shivered each time it howled, and she was shaking noticeably on her horse. Her eyes teared due to the piercing blasts that cut her face with no mercy whatsoever. She questioned if everyone else was feeling this way, as if they were being invaded by the wind and getting lost inside their own minds. As if that wasn't enough, the strong gusts were also making the journey harder for the horses. Their efforts to run were much harder now, and the pace had slowed slightly.

"We must respect the horses, Cordella," protested Orion loudly so Cordella could hear. "They either need to slow down or to rest."

Cordella stopped and looked back.

"Let's slow down and keep going for three more hours, then we rest. Traveling through this forest in the deep of the night is not reasonable even in normal conditions. Imagine now." She guided the group again, now galloping slower and more rhythmically. Sometimes, Alegra and Cordella would exchange words and looks, probably deciding the best way to go, the best path to follow. Olivia could barely hear anything from where she was. She was once more following Cordella blindly.

"Olivia, put this on." Bran got closer to the girl and handed her a plaid wool blanket. "You are shivering, and it's only going to get colder from here on. You need to stay warm."

"Thank you, Bran. But I feel like this cold is coming from inside of me," said Olivia, throwing the blanket over her shoulders and giving Bran a half smile.

"I know this will be hard for you, but try not to pay attention to what happens in the forest, or what happens with the wind. That will make it easier for you," advised Bran. "These are the Murmuring Winds. They protect the forest. But they must do you no harm." He looked to the horizon of trees surrounding them. "Let's go, we don't want to be left behind."

The blanket was warm and made it easier for Olivia to keep going. The group got back to the usual formation at once, and Bran was galloping a little bit behind her again. The wind still seemed to be whispering messages in the dark, and wolves were howling at a distance. The truth was that, if she wasn't with these incredibly gifted and strong people, she would be crying in despair. She loved the forest, but these surroundings were giving her nothing but the creeps. And, as she'd told Bran, that wind was freezing her from inside out.

They stopped again after hours of galloping. Once more, Cordella chose a place full of trees that could serve as shelter for the night. A night that was cold and had no stars. The weather once again seemed to reflect the mood of the mission. Those fresh days that smelled like wildflowers with clear skies full of stars appeared to be in the past. A moment that was long gone, lost in a happier time. The weather grew sinister as they got closer to their destiny. And nothing could make more sense.

"My butt hurts from all this riding. And I feel like Skyscraper doesn't want to look at me anymore," complained Trevor, feeding some carrots to his horse, who really seemed to be in a bad mood.

"Yeah, Trev ... And that was only the first day," said Olivia.

"Don't even talk about it. By the way, if the Portals were meant to share knowledge, why are there no cars in Tartae? Or something that would make our travels easier? No offense, Skyscraper, but horses are not very fast or comfortable," said Trevor, petting the horse, who was already looking happier.

"Some of the transportation you use in your world is not good. They mess with our environment. That's what I've always heard. They fill the skies with dark clouds and make it harder to breathe. Tartae was never interested in that." Bran jumped into the conversation, answering Trevor's question. "How are you two feeling? Is it too hard to keep up with the pace?"

"Easier than I thought," said Olivia. "It was tiring and challenging sometimes, but far from impossible."

"Speak for yourself, Olivia. I'm broken. I need to sleep now!" said Trevor, walking to his improvised bed, right under an ancient oak tree and right next to Alegra, who was already sleeping.

"I can already imagine how it's going to be tomorrow ... Trevor after a night sleeping on the forest floor!" laughed Bran.

"I must admit that this isn't my first choice for a bed either ... I confess that I'm not looking forward to it, and it's an experience that I'd gladly not repeat!" said Olivia. She continued in a more serious tone, "Bran, why is this forest ... so strange? And why did Cordella say it's not wise to travel around here, even not considering Lars?"

"Maybe it's not wise to travel anywhere in the dark of night. But usually, the Ancient Forest is a safe place, and even a nice place to visit. I used to come here with my dad when I was little. Cordella probably suspects that Lars is already experimenting with the Portals, and the forests are the first to feel this."

"But it wasn't like that when we were in Belenos."

"You are right. But this is because Belenos is a good and powerful wizard. His magic protects that place more than we can measure or imagine, and it was protecting us too. He is the one the forest chose as a son. Lirianthis also vibrates with a different energy. If it comes to a day when these two places start to feel cold and unsafe like here, for example, there won't be much hope left for Tartae ... or for all the worlds." Bran said. A heavy silence fell over them.

"I felt as if the wind was whispering something."

"It's normal, and that's why I told you to ignore that. It will make your journey easier. Around here, the wind blows in the trees and seems to tell secrets. But it's only a trick. A way to keep the dark out of the forest. You have no reason to worry, but the ones with evil intentions can go mad listening to the night whispers."

"One of those things you should have warned us before, don't you agree?" challenged Olivia, smiling. Bran smiled back, and Olivia's whole body warmed up for the first time since they entered these weird parts of the forest.

The night was dark, different from when they'd arrived in Tartae and the two moons had brightened everything, making the night almost day. The wind was not howling anymore, but the weather was cold and humid, and the earth where they lay down to rest was freezing. However, Olivia slept much better than she expected. Maybe because she was so tired. But considering everything, this was almost a good night of sleep. No disturbing dreams or unsettling sensations. She just slept and rested like a tired child.

CHAPTER EIGHTEEN

THE STORM

T hey woke up easily the next day. Apparently, sleeping on the bare ground and without all the comfort that Belenos' house had to offer made sleeping in less interesting. They took only a few minutes getting ready to leave the campsite, and then they were quickly back to their journey. No one was up to conversations this morning; they exchanged only a few words while still on the improvised camping site. Even Kirk seemed serious and focused. The idea of keeping the same demanding pace for eight days and then facing Edmund Lars wasn't very relaxing for any of them. Sometimes this realization seemed to suck all of their energy away.

One of the biggest problems about the way they traveled in Tartae was that no one was given any time or opportunity to talk to anyone else. The horses would gallop fast and the sound they made was loud, making it too hard to carry on a decent conversation. Olivia could hardly remember the last time she talked to Cordella, but she couldn't forget some questions she had for the witch. Cordella seemed to know so much more than she was sharing with Olivia, and Olivia couldn't decide if Cordella didn't have the time to tell her those things or if she simply chose not to do it, which would make more questions arise. If Cordella decided not to share all her knowledge, what were her reasons? Why she was exposing Olivia and Trevor to unimaginable dangers without giving them all the knowledge they needed? Olivia kept looking at Cordella from a distance, thinking about the conversations the two of them would probably never have, the things she would never learn from the witch. After all, if everything from now on went according to their plan, there would be no time for anything of that sort anymore, and Olivia and Trevor would be back to their homes in just a few days. They would be safe in the City of Leve, far away from any kind of magic, with no Portals to worry about and no Edmund Lars.

They rode for long hours until Olivia could barely feel her legs. From time to time, she would exchange a deep look with Trevor, who clearly shared her worries and the same pains. Once again, they took a break to rest and eat. It was afternoon already, and Cordella chose a place on the edge of a thin stream so they could all fill up their water bottles and freshen up.

Olivia and Trevor climbed down from their horses and went quickly to the river. The cold water was a breath of life for them. As Olivia washed her face, a peaceful sensation filled up her whole body. The river flowed quietly and got lost into the thick forest and on both edges, she could see some rocks and green plants that grew wildly.

"Let's keep following the river for a while, so we will have fresh water for at least part of our journey and we won't get lost," said Cordella, who was getting ready to leave. "Keep this in mind: if you get lost, follow along the river and you will find the rest of us. But try not to." She was now looking at Olivia and Trevor exclusively. Both of them were still sitting and eating some pieces of banana and honey cakes.

"We are in the heart of the Ancient Forest. This place is full of history and power, but also an easy place to find yourself completely lost," warned Belenos. "Don't listen to the howling winds or the wolves and you will surely be safe."

"I must say that I'm happy to learn that there are wolves in this forest," joked Trevor.

"Wolves and tricky winds. Feels like a great combination ... Let's just make sure that we don't fall off our horses." Olivia got up, offering a helping hand to Trevor. There was something about this forest that was out of place. Even though these woods didn't feel evil, everyone kept warning them about the dangers, and Olivia had this increasing sensation that she should be extra careful around here.

The group soon left and went on along the river. Even when

they couldn't see it, they could still hear the water tinkling, following the flow. The forest didn't seem to change much as they got deeper into its wilder parts. The trees and plants all around were the same. However, something in the air was getting heavier, and it was almost palpable. The forest was becoming less and less inviting and comforting. It was as if at this point, this was a place intended only for the forest beings and no one else. Anyone who would dare to go this far was an intruder. And the forest would make sure to treat them as such.

Since they were now so deep in the woods, they were galloping slower, but it was still quite fast. The afternoon became night in the blink of an eye, and when they finally stopped to rest for one more night, the river noises were behind them. Too far to be heard or followed.

After the day by the river, they journeyed for three days that went by almost uneventfully. They rode between trees and rocks and flowers. They saw the wild animals living their lives in the forest, swinging on tree branches and gathering food from the forest floor. They made short breaks and tried to keep their insanely fast pace. After being on the road for five days, they all felt it in their bones. Some more than others. They traveled rapidly through the Ancient Forest, which covered the whole way until the Tria City, where the Tria Plains were located. By the time they arrived in Tria, they would be only a day and a half away from the ruins where Edmund Lars was hiding. They were getting closer now.

On the morning of the fifth day, they traveled relentlessly until they finally stopped for lunch. Everyone had deep dark circles under their eyes, except for Belenos and Orion, who looked close to perfect. As if the tiredness didn't have the same effect on them as the others. It was a cloudy afternoon, which was good, because there was now a cool refreshing breeze, and it made the once warm way much more agreeable.

As soon as they stopped, everyone sat down and ate silently, resting from the long hours on the back of a horse. After a while, Alegra and Kirk started to discuss some battle techniques and got up to try them. Even when extremely tired, those two were restless. They seemed to have trouble keeping still for more than a couple of minutes. Olivia was getting more tired just seeing them practice; to her, it seemed almost painful. But one could tell that they were not in their best shape. Their once fast moves were now slower, and their response time from each attack was taking much longer.

Alavro quickly fell into a nap under a tree, slightly snoring and breathing very loudly. He was enjoying the fresh shadow of the oak, and everyone was almost jealous that he could manage to sleep so easily. Alavro would take a quick but powerful nap on pretty much all their stops, and later wake up refreshed and recharged.

Cordella had been feeding the horses at each stop they made. She also gave them some kind of magical elixir called tourmaline potion that would make them stronger and more relaxed so they could bear the heavy journey. And they were doing well. Actually, they were the only ones that seemed able to keep up with Belenos and Orion.

"Olivia," called Cordella, who was still feeding the horses under some trees, quite far away from the rest of the group. "I think it's time for us to have a tonic too. We must have our strength when we get to Lars, and right now we are all as worn out as a pair of old and used leather boots. We are also almost through our food provisions. I need you to get the ingredients for the elixir. We need allandrio leaves, lazuli nectar, artemisia branches, and chamomile flowers."

"Of course, Cordella. And can I find everything here?"

"Yes. All the plants that exist in Tartae exist here in the Ancient Forest. No exceptions. Please, don't go alone. The forest is well protected, but it doesn't hurt to be extra careful ..."

Olivia nodded and went back to where the group was resting. Thanks to Emma and to some books in Belenos' library, Olivia now knew how to find all the herbs they needed for the elixir, but she didn't recognize this particular combination of ingredients, even though she had learned how to make tonics herself. After some lessons, she was even able to brew a tonic for better sleep, for visions in dreams and to heal small wounds. Probably, some elixirs required more skills than the ones she had, or a longer period of study.

Olivia grabbed a small white linen bag from her backpack and two small glass bottles so she could collect the lazuli nectar. It felt good to be useful and do something other than just ride through unknown places for hours and hours.

"Trev, can you help me get some herbs?" asked Olivia. She was now tying the linen bag to the same belt on which she carried her sword. Trevor said yes and got up at once.

"What do you need?" asked the boy, getting his bow and arrow.

"I think I can help you. And I don't believe you two should be walking around by yourselves. May I join you?" said Belenos with his always-solemn tone before Olivia could even answer Trevor's previous question.

"I'm going too. We need more food, and I can find some fruits and mushrooms, I'm sure." Bran got up in an instant and joined the group.

"Come back soon. The weather is changing, and I feel the rain coming," warned Cordella.

The group walked through the Ancient Forest, and Olivia explained to the others what she was looking for. In order to find everything they needed, they separated and spread out in the woods, but they would always keep an eye on each other. Even Bran, who was looking for food instead of herbs, was always in sight. He was currently looking for things that could be eaten without the need for cooking, and a fire of course.

After a while, they reached a small forest clearing that had a number of trees lying on the ground. Trees that had fallen down at some point in time and were now being enveloped by other plants. This place resembled the ruins of some lost city, the remains of an ancient time that passed and left only vestiges of itself, vestiges that nature was now reclaiming. The energy of that clearing was strong, pure, and there was something epic about it. Everything vibrated around Olivia. All of those plants were trying to tell a story, an unintelligible story to the beings that weren't part of the forest, a silent poetry. Before stepping into the forest clearing, they all stopped and contemplated the place. There were branches everywhere, and somehow the forest was being born again. The branches were covered in flowers, grass, clover, moss, and mushrooms. All was becoming green, glistening with life.

"What is this place?" asked Trevor, more to himself than the others.

"We're in Rtirsoo. This is where Tartae started to fall when Miniso Lor tried to dominate the Portals," answered Belenos, looking around. His eyes were a bit watery, his voice was soft, and he said the words slowly and contemplatively. "This clearing was opened many years ago. Much before you and I. Tartae was changing. Her trees, Her life was fading away and giving room to evil things, which I don't dare to talk about in here. The Ancient Forest is strong and protective. We are here, and we are safe because the forest knows the Clan; she recognizes you two. Rtirsoo teaches us that little by little, nature will take back what's Hers."

"I'm glad that we're about to close the Portals forever," said Trevor, looking around and pondering the mess that had been caused by that pursuit of power.

"I don't know if what will happen to Tartae after we destroy the Portals will be much different from this, Trevor."

"What are you talking about?" he asked. It was the first time Belenos had said something about this directly to Trevor.

"I really don't know, Trevor. Nature has created the Portals, and I feel that destroying them could be a serious mistake. I don't know what our futures will hold without the Portals."

"But if you think something bad might happen, why don't you do something?" asked Trevor.

"There's not much else I can do. I tried discussing this with the Clan, and it didn't help. And I truly believe that at this point, stopping Lars and trying to destroy the Portals is a priority. It is the best solution. I can only hope that our future isn't a disaster. It would be sad that all of these efforts be for nothing." Belenos was still admiring the forest around him, filled with pain. It seemed that he felt that future happening, that he could foresee an ending to all of this that was much different from what the Clan was hoping for. "I'm here," he continued after a brief pause. "I believe in this mission. I wasn't planning on being part of it, but here I am, and we will make it. Let's move on." Belenos walked away from the clearing and bowed as he left that place.

"My dad always told me that we must respect this place. We shouldn't harvest anything here," added Bran. "Come on, I think I saw some fruits over there."

They all bowed lightly as they left the forest clearing. A cold wind blew and brought with it some even darker clouds. The rain was coming, as Cordella had warned them.

Olivia and Trevor got a little behind. They started to look for more artemisia leaves on the edge of the forest clearing.

"Olie," whispered Trevor, doing his best not to be heard by the others. "What do you think about this? About what Belenos was talking about before?"

"I honestly don't know what to think, Trev. Did you notice his eyes? I told you about this. His heart is not in the destruction of the Portals, and he doesn't seem to think that the future of Tartae will be a good one without them. I don't know what to think ..."

"I don't agree with Belenos. I believe there's nothing to be afraid of. Cordella and Alavro have been studying the Portals for years. They know what they're doing. And last time I checked, Belenos wasn't even a Guardian."

"But he protects the Portals any way he can. And he protects us too. Or have you forgotten about Strage? Belenos is all about the natural circle of things, the powers of nature. He can't accept this violation, and I understand this must be hard. Must be conflicting."

"I don't know ... Do you really think we can trust him?" asked Trevor. His eyes were full of doubt, and his hands shook.

"Trevor, Cordella told us that she would trust her life to Belenos. He's here, isn't he? He saved us." Olivia had a serious look on her face. She couldn't understand how Trevor could doubt Belenos, who had helped them until now. "I guess we have what we need. Let's head back," said Olivia, putting an end to Trevor's questions and walking toward the others. "Bran, did you get what you want?"

"Yes, let's go back."

"Very well. Let's head this way. Follow me," said Belenos, guiding them in the camp's direction.

They followed Belenos through the path of dust and plants for a while, until they all could sense the weather shifting. Suddenly, the day became night, as if a dark shadow had taken over the sky at once. Rain started to fall, and the raindrops were getting bigger and heavier quickly. The rain became a storm. The wind was so strong now that it made the simple act of walking something that required a lot of strength. The powerful blasts broke some of the small branches over their heads, and the water fell so aggressively from the sky that it became almost impossible to see the path in front of them. The weather conditions made the path more and more challenging.

"STAY CLOSE!" yelled Belenos.

They kept walking as fast as they could, fighting the frigid conditions and looking forward to joining the others so they could find shelter. Resuming the journey was impossible with these conditions, so they would have to wait at least for a while.

As they kept going, the rain grew worse, and the raindrops were now so large that they were hurting their skin. A white cloud formed in front of the group, making it harder to see the path they needed to follow. Olivia wanted to stop and wait. She could hardly see anything around her; her eyes could barely stay open under that rain. But at the same time, she just wanted to get back to the camp safely with the others. The mud made their way even harder, and the water was now up to her ankles.

Without any warning, Olivia was pulled back abruptly, a colossal tree crashed down right where she had been just a second ago. There was a loud noise followed by a splash of mud. Olivia looked back and saw that Bran was the one who had pulled her away. She squeezed his hand tightly in a silent thank-you, and then she found Trevor's desperate gaze. He was petrified in terror.

"Where is Belenos?" asked Trevor.

"He was in front of us. The tree fell down between us and him," answered Bran.

"Did you see if he got hurt?" There was despair in Olivia's voice. The tree was immense.

"Don't worry, Olie. He's okay. I'm sure he's on the other side, still waiting for us. Come on." Bran started to climb over the tree. The thing was so big and its trunk so wide that it created a wall of sorts.

The three of them managed to jump over the tree, but they couldn't find Belenos. They yelled his name as loudly as they could, but in the torrential rain, it was impossible to hear anything other than themselves and the water. They couldn't hear an answer, and they didn't even know if Belenos was yelling back.

The rain, the wind, and the mud finally won. They walked and walked in the direction that they believed the camp was, but they got nowhere.

"I think we should stop and find shelter," said Bran, looking around for something he recognized in the forest.

"NO! What if we get lost, Bran? What if they think that something happened to us? WE MUST GO ON!" insisted Olivia. She was deeply disturbed by what was happening. Her legs shook. She looked around and couldn't recognize a thing. The rain made her more desperate.

"Olie, I agree with Bran. We should wait for a while. They will wait for us. They're okay."

"But we could get lost! It's better if we keep going now," said Olivia.

"Olie ... we're already lost," sighed Trevor.

CHAPTER NINETEEN

A CABIN IN THE WOODS

Olivia, Trevor, and Bran took shelter inside a small cave. They stayed there in complete silence until the rain wasn't so intense anymore, which took an hour at least. They didn't know where they were, or even where the rest of the group would be by now, and they were worried about what could have happened to them, to Belenos.

"I just hope that Belenos isn't hurt." Trevor broke the silence as soon as the rain and the wind weren't so strong anymore.

"He isn't. I can *feel* it," asserted Olivia. Bran peered at her with a puzzled look, and he seemed quite disturbed by her affirmation.

"You can *feel* it?" asked Trevor, sounding confused.

"I can't explain ... But I'm sure he's okay. I'm pretty sure now that everyone is okay. We're just ... lost." She took a pause and got up to her feet. "What are we going to do now?"

"We'll get back and join the others. I'm sure we can find our way," concluded Trevor.

"No," interrupted Bran. "We will go on our own way now."

"WHAT?" Olivia and Trevor protested.

"We have agreed not to come back if we got lost. We will stick to the plan and keep moving forward. The others will do the same and we'll meet eventually along the way," said Bran resolutely.

"We didn't agree on anything like that, Bran. We don't know the way to the Tria Plains. How are we supposed to follow a path we don't know?" said Olivia.

"Olie, trust me. This is what we have been doing on our

journeys since the beginning. We probably forgot to tell you this. And think about it, it wouldn't be the first time we forget to tell you two something important."

"He has a point, Olie. If there's something that everyone here always seem to forget, it's to tell us small details that make all the difference," said Trevor sarcastically. "How are we supposed to keep going without our horses? We still have some days of travel ahead of us."

"We'll walk. Let's keep heading to the Tria Plains and try to find the path the Clan chose for our quest. Hopefully, we'll encounter them at some point before we get to where Lars is hiding."

"Trevor, what about your medallion? You can use it to send a message to Alegra," reminded Olivia, a glimpse of hope growing in her heart.

"It's in my bag, Olie. I only brought my bow and arrows with me. And I was lucky I did so."

"We will make it, guys. We have been through things like this before, and we managed to get out of it just fine, trust me. We're all together, and we have each other," said Bran, putting his hand lightly on Olivia's arm. "We'd better go."

"And do you know the way?" asked Olivia, still unsure if that was the best decision for the now-small group.

"Like the back of my hand," answered Bran, smiling.

"I just hope you know the back of your hand very well," concluded Trevor, getting up and leaving the cave.

Olivia and Trevor started to follow Bran, who actually seemed to know where he was going, and that made Olivia and Trevor a little calmer. Even now that the rain had completely stopped, their wet clothes and the muddy ground made their path much harder than it had been before. And they were walking fast, almost running through the woods.

The afternoon was coming to an end. They had spent too much time getting lost and that made their way even more complicated, but they couldn't stop. Every break would take them further away from the rest of the group. They didn't know how long they would walk or if they would really be able to find the rest of the group, but giving up wasn't an option. At least Olivia felt in her heart that everybody was well. She was only hoping that they were following the plan and that no one was left behind looking for them in that muddy, thick forest.

They walked non-stop for hours. Since the others would be riding horses, they should avoid wasting time and getting too far behind the rest. Obviously—and hopefully—the group would be going slower than the usual, but that would still be faster than them. It would mean nothing getting to the Tria Plains without Olivia and Trevor. Nothing could be done about the Portals without them.

Bran now felt responsible for Olivia and Trevor, more than ever before. It was possible to see the pressure he was putting on himself. He frowned the entire time while he was running, and his whole body seemed rigid with the responsibilities he was now carrying on his shoulders.

They had a long way ahead of them. And it would be a hard and sad way too. Olivia, Bran, and Trevor didn't want to talk and felt as though all of the muscles in their bodies were tense. As the night came, making the already dark day even darker, there also came a mist that rose quickly and spread between the trees. All the things the night brought with itself seemed to be an invitation to nightmares that want to become true, to unknown creatures that wished to follow them in the shadows. In the dark of the night, the Ancient Forest was still making even the simplest things frightening.

When the night was high, they finally stopped to sleep. Their clothes were still quite wet, and so was the forest floor, which made sleeping very difficult. Olivia caught herself looking at an owl with deep red eyes that was resting on a branch right above where she was lying, hooting incessantly. The owl's hypnotic gaze and the soothing noise finally made Olivia fall asleep, as though she were hypnotized into her dreams.

***

Olivia woke with something cold dripping on her right hand. The sun had risen and apparently, they had slept too much. For days they had been waking up before the sun. She checked her hand, trying to figure out what had awakened her, and saw some water drops that didn't dissolve. Like very resistant, almost solid dewdrops.

"Trevor, Bran, we need to go." Olivia tried to wake the two boys up.

Bran and Trevor looked tired. Their night of sleep seemed to have been as bad as Olivia's. The huge, deep, dark circles under their eyes were the biggest proof of that. The clothes they wore were still damp from the previous day, and it took Olivia a while and some complaints from her friends to remember that she could do something about it. She had learned some spells to manipulate the air element and was able to conjure a warm breeze, which dried their clothes and made their journey less awful.

"Couldn't you have remembered this before? Like before we slept?" said Trevor.

"I still have a hard time remembering this stuff. I'm sorry, Trev. I still don't feel comfortable using magic; it's not something that comes easily to me. And if it helps, I had an awful night of sleep too."

"What matters now is that you remembered," continued Trevor, who had a fraternal smile on his face. "Any chance of bringing some horses to us?"

Olivia laughed and thought about how that would be amazing. But, even though magic was wonderful and full of possibilities, it didn't work that way, and she still didn't know most of it. The three of them started to walk, and their breakfast was an apple, which they ate while on their way. All they had now were fruits, mushrooms and leaves that the forest had to offer. It wasn't bad, but sometimes it didn't seem quite enough.

They walked in silence almost the whole time, exchanging only a few words here and there. No one seemed to be up for conversation. They were tired and still quite disturbed by what had happened the previous day. Somehow, those unexpected events made them feel that they should be prepared for everything and that they should always stay together. No one else could get lost. The day was passing and the sun getting stronger, making the temperature rise. At least there wasn't a single cloud in the sky anymore, and the possibility of another storm seemed blissfully distant.

"Bran, be honest with us. How long do you think we'll take to get to where Lars is hiding by foot?" asked Trevor. Bran took a deep breath, and his eyes lost a little bit of light.

"I don't know for sure, Trev. It will take longer ..." he answered, clearly disturbed by his own response.

"I have an idea," continued Trevor. "Tria is a city, isn't it? We

144

need to go there and find ourselves some horses."

"We can't expose ourselves, Trevor. No one can see us or recognize us. It could put our plan at risk," said Bran.

"Bran, I really think we should consider Trevor's idea," said Olivia, meeting Trevor's eyes, which were full of expectation. "We are losing time and energy walking for so many hours. What will happen when we finally face Lars? Not to mention that we can't carry much and we don't have any provisions. And frankly, I don't think we will catch up with the others anymore. There's no sign of them; we are too far behind."

"And if we are late, the whole plan will be late," completed Trevor.

"I don't think this is a good idea ..." stressed Bran. He was trying hard not to look directly at Olivia and Trevor. He knew that once he did, it would be hard to say no. As if even a simple look was enough to make him change his mind.

"It's risky, Bran, but some risks are worth taking," said Trevor. He knew he was almost winning.

"Anyway, we are far away from any kind of civilization right now. It's pointless to try to convince me."

"Actually, there isn't a lot of convincing to do. We are two against one. It's pretty much settled," declared Olivia firmly, raising her eyebrows.

"And who said this is a democracy?" said Bran, smiling.

"Oh, don't freak me out even more now, Bran. The last thing I want is to find out that we are trying to help someone who believes in oppressive governments!" joked Trevor.

Bran paused and still looked quite bothered by this idea, but apparently, going by foot all the way to the Tria Plains didn't sound very inviting, even to him.

"All right then. We will need to divert considerably from our way to find somewhere where we can get some horses. If we take a left now, we will get to a village called Lotrium. The only problem is that it's not that close either," said Bran.

"How far?" asked Trevor.

"About forty miles. One day of travel, give or take," answered Bran, and Trevor looked a little bummed.

"It's not that bad. Come on! If we don't start, we will never get there." Olivia tried to sound upbeat. But the truth was that taking that detour would make them lose hours and get further away from

MARCIA SOLIGO

Edmund Lars when they were supposed to be doing the exact opposite.

"I don't think we have another choice ... Not a good one, I mean. We should go, Bran," said Trevor.

Bran nodded and took a deep breath. He seemed a little upset but began to guide Olivia and Trevor once more. And off they went through the Ancient Forest, heading to Lotrium.

Lotrium was a small and humble city of farmers, where Bran hoped that no one would know who they were or who Edmund Lars was. Bran could barely imagine the size of the problem if something went wrong.

They walked for hours. And since by now they didn't have a lot to eat, they wouldn't take long breaks to rest. Normally, they would just grab a fruit from a tree and keep walking and eating along the way. They were now like wild animals, living from what the forest had to offer, like birds and bats. Olivia couldn't help but think that maybe in Lotrium there would be bread, cake, and potatoes. Things that could give her a little more sustenance.

Even though the Ancient Forest wasn't very inviting, it seemed welcoming enough. Other than the storm, they didn't have any kind of trouble walking around there. And according to Bran, that would happen sometimes. Word had it that people would get trapped, go hungry or lose their minds trying to find their way out of the woods. The forest eagerly wanted to protect itself, but only against those who had bad intentions. However, it made one wonder what the forest judged as a bad intention, and how it would choose to punish them.

Of course, all of those stories didn't make their way any easier. Bran tried to hide, but he was a little bit afraid of what might happen between those trees. But the reality was that things were going fairly smooth for them. They were able to find a good amount of fruits any time they wanted, all the paths they chose were clear, they could find water even on leaves, and they didn't see any dangerous wild animal prowling. If it wasn't for the stories or the murmuring winds, the forest would seem light and pleasing enough at this moment.

As for Olivia, she couldn't help but feel that the forest was hurting somehow. She wished that she could heal it and make it breathe a new life with no fear. Olivia didn't even know if the forest was once that way, carefree and just wildly living. However,

146

she longed for such a time.

Olivia and Trevor kept following Bran around. The two friends had no idea how Bran knew the way, as it all seemed pretty much the same to them. Finally, after a long time only seeing trees that looked the same, something different created a shadow inside the woods.

"Look, standing stones," said Bran, pointing to three standing stones in the middle of the forest, almost hidden between the trees.

"What is that?" asked Trevor, and they all stopped to admire the stones and the shadows they cast on the forest floor.

"They were put there by old forest folk, who lived in older, much older times. They are some sort of reverence to nature and a place of meditation, or a temple. I read about them when we were at Belenos'. Nowadays, they are not as common, that's why we don't see them very often," said Olivia. "People believed that the first Portals would happen there. They would appear inside the circle of standing stones because of all the energy they channel. But that is just an old saying. No one is sure about that."

"They are usually hidden in the forests, sometimes built inside a clearing, sometimes like they are here. In between the trees. Here in Tartae, we take good care of them. We don't dare to put them down. Which is great, because they sure are magnificent," said Bran.

"Wow. I've never heard about it. They feel old, that much I can tell." Trevor was analyzing the stones from afar. The stones were strong and full of energy. They were magnificent, as some kind of a portrait of old times. A picture of old lore and beliefs that had been forgotten.

Olivia walked toward the stones, stepping into the carpet of tiny yellow wildflowers on the ground.

"Olie, we don't have time. We must keep going," said Bran.

"I know, but it'll only take a minute. I need to get closer. I'll probably never have this opportunity again." Olivia got closer to the stones while Trevor and Bran only watched her. The scent of the wildflowers got so strong that she could almost taste them, and then, when she was already under a stone's shadow, she touched it. Immediately a rush of energy ran through her body, and she felt loved and full.

"Can we go now, Olie? I'm worried. We must go on," insisted Bran. Olivia looked at him and wished she had more time.

"Okay, okay. I'm going!" said Olivia, smiling. She turned her head briefly to the stones and whispered, "Thank you." She had no idea why she said that, the words just jumped out of her heart.

As they kept moving forward, the energy in the group got a little lighter. Maybe because the stones were truly powerful and gave them more stamina to keep going, or because Olivia, Trevor, and Bran had a little time to chat, and that alone already made them happier and less tense.

They had been walking and running the whole day, and now the sun was almost setting. Every night in the forest was a challenge: the blasts of wind were harsh and loud, and the mist would come up and cover the grounds quickly. By now, Olivia truly believed that there was no danger in all of that, but she would still get goosebumps. And they knew that as soon as the mists were born, they couldn't run through the forest anymore. It was hard to see even a foot in front of them when that happened; it was as though the forest was telling them to stop and rest and keep on only tomorrow when it was day and warmer.

Olivia, Bran, and Trevor saw one more dusk from inside the woods. Now that the close of the day was near, they were running fast, trying to get the best of the time they still had today. Olivia was exhausted, her heart pounding and her throat completely dry. It was time to stop and rest, but she didn't dare to say anything. She knew what was at stake now; they had no time to lose.

After a while of running like three crazy wolves through the dark forest, they stopped.

"We can stay here for tonight. Let's rest now ... I'm sure we all need it," said Bran, almost out of breath.

They all sat down next to a giant fallen tree. Its big trunk and roots would make a good shelter for the night, and the place looked fairly cozy, considering the conditions provided in these surroundings. All around them were more trees and ferns, and now the mists were already very tall and thick.

"That was a good call to stop," said Olivia, studying the rising mist.

"Sure was ..." agreed Trevor. "Bran, have we been here before? I mean, me and Olivia."

"No, this is the first time for you two. So, no need to blame yourselves for not knowing the way."

"I'm not blaming myself for anything ... I had no say in any of this," said Trevor.

"You say that, but I understand that you two put too much pressure on yourselves. I wish I could help more, truly."

"Were you always with us when we came here before this time?" asked Olivia. Intrigued by what they could discover. The night was young still, and they weren't feeling that sleepy yet. There was time for a conversation, something that seemed very rare in Tartae. At least for them.

"Pretty much," answered Bran. "But you were just with Cordella sometimes, especially in the beginning. I believe she was teaching you more about magic, Tartae's history, and even heavier and more dangerous stuff. You two would always look more serious after those times with Cordella, and I know that learning some things about our history might be quite depressing. I've been there too."

"Yeah ... I guess if I learned all at once about what happened in our world, I would be bummed too. There's so much darkness that sometimes it's hard to believe there's also light," said Trevor. After a brief pause, he continued, changing his tone a bit. "And what have we done all those times? Because sometimes, it doesn't seem that we helped at all. Everything is still so lost. Edmund Lars is still around."

"Everything is not lost, Trevor. And you two had helped a lot. At first, you would come and train, learn things about the Portals and magic; you were getting prepared for all that was going to come your way. And you did that for a long time. You see, you had to be prepared for everything. Really, truly prepared. And then, when you were ready, we went on a quest to find the lost Key of the Portal."

"And that's when I got hurt?" asked Olivia, putting together the pieces of the story she already had.

"Yes, but not as soon as we started," answered Bran. "We weren't sure of where the Key was hidden. We were looking for it, asking about it and studying the traces the Keys can leave behind. After a while looking for it, we probably got very close, but we were hunted by trolls. And that's when you got hurt. But you were not the only one. That was a harsh fight. We must have been pretty close." Bran seemed sad and a little disturbed by remembering this. Olivia's eyes were getting heavier as he told the story. She was so tired at this point that not even that could make her stay awake.

"And there I was in Leve, worrying about my final grades and the fact that my dad couldn't bear me living at the university dorms … That sounds so stupid now," said Trevor, shaking his head. Their life in Leve was so distant at this point that it felt like something they read in a book a long time ago.

"That was your life, Trev. We can't compare to what we are living now. We didn't even know that this existed … Sometimes I wished that there was only one world, and Tartae could be shared with everybody from where we came from. But other times, most of the time actually, I think it's best to keep them separate," said Olivia, but she was under the impression that she had lost track of her thoughts and nothing was making much sense anymore. "I'm gonna sleep. I can barely keep my eyes open."

Trevor and Bran followed her cue, and they spent some time still thinking about the conversation they'd just had. Olivia and Trevor couldn't help but wonder how all of this would be going if they still had their memories. However, by now, after all this time in Tartae, they had almost no hope that this could ever happen. They would have to face everything that had to be faced exactly how they were now.

They managed to wake very early the next morning. The sky was still dark, but there was no more mist covering the forest ground. They ate some of the fruits they have gathered the day before, and they were soon on their way again, heading to Lotrium.

Olivia, Bran, and Trevor walked for half a day until the Ancient Forest got less dense, but this change was still very subtle. There wasn't a sign of civilization yet or any sort of demarcation or trail on the ground. And as for the three friends, there was just a reigning feeling of hope hovering over them. They hoped with all their hearts that there would be someone with horses to spare and maybe a very warm, out of the oven, delicious honey cake. As the path they were on got less wild, the tree roots were getting smaller, and they didn't jump out of the earth creating obstacles like before. Everything was getting easier, and if not for the weight they felt constantly on their shoulders, they would be relieved and fairly more relaxed with the success they were having until now.

After a long time marching between pine trees and beeches, the trees were getting spaced out. The sun kissed the forest and passed more easily through the leaves, and the air was not so humid anymore. They walked through somewhere with just a few trees that was full of bluebell flowers, and in the silence of the forest, the sound of swords clanging got louder. Olivia, Trevor, and Bran looked at each other and ran toward the noise, already wielding their weapons.

They tried to hide between the bushes and tree trunks and slowly got closer to the noise. It didn't take long for them to see a stone cabin and two children playing with swords that were clearly too big for them.

"It's now or never!" exclaimed Trevor, walking toward the hut. But he was quickly held by Bran.

"No. You two stay here, and I will go," said Bran. Olivia and Trevor started protesting, only to be interrupted by Bran. "Listen to me. You two are not from Tartae, and it's pretty noticeable. You stay here, and I will get us some horses."

"Try to get some food too! Not that I don't appreciate fruits, but I'm really hungry. And I wanted to eat something heavier ... you know, heavy carbs," Olivia said, and Bran nodded, putting away his sword.

"If something happens to me, you two need to keep moving. Head north and you will eventually arrive in Tria." Bran then left and walked to where the children were playing.

"Eventually. Quite encouraging," said Trevor sarcastically. He and Olivia were now observing their friend from afar, and they were alert, in case those children were not that innocent. They were playing with real swords, for crying out loud. Something could definitely go wrong.

Bran was talking to the kids, and one of them went inside. It didn't take long for a middle-aged, short man to come outside the hut. He had just a few hairs on his head and a big round belly that was squeezed inside a blue vest with its buttons about to explode. The man had an inviting smile, making it clear that he didn't see in Bran any kind of threat and that he didn't recognize him at all. Bran walked inside the cabin and stayed there for a good thirty minutes until he appeared again, coming from the other side of the hut bringing two horses and a brown paper bag.

Bran made a discreet sign to Olivia and Trevor. They ran in the direction they had come from and found Bran feeding some carrots to the horses by the shadow of a tree, far enough from the stone hut. The animals were strong and well taken care of.

"There you go. Now we can continue. I hope you two are

happy!" said Bran, handing the rein of one of the horses to Olivia, who was already petting the animal.

"What about my horse?" asked Trevor, looking around.

"We didn't have enough money to buy three horses, and that would also draw more unwanted attention. You will need to ride with us, and we can take turns," suggested Bran. Trevor seemed a bit upset, but he didn't protest.

"And how did that go?" questioned Olivia.

"You took your time, that's for sure. You should have gotten a better price for the horses and got three of them ..." exclaimed Trevor.

"Nothing out of the ordinary. The farm belongs to Mr. Ribaldo Fesster. He and his family have been living here since forever. I negotiated a fair price for the horses, and I also got us some pieces of cake and fresh water."

Olivia's eyes sparkled when she saw the banana and the honey cakes. Trevor took a piece and continued with his mouth full, "That was good that you had money with you. I have nothing."

"I don't have any money either. But you know, I can always make some magic tricks and get us some money!" joked Olivia. "If it comes down to that ... I make a mean small fireball."

"Actually, my pockets were empty too," said Bran. "I exchanged the horses for a silver compass I had with me." He said it quickly. He seemed quite upset about it.

"What is it, Bran?" asked Olivia. "Was it valuable?"

"We are not supposed to get attached to stuff. It was for a greater cause," declared Bran, who evidently wanted to leave this subject behind. "Are you ready? We need to keep going and take advantage of the few hours with sunlight we have left. We will find shelter for the night in the deep of the forest again, where we will be safer."

Before getting back on their horses, Olivia touched Bran's hand lightly and whispered, "I'm sorry."

The boy smiled at her and squeezed her hand in a silent thank you. Olivia and Trevor climbed onto one of the horses. The journey would be less comfortable this way, but that was their only choice, and surely this was better than walking for who knew how many more days until the Tria Plains.

"I miss Skyscraper ..." sighed Trevor, who was finally showing his affection for his horse.

They headed to the heart of the Ancient Forest, and little by little they saw the scenery change once again. The surroundings were getting wilder, the trees bigger and older. And they were finally getting closer to Edmund Lars.

CHAPTER TWENTY

THE EARTH ELEMENT

Olivia was awakened by the hooting of an owl. She got up slowly, her back aching, and saw the animal perching on a tree right in front of her. It seemed to be the same owl as before, with deep red eyes staring at Olivia relentlessly. She stared back for a while, and for that brief moment, her mind was empty. It was just filled with the calm gaze of that owl.

It was time to wake the others. If they wanted to make up for the time they lost, they would have to go on extremely fast. They were now only three, and that would already make the journey easier.

Bran and Trevor had no problem waking up. If there was anything that Olivia had learned from sleeping in such poor conditions, it was that waking up was not that bad. When you are sleeping on the bare ground after hours riding a horse or walking, five more minutes sleeping doesn't sound as inviting. It only sounds like the prelude to more back pain.

The three of them got back on their horses as quickly as they could, but the incredibly dense forest wasn't allowing them to ride fast enough. There were too many roots jumping out of the ground, too many rocks in their way.

"Olie, you need to do something about this. If we keep going at this pace, with this many obstacles, we won't be able to ride into the woods at all at some point," said Bran. A shiver came down Olivia's spine instantly and she started to shake.

"Olie, can you do it?" asked Trevor. His tone was nice and

reflected how much he understood the pressure Olivia was feeling. Using magic wasn't easy for her, and Trevor knew that better than anybody else.

Olivia didn't answer right away. She didn't even know what to say exactly. She kept thinking about how many times she wanted to ask Cordella and Belenos about the spell they used. How could they make their path clearer? She thought about how many times that question came all the way to her lips, but due to their crazy pace, it never really jumped out. This experience in Tartae was teaching her a lot. And it made Olivia understand the urgency of all things. Life and odd circumstances don't wait for you to have time or courage.

Olivia closed her eyes, trying to remember everything she had learned about trees and the earth element. She was aware that the trees had strong personalities, and they could be quite resistant to the efforts of the witch or wizard, requiring a great amount of stamina from them. She figured that a place like the Ancient Forest would be just like that.

"I'm gonna try," she declared finally, and no one said a word. Olivia looked into the forest for a while and took a deep, calm breath, smelling each plant and noticing all the life that was blooming in that place. She closed her eyes again and, for a moment, there was no doubt in her heart anymore. There was just the forest. She was feeling the Ancient Forest, and it was as though everything that surrounded her was a part of her, and that connection guided her senses. To her surprise, it wasn't that hard. It felt as if the forest wished to help her, and Olivia didn't find any resistance from it. Inside, she heard words that she didn't know, and she felt larger than life. She opened her eyes and the path in front of them was open, cleared from all the obstacles. She smiled and spoke solemnly: "Let's go!"

From that moment on the trip completely shifted for Olivia. She wasn't running through the forest anymore, she wasn't only seeing the blurry scenery passing by. She also saw herself passing by. The wind touched her face, the smell of the horses was stronger than ever. She was the ground trembling under the weight of the horses and what was ahead of them was already inside of her. Instinctively, she started to guide the group, and they were able to advance considerably on that day.

At night, Olivia slept much better. However, her dreams felt quite different from what she was used to, so much that she couldn't even explain them to anyone. There was no nightmare, no darkness, only plenitude.

She woke up the next day feeling rested and not at all tired.

"We are one day from leaving the Ancient Forest and getting to the Tria Forest border. We will be at the Plains soon enough," said Bran, tying up his black boots and looking ahead, like he could see their destination right in front of him. "We must take turns with the horses, so they don't get too tired."

"Now it's my turn to go alone! That's for sure," said Trevor, already approaching one of the horses.

"Let's go then, Bran. But I think it's better if I guide us," said Olivia, climbing up on her horse.

"Trevor, you will need to go fast to keep up with us," warned Bran, mounting the horse and wrapping his arms around Olivia's waist.

"I know!" laughed Trevor, already following the other two.

Quickly, Olivia got back to the rhythm she'd had on the previous day. Trevor was having a hard time keeping up, she could tell, but he wasn't complaining. Although he would whine a bit sometimes, Trevor wouldn't shy away from challenges. And he jumped with his whole heart into this one. He wanted to save Tartae; he wanted to get back to his world.

The ninth day of the journey went by in the blink of an eye. Nothing special happened, except the way Olivia was now experiencing the forest. This was quite new and exciting for her; she felt as though her senses had evolved somehow.

The group was now back to their non-conversational mode. The galloping of the horses didn't allow anything other than that to happen, and to Olivia, not speaking was good. Immersed in the silence, she could enjoy things around her through a new light. She could let it all sink in.

If everything had gone according to what Cordella had planned, they would have been in Leve by now. This whole reality would probably be behind Olivia and Trevor, and maybe things in Tartae would be different, much better.

At the end of the day, they chose a tree to sleep under. They were now getting used to this routine, and things were not quite as foreign for them anymore. They would know what places to avoid, what kind of trees the snakes and spiders liked the most. At the first light of the dawn, they were back again on their horses.

The sun was still fresh when they arrived in the Tria Forest. It was brutally different from the Ancient Forest. The trees were younger, and the connection Olivia felt with the place was also very distinct. The smells were different, and the species that lived there were too. Olivia could have sworn that the Ancient Forest said good-bye to her, and she made sure to also say her farewells and thank the Ancient Forest for making their journey so secure.

They stopped briefly to eat and rest. The Tria Forest was definitely lighter and less intense than the Ancient Forest. The birds were singing a different song, and nothing was as tempestuous. They sat down by some big rocks that had plants climbing on them, and for some reason, the fruits were making Olivia feel fuller than before; she wasn't as hungry.

"Olie, did you see this?" asked Bran, sitting by her side and showing Olivia a lock of her hair, a simple movement that made butterflies dance in her stomach. At the end of the lock of hair, now quite tangled, there was a pink flower, which was slowly blooming as they observed. Olivia looked at her own hair with her mouth open in amazement, until she finally realized that her arms had a slightly greenish tone now.

"Is this normal?" Olivia's eyes were wide, and she looked for confirmation from Bran, who was just as surprised as her.

"I ... I have no idea." Bran was fascinated. Trevor got closer to them and let the apple in his hand fall onto the ground.

"OLIE!" exclaimed the boy. "You're becoming a tree!"

Bran gave Trevor a nudge in the ribs as if he'd said something forbidden. But Olivia didn't seem to care or worry about becoming a tree.

"I guess so! I just hope I don't grow roots yet. That would be potentially problematic." She said, bursting into a laughter that made them all keep laughing for a while. Olivia didn't even remember the last time she had laughed this hard, so genuinely and spontaneously.

They resumed their journey between giggles. From time to time, Olivia would look to her arms and still see a greenish color. For a moment, she thought that maybe this was something that she should worry about. But since she was so deep into the forest and so connected to it, she had a hard time listening to her own thoughts. It was as if the whole forest lived inside her, and that was a strange feeling that didn't allow much space for her own wonderings or obsessions. It was as though she had become too big to fit inside herself.

Bran had just announced that they were getting nearer to the Tria Plains. They would have to spend one more night in the forest, and if everything went according to what they had planned, they would soon find Cordella and the others waiting for them. That thought alone gave them strength.

Once more, Olivia's sleep was calm and uneventful. She dreamed that she had roots that grew into the earth, and then she lived there, in the forest. Forever in the soil as a tree. She woke up and checked her arms and hair. Everything was still the same, but there was no sign of roots as of yet.

Finally, it was the last day traveling. Olivia, Bran, and Trevor couldn't believe that they would see the others shortly and were indescribably eager for that. During that time, when it was just the three of them in the forest, they felt quite alone and lost sometimes. So, the idea of being reunited with the others was beyond comforting.

They got ready and soon left to the trail that would lead them to the Tria Plains. Olivia now guided the group while riding alone, and Bran and Trevor shared the other horse.

Everything was as usual, but Olivia's heart shrank in a way she couldn't stand. Her eyes were darkening, her hands got cold, and her head started spinning. Everything happened much faster than she was expecting. Her body collapsed, and everything that surrounded her immediately disappeared.

CHAPTER TWENTY-ONE

THE SHADOWS OVER THE PLAIN

Trevor and Bran looked at Olivia with despair in their eyes. Olivia woke up on the ground, and Trevor was splashing some water carefully on her face. She took some time to completely grasp what was happening, but as soon as she regained consciousness, her chest began hurting again, a piercing pain that left her almost out of breath.

"Are you okay, Olie?" asked Trevor, helping Olivia to sit.

"No." Olivia spoke in a low tone, almost a whisper, bringing her hand to her chest. "There's something wrong. My... chest... hurts." Bran looked from side to side and then back to Olivia, who looked as pale as the winter sun.

"It's Lars. His influence is here already. You are connected to the forest, Olivia." Bran looked up, the trees were leafless, dry and weak. "Look, Trevor." He pointed to the branches.

"Trev, Bran, we need to hide," warned Olivia with shortness of breath.

"What?" asked Trevor.

"Hide ... NOW! There's someone in the forest." Olivia was trying to get up.

Trevor and Bran helped her, and Bran took the horses quickly and quietly with them. They climbed on a slight elevation that led to a denser part of the forest, where they found a hiding spot behind the large trunk of a tree. They hoped that the horses wouldn't make any noises while they were there, and then they waited.

Shortly after, they could see the creatures approaching. They were tall and curved, covered in very dark fur that shone when touched by light. It was hard to tell if they looked more like wild cats, rabbits or giant flies. Their faces were catlike, with big eyes. Their ears were tall and pointy, alert and scanning for noises in the forest. Their bodies were slender with a protruding belly and short legs. On their back, two small wings that looked under-developed and a long tail, which was spreading across the ground. The creatures had a putrescent smell, and their looks were horrifying. As they walked by, they jumped from side to side, leaving a trail of shadows on the ground. They laughed frenetically, making an annoying sound that was almost deafening. Happily, they didn't see Olivia, Trevor, and Bran, who were doing their best to stay silent. They were static, still as statues. When the creatures finally disappeared into the forest, they started to move bit by bit, carefully.

"They are Phookas. They sided with Lars for sure," said Bran.

"They're sadistic shapeshifters. Emma told us about them. They always side with evil, for all that history can tell us," continued Trevor, still observing the path they took. The Phookas' shadows were still dancing on the forest floor.

"It's comforting to know that you are familiar with something in Tartae!" joked Bran. "Olie, how are you feeling?"

"Not very well," said Olivia, who had almost no color on her lips anymore.

"You need to break the connection with the forest now," said Trevor.

"But how are we going to keep going?"

"We will go slower. There's no problem. We're closer now, almost leaving the forest. Isn't that right, Bran?" said Trevor, and Bran nodded.

"All right. I need a minute. I'm not sure how to do this." Olivia took a deep breath and focused, which was extremely hard with all the pain in her chest. She had this weird sensation as though she were abandoning someone she loved in a moment of need. She was filled with deep sadness and soon after, relief. Olivia's face recovered its color quickly, and her arms were no longer green. However, with normality came also a feeling of guilt.

"How are you feeling?" asked Trevor.

"Better ... I'll be better."

160

Bran and Trevor helped her get up. She saw that the flower that bloomed in her hair was now on the forest floor, and the tips of the petals were drying out. Olivia took it from the ground and put it inside the linen bag she was still carrying on her belt. Trevor observed her without saying a word, and they went back to their horses. The day was passing, and they were still hoping to meet the rest of the group.

It was strange to walk through nature without feeling a part of it. However, Olivia now was more capable of understanding certain things, of understanding the Portals and Tartae. She remembered something her father used to say when she was little: "We grow when we find adversities. It's in the solution to our problems that we find ourselves." And this would fit perfectly with what she was living now.

There were fewer and fewer trees surrounding them at this point, and they could already see a huge green field dotted with some rocks and trees here and there. Finally, they were arriving at the Tria Plains.

When seeing the Tria Plains, one would have the illusion that the green fields stretched out of sight. Surrounding it were tall mountains so close together that they seemed to become only one. The plains were peaceful and almost symmetric, and the greens were only broken by bluish, yellowish, and reddish flowers that grew in the ground, dotting the field with some color. Miles and miles of the same scenery. It was almost tiring, especially for those who don't find amazement in nature.

At first glance, the Tria Plains appeared to be anything but threatening. However, during times like these, they weren't the best path to take. In an open field with no trees or shadows to offer cover, everyone was an easy target.

Those who dared to venture through the roads of the Tria Plains were surprised by a sudden change of scenery if they insisted on carrying on. And that surprise would soon be followed by their last breath. The terrain was burned from a certain point on, as if a fire had destroyed all life there. The green was suddenly gone, and there weren't any flowers. Only ashes covering the ground and a putrid smell all around. Even on better days, only a few people would choose that route; it wasn't an important one for trading, and a lot of people were afraid of the hawks that flew over that region.

Bran stopped and made a sign to Trevor.

"How do we know where the others are?" asked Trevor, mapping the whole place with his eyes. The temperature was dropping drastically.

"I'm not sure. Alegra said that Lars' hiding place was after the Plains. We will probably find them there, or somewhere near there," answered Bran. "Olie, how are you feeling?"

"I'm much better. Thanks. The sun is about to set. I imagine that this isn't a good place to be in the dark. It wouldn't be a good place to sleep and wait until tomorrow either."

"You're right. We need to keep going and cross the plains as fast as we can," said Bran.

"And can we do it before nightfall?" asked Trevor.

"I hope so. Riding through the plain terrain will be faster." Bran was already getting ready to leave again when he turned to the others and said, "Be careful. Things around here will not be as tranquil as they seem. Our path can become tricky." As soon as he finished his sentence, he headed west and guided the group.

Trevor followed Bran, galloping fast. The sun was setting, and most of the Tria Plains were behind them; as they rode, the plains changed into a burned wasteland. Little by little, they were getting closer to one of the mountains, and they could see a concentration of trees, and plants at the bottom of it. They kept going and going, but there was no sign of Cordella or the others.

As they got closer to the mountain, another forest began. A place none of them have ever heard about before. A black forest that was apparently impenetrable. They couldn't see much from outside, since the forest edge resembled the walls of some sort of fortress. There were trees all over the place, and they were very close together. Between them were tangled ivies and other creeper plants creeping up, creating some kind of web that made the pathway completely impenetrable. And even though the purple light of sunset was still shining over the Tria Plains, it was all dark inside that forest, as though the night had already arrived there–or had never left.

They stopped their horses and studied what options they had. And as of yet, not a sign of the Clan or anyone who should be waiting for them. Olivia climbed down from her horse and got closer. There was a border, something marking the end of the plains and the beginning of that strange forest. Trevor and Bran followed her and also studied the place for a while. Bran wielded his sword and was about to cut his way in to create a path for them.

"I wouldn't do that," warned Olivia. "I believe that pretty much everything we do here will have consequences we don't want to deal with. We must find another way."

Bran took a step back but didn't lower his weapon. There was something unusual about that forest, and Olivia felt in no way connected to it.

"Any sign of Cordella? Or Alavro?" asked Trevor.

"No," answered Bran and Olivia at once.

"And how do we know if they are here? Or if this is the right place?" continued Trevor. His face was full of doubt and fear.

"They have to be here," said Olivia, exchanging a hopeful look with Trevor.

"I hoped they would leave a sign of some sort. Or that they would be waiting for us before the plains ..." said Bran, looking from side to side. Trying to find something that probably not even he knew what it was.

"I just wanted to go home ..." Trevor mourned. He said it so low that he might have been talking to himself. For a moment, he who looked older each day they were in Tartae sounded like a child. A lost child that was eager to find their parents, who longed for home and their toys.

Olivia held Trevor's hand tightly. A million things passed through her mind. She was desperately trying to find a way to safely cross those weird-looking plants. But, even if she managed to do so, where was the Clan? What if they never made it there? What if they waited for Olivia, Trevor, and Bran? What should they do now? If this was it, and she was by herself now, she was far from knowing what to do. She had not the slightest idea how to destroy the Portals, how to look for the Book, or how to deal with Edmund Lars.

Olivia sensed something hovering over her head. A shadow was flying fast over the three of them. They were all scared and ready to fight when they saw Atlas, the Eagle Guardian. She landed on one of the horses and stared at them with piercing brown eyes.

"This is Atlas, isn't it?" asked Trevor.

"Yes!" answered Bran.

The eagle looked at them and flew further away from the group

163

and then started to go in circles over a certain point at the edge of the black forest.

"I guess we must follow her," said Trevor.

"What are we going to do with the horses?" asked Olivia.

"We will let them go. They will be fine, Olie. They like the forest," answered Bran.

Olivia petted both of the horses and thanked them. Bran took off their saddles, and they rode toward the Tria Forest, far away from the group.

Olivia, Trevor, and Bran followed Atlas. The bird was spiraling in the air, pointing at something, showing them a way inside the black forest. There was a small opening in the ground. Someone had dug their way through the dirt and underneath all the plants. It wasn't large, only big enough for an adult to slide inside. And it wasn't very inviting either, since they couldn't see anything inside.

The eagle quickly dove into the hole and was followed by Olivia, Bran, and Trevor. They slid and landed inside a tunnel, also quite small and claustrophobic. Its walls were all dirt, and the place didn't look safe; it looked like an improvised pathway whose walls could crumble down at any moment.

They walked for some minutes in the complete darkness until a beam of light came in the tunnel, showing an exit. They were now inside that strange forest. There, the plants weren't as tangled as outside anymore, and the vegetation was more similar to what they were used to, even though the place was still quite sinister and dark. Olivia was under the impression that the plants there were lifeless. They didn't emanate any kind of energy. Nothing good or bad. They could very well be made of plastic.

Atlas was still guiding them through the black forest. It was night, but the two moons weren't shining, making the path very dark and difficult. However, Olivia wasn't even sure if the light would touch that place. Everything was so gloomy and hopeless. Suddenly, Atlas began flying faster. Olivia, Trevor, and Bran started to run, but it was hard to keep up with the animal.

"Bran, Trevor, can you hear it?" asked Olivia, stopping her friends abruptly. Trevor and Bran paused for a moment to hear screams and the clanging of swords at a distance.

"Alegra!" said Trevor, already running.

Olivia and Bran followed him as fast as they could, their weapons in their hands. As they got closer, the noise got louder, and what was happening became clear. There was a glimpse of hope inside Olivia that maybe those screams belonged to someone else, to some other fight. They finally got to some sort of a garden, and there they were: Cordella, Alavro, Belenos, Alegra, Kirk, and Orion fighting with trolls, phookas, and Baltazar Fletce.

CHAPTER TWENTY-TWO

THE SHAPESHIFTER

The blood seemed to have left Olivia's body. Her hands were cold, and her heart was beating faster than the wings of a hummingbird. It was time, and again nothing was happening as they had planned.

A number of questions flew inside Olivia's head. What had happened there? Was Lars waiting for them? Was it all a trap? She was completely paralyzed by all that was happening around her. And she had no idea what to do. Bran caught her by the arm, and it was like waking up from a dream.

"Olie, we must go!" urged the boy. His eyes were wide open and serious.

Trevor was already somewhere in the battle. Olivia couldn't see him. There were bits of fire scattered all around, smoke, blood, and dirt. Olivia finally managed to find Cordella; the witch was fighting with Baltazar Fletce, which was impressive to witness. The way Cordella moved was almost choreographed, resembling a brutal ballet in which she would escape gracefully from each and every strike or spell Baltazar threw at her. Cordella looked tall and majestic, as if magic were making her grow and reach a level of stamina that didn't agree with her age. On Cordella's face, there was the strength of an amazon. She was glowing.

Olivia smelled the putrid breath of a troll creeping behind her neck. She turned and struck her sword into the creature's chest, while a phooka was already attacking her on her right. She raised her arms and closed her eyes, enveloping the creature's body in flames that came out of the ground in a brownish blaze. Some other trolls attacked her, but Olivia managed to fight them back successfully, either striking her sword or doing some spell she had learned. She was fast and mindful, fighting back every troll or phooka that came her way. She finally understood what Bran told her when they began their training: in order to succeed in a battle, you must empty your mind and find an almost meditative state. And that's what she was doing now. She was all there in the battle. All there in those loud sword strikes.

A phooka yelled and jumped in her direction, making too much noise for someone who wanted to strike her from the back. She turned around and made the fire on the ground chase the creature, who ran away screaming even more.

At this moment, Baltazar's gaze looked away from Cordella and searched for Olivia. As their eyes met, Baltazar smiled and ran. During that brief moment in which they looked into each other's eyes, Baltazar's face looked even further from human. If his monstrous appearance was hidden by tidiness and an exacerbated effort to look groomed before, now he was completely revolting. His hair was disheveled, and blood was all over his pale face. His teeth were now big and pointy, and his mouth seemed too wide to be real or even part of his face.

Cordella followed Baltazar's gaze and found Olivia. As soon as the man ran away, she went in Olivia's direction and hugged her.

"What happened, Cordella? What are we gonna do now?" Olivia asked with despair in her voice. The battle sounds were deafening: screams, growls and the clanging of swords.

"There's no time. It doesn't matter how it happened, Olivia. We need to go inside now and look for the Key and the Book." Olivia tried to say something but Cordella interrupted her. "WE MUST GO NOW!"

Cordella took Olivia by the hand and ran through the garden toward a staircase made of stones, which were fairly destroyed either by the fight or erosion. The witch looked for Trevor, who was fighting a troll, and waved her hand, guiding one of Trevor's arrows into the troll's heart.

"TREVOR!" yelled Cordella. "WE MUST GO NOW!"

The boy didn't hesitate and followed Olivia and Cordella to the stairs. They went up quickly, arriving on a facade made of old stones that were almost completely covered by the most odd

167

looking plants. Here, the moss wasn't green. Everything was as red as blood, and the plants were moving, crawling over it all slowly, like snakes.

As they crossed the portal, Cordella stopped abruptly. Gradually, walls were forming all around them; the ruins were disappearing right before their eyes and making way for a majestic house, as though a curtain had been lifted from the rotten ruins to reveal the most sophisticated palace.

"That was a surprise ..." said Trevor, studying the place.

"Edmund was always a fan of luxury," Cordella pointed out. "He wouldn't change now."

Right in front of them, a huge common room appeared in a matter of seconds. The floor was made of dark stones that shone brightly, showing that they were too clean and expensive. An enormous crystal chandelier was now hanging over their heads, adding even more luxury and weirdness to that room.

"How are we going to find the Book of the Portals, Cordella?" asked Olivia.

"You two must find it."

"How? Aren't you helping us?" asked Olivia.

"I am, but the Book has a stronger connection with you two. Try to sense it. I'm afraid there's not much we can do other than this," Cordella confessed, killing the little hope they had that the witch would have all the answers they needed. "This place is enormous, and we can't waste any time. You ought to do your best to find it. Use your connection. NOW!"

"All right ... What about heading this way?" Trevor pointed to a huge set of double doors on their left. One of them was open, showing a glimpse of the hallway behind it.

"Not without me!" shouted Bran, running toward them. "I'm coming with you. The group is doing all right out there," he joked lightly as he caught up with Olivia, Trevor, and Cordella. He was clearly trying to make the tension a little better, but no one really laughed at his effort.

The truth was that everyone knew that the fight might well be going horribly, but they were too afraid to ask or to even think about it now. They were a small group, and they had no idea how many allies Edmund Lars had. At least they could count on skilled warriors and wizards.

The whole mansion had that same luxurious and modern design

of the grand hall. Most of the halls that they walked through were wide and well-lit by fancy fixtures. But the place was cold, and there were so many entrances, and hallways, and turns that it felt like a labyrinth. And it seemed that there was no soul living in the place. They couldn't hear any voices, steps, nothing. Oftentimes, Olivia would think that this was all a trap, especially considering Baltazar's reaction when he put his eyes on her. Surely, Lars' most trusted ally had run to tell his master that Olivia was there, that killing her was urgent.

They kept walking fast, passing through hallways that sometimes seemed to have no end. They walked aimlessly, turning right, left, again and again, hoping to feel some sort of call, but nothing changed. There were only hallways without doors, with bare walls painted in a dark shade of gray.

"This place is odd. I feel like we're trapped," said Olivia quietly.

"And you're surprised because ..." Trevor had a somber and mocking tone in his voice, as if he wished to tell Olivia that they should have known that this wouldn't be easy, because nothing ever was in this whole experience.

"This is Lars' home. He built it with this very day in mind. He is protecting himself, his treasures. This is Lars' home, but he made it into a trap," said Cordella. "Come on, Olivia and Trevor. Put your hearts into it. We must find the Book now!" Cordella was assertive, but Olivia and Trevor only felt more cornered. They had no idea if they could manage to do that.

Until this point, after long minutes that would soon become hours walking around the house, they hadn't heard a thing. Not even a faint sound of someone closing a door at a distance. There was no vestige of life in the house.

As they walked through one of the hall doorways, Olivia and Trevor hesitated and suddenly stopped.

"Do you think—" Trevor didn't complete his sentence. His eyes were wide open when he found Olivia's.

"Yes. I do," interrupted Olivia, opening the black wooden door on their left side.

"Careful," warned Bran, wielding his sword.

Inside the room, they found a number of chairs aligned in a circle. In the middle, some kind of wooden altar stood tall and pompous as the main piece of decoration. The place barely had any light whatsoever, only two tall weak lamps located right out of the circle of chairs. As they got closer to the altar, they could see a small key over the wooden structure, resting on a velvet cushion. It was fairly rusty and engraved with a symbol that resembled a leafless tree.

"It's the lost Key!" said Cordella with relief. Her voice was full of hope and contentment.

This was the first time Olivia had set her eyes on a Portal Key. She never knew exactly what to expect, but the thing was small, simple, rather rustic. Only a few would think that such an ordinary artifact would carry so much power, would have such a crucial place in the lives of so many people, of so many worlds.

Cordella took a silver chain from her neck and lopped it through the hole at the base of the key. She then put the necklace on Olivia. It felt unexpectedly warm when it touched Olivia's skin.

"It doesn't matter what happens to the rest of us. You two must destroy the Portals. So you should keep that, and keep it safe. Now let's go. We still need to find the Book."

"You really didn't think it would be this easy, didn't you?" said a thin, mocking voice coming from the shadows in the room. The group promptly got their weapons and two phookas came out of the shadows.

"This key is not going anywhere, old grumpy Cordella," said one of them.

"It's time to retire, old Cordella. You don't know how to create plans that don't kill people anymore, old Cordella!" continued the other one, laughing like a hyena.

Cordella threw her body in front of Olivia, Trevor, and Bran, protecting them and walking slowly backward while the phookas got closer. When Olivia, Trevor and Bran were right in front of the door, Cordella turned to them abruptly and blew hard, making the three of them fall on the hallway floor, pushed by the strong blast of wind. In that fraction of time, before the door was closed, Cordella yelled, "GO!"

Trevor stood quickly and tried to open the door, which was already locked. They could still hear the noises coming from inside the room, the strikes, and the phookas' perverse laughs.

"Let's go!" said Bran. "She knows what she's doing, and we need to find the Book. Come on!"

Trevor and Olivia hesitated for a moment. But there wasn't much they could do. They finally ran through the mansion, looking for the Book of the Portals. They got into a number of rooms, and the place only seemed to stretch. They were getting lost inside those walls, rooms, stairs, and shadows. Olivia felt stuck inside a luxurious maze, impregnated with a weird and agonizing energy.

Stairs seemed to appear out of nowhere all around. They would go up and down, and Olivia's head was already turning. The house was dark, pretty much all painted in gray and black, and even though everything was supposed to be very beautiful and sumptuous, that was not the feeling they were getting inside the peculiar mansion. Olivia, Trevor and Bran were deeply, intensely, greatly lost. And the fact that Cordella was not part of the searching party anymore made them panic a little.

Olivia and Trevor tried to keep in their minds that they would *feel* the Book. That their energies were connected, and maybe that would be a calling of some sort. The fact that they had just felt the Portal Key and managed to find it was making them feel more confident about their unique task. After one more sinuous corridor, they stepped inside an oval room where a fireplace was crackling soundly; they saw a wide staircase at the end of it and headed upstairs. Edmund Lars' entire house was freezing, and the fireplace seemed to have accepted a challenge that was way beyond its capabilities. The energy in the place was only getting worse and worse, and there was no sign of the Book of the Portals yet. Olivia was already asking herself if the thing would really be hidden in that vile place.

The room upstairs was full of mirrors. One leaning over the other, and all leaning against the walls. Every single mirror was adorned with elaborate frames and apparently made of gold and silver, carved with colored gems that reflected the faint light inside the room. A dark shadow moved through the mirrors.

"WATCH OUT, OLIE!" yelled Trevor.

A number of phookas came out of nowhere, and Olivia could barely see them, as they were blending into the shadows of the dark room. The creatures jumped from side to side and used the shadows as an advantage to attack the group by surprise. Trevor threw arrows almost without thinking, but it seemed that for each phooka he hit, two more would appear. Olivia and Bran fought the creatures fiercely with their swords, trying to strike them any way they could. The creatures would jump and push them around the room. Oftentimes, Olivia felt as though she were being shaken from side to side. Her head was spinning, and it was almost impossible to concentrate with all that horrendous laughter and the shadows that crawled everywhere in the place. Suddenly everything went silent, and the room seemed to have completely emptied out. All the phookas disappeared, and their laughter faded into the distance until they were completely inaudible.

Olivia looked around, searching for her friends, and she heard Trevor. He was screaming, resisting. Her eyes studied the room until she finally found Trevor fighting with a phooka. The creature was all over him, biting his arms and neck, clearly winning, and Trevor was slowly giving up.

Olivia was taken by a wave of anger. The thought of losing her friend made her heart shrink and explode at the same time, as if her life was also being lost. Or, even worse, as if she were going to live a life without light. Without purpose.

She wielded her sword and moved toward the phookas with all her strength, only to be stopped. She couldn't move anymore. She looked back and Bran was holding her strongly.

"WE MUST HELP HIM!" Olivia yelled, her eyes fixed on Trevor and the phooka.

"No. He must go alone."

Bran held Olivia even more strongly now until he wrapped his arms around her in an unwanted embrace. Olivia took some time to process what was happening, and then she started to scream. She needed to break free, she needed him to let her go.

"I MUST HELP HIM, BRAN! WE NEED TO HELP HIM!" Olivia screamed. She didn't understand why he wouldn't let her go. She didn't understand the reason for all that protection. If they worked together, they would figure out a way to defeat the phooka. To get out of that place. "BRAN! WE NEED TO HELP HIM!" Olivia fought Bran's embrace, screaming and clenching her teeth. She did her best to free herself, and Bran only seemed to hold her tighter.

And then, Trevor stopped resisting. His screams were getting weaker, and the noises made by the phookas took their place. Trevor was gradually surrounded by the creatures, who came out of the shadows once more. They danced around the boy as in a sinister ritual. Trevor's body was dragged out of Olivia's sight and disappeared into the shadows of that mirrored room. Now, there was just an emptiness in her heart, an abyss. Little by little, she quit screaming and fighting Bran's arms, and he finally let her go.

"WHY DID YOU DO THAT? WE MUST FIND HIM! BRAN, WHY DID YOU DO THAT? I COULD–WE COULD HAVE HELPED HIM!" Olivia was yelling again. Tears ran down her face uncontrollably, making her cheeks and her mouth wet. "WE CAN'T GO ON WITHOUT TREVOR! WE MUST FIND HIM, WE MUST HELP HIM NOW!"

For an instant, she didn't recognize Bran anymore. Olivia paused, took a breath, and looked the boy in his eyes. He seemed different ... strange. She didn't find that sparkle that she loved so much in there. His eyes were cold and satisfied. Slowly, a discreet smile was growing on his face.

"You are right, Olivia Halin. We can't go on without Trevor." There was a different voice in Bran's words. Something screechy and full of mockery. And she knew that voice.

Hearing that voice that she hated profusely coming out of Bran's mouth was unbearable, repulsive. Gradually, Bran's face began to shift, giving way to someone else's features. His smile was not gentle and kind anymore; his eyes were now filled with hate. The Bran she knew and loved so much was being replaced by the one who haunted her since she was in her world. Bran was shifting into Baltazar Fletce.

CHAPTER TWENTY-THREE

THE CONSEQUENCES OF WAR

Seeing Bran's face transform into Baltazar's was deeply disturbing. The change happened slowly; Olivia witnessed every inch of Bran's skin change its color, his delicate features invaded by Baltazar's. Someone who Olivia feared, and who represented all that was wrong in Tartae. Thinking of Baltazar pretending to be Bran for those last hours was disgusting. Olivia was nauseated, anger and revulsion were taking over her body.

Once again, she found herself alone with Baltazar, and there still wasn't a sign of her memory. And once again, he was between her and the Book of the Portals. When that specific thought crossed her mind, she figured that she should be close. She couldn't give up now. Baltazar was there to protect his master and the Book, and she wasn't going to leave this dreadful place without it.

"Did Lars send you to do his job again? It must be tiring to serve someone so lazy," mocked Olivia. Her voice was firm, and she put all that she had into not showing any trace of weakness. In her head, she was gathering all and any memories she had of the lessons she had learned about magic and fighting.

"I see that you lost your memory, but you're still a brat, Olivia," said Baltazar insolently, and Olivia was puzzled; she couldn't hide her surprise and the question burning in her eyes. "Yes, I know you don't remember anything about Tartae and the Portals. As you can tell from today and your last failed attempts to get your hands on the Book, we are always a few steps ahead of you and your little group. It's even sad."

"No, it's not. Being you must be sad. You do all the work and never get the glory. No one even knows who you are. No one ever heard your name," said Olivia. Baltazar's expression changed, and Olivia knew that she'd gotten where she wanted.

"Lars doesn't get involved with things that don't require his attention."

"So, you're saying that you're in charge of the things that don't really matter? That's good. And here I was, thinking that I could be in danger. That he sent his best buddy to fight me. Allow me to give you a piece of advice, Baltazar. I really think you should call him Master Lars. Or even better, Master Edmund Lars. I guess he won't like to be treated disrespectfully by one his lackeys. You must call him properly. Maybe you shouldn't even say his name."

"Oh, Olivia ..." laughed Baltazar. His teeth seemed to be getting bigger by the minute, achieving now unimaginable proportions. His face twitched with that morbid laugh, which still looked like a foreign movement on his face. "I only have one thing to say. This time you won't be so lucky."

Baltazar Fletce moved his hands, stretching his arms in front of him as if he were trying to reach for something. His long fingers stretched and widened, and his veins popped out of his skin. All of the mirrors in the room broke at once, and the pieces flew in Olivia's direction. She ran and quickly hid behind one of the biggest frames in the room. However, she couldn't avoid all the broken glass and was cut on her arms and face.

Olivia got down on one knee and put both of her hands on the floor. Rapidly, the black stone started to crack until it opened completely, caving in where Baltazar stood. He fell with the stones, landing clumsily on the first floor of the building. But Baltazar got back up quickly, jumping as high and precisely as a monkey, returning to where Olivia was.

Baltazar's face was far from human now. And it was only getting worse. His eyes were big and incredibly wide, and his pupils were bright red, giving the impression that they would jump out of his eyeballs at any given second. His mouth was open and his teeth completely humongous. Craving destruction. Longing for blood. It was evident that killing Olivia was important to him. He was being tested.

As he got face-to-face with Olivia, Baltazar studied her for a while and then proceeded to attack her once more. His hands reached for Olivia's neck, but she grabbed her sword in a quick movement, wielding the weapon fearlessly. The man took a step back but didn't seem too frightened. He still carried a threatening look on his bizarre face. It was clear that Baltazar didn't think much of her, maybe because he knew she wasn't the same as before. Maybe he never saw her as much of threat. It didn't matter now. The only thing that Olivia had in mind was to finish that fight and carry on. In all that insolence and confidence, Olivia found his weakness.

They only looked at each other for a second or two, both trying to figure out what the next movement would be. Baltazar was slowly losing bits of his once unshakable confidence. Something had changed in Olivia, and he was now being careful. Time seemed to have stopped. However, Olivia knew that the clock was still ticking, and with each second that passed, Trevor's life was in more danger. This wasn't the time to hesitate.

Olivia took a deep breath and remembered what Cordella and Bran used to say about balancing mind and matter. She advanced toward Baltazar with an aggressive strike, which the man dodged, moving in her direction as soon as he recovered his balance. Baltazar dug his pointy nails into Olivia's arm in a movement that was so fast it made her drop her sword. She put her hands on Baltazar's fists, trying to break away from his grasp. The man's arms were hot as if his blood was pulsating to the point of boiling inside of him. She tried to break his hold using all her strength, but his hard nails seemed to only get deeper into her skin. In his eyes, the confidence was growing again.

The pain started to take over Olivia's body. It all could end there, and it would all have been in vain. Clearly, Baltazar was acting like a wild animal who had to weaken its prey until it was the right moment for a final strike. He would definitely look for something more frail and vital than her arms ... and that would be it.

Olivia closed her eyes and gathered all the strength she had left. Her movements needed to be precise and strong. She would probably only have one chance. She needed to get out of there and save Trevor. They needed to save Tartae. Baltazar's arrogance made him weaker and more vulnerable. She made a quick plan in her head, and she had one shot to make it work.

She knocked her head with all her strength onto Baltazar's nose, who took a step back and released his grasp a bit, just enough for her to kick him in the stomach. The man, who was now bleeding through his nose, lost his balance and staggered, taking another step back. "You stupid girl!" he said, and before he could do anything else, Olivia took her sword from the floor and, with her eyes closed, aimed it at the man's chest. The blade perforated his flesh and slid through it until it was completely out again through the other side. For a split second, he stood still, looking at her. The rage was slowly leaving his eyes. They were all blank now. Baltazar fell like a rock onto the floor.

That moment went on so quickly that Olivia didn't know exactly how it all happened. There was an incredible amount of blood coming out of Baltazar's mouth and wound. Around him, a pool of blood spread on the floor, touching Olivia's feet. Baltazar Fletce was dead, and Olivia was the one who had killed him.

Olivia didn't have the guts to take the sword out of Baltazar's chest. Even though she was fighting for her life—and her friends' lives—the realization that she had just ended someone's life took over her body like a poison. She was about to throw up and cry. Her heart sank with guilt.

CHAPTER TWENTY-FOUR

THE FINAL CHALLENGE

A fter a minute or so of staring at Baltazar's lifeless body, Olivia shook her head and reminded herself that she needed to keep moving. She ran into the shadows in the room, heading in the same direction where the phooka had vanished with Trevor some time ago. She walked between the mirrors and, where she thought there would be a wall, there was a dark, long corridor. She materialized a flame in her hand, strong enough for her to see a couple of steps ahead. She kept walking almost blindly through the hall for some minutes, listening only to her own steps. It took her some time to come to her senses and realize that she had left her sword behind. From now on, she had to count only on her young and inconsistent magic.

She kept moving forward until the construction changed, the walls were now quite rustic. Olivia had arrived in a stone corridor, a place that resembled a cave. From a distance, she started to hear the familiar noises made by the phooka. All that annoying laughter and incessant jumping. Olivia walked faster, being extra careful not to be heard.

Olivia saw a doorway some feet away from where she was now, and the phooka sounds were getting very loud. She made the flame in her hand become small and weak so she could get closer without being noticed and the flame would be ready for what she had in mind. As she got nearer to the doorway, Olivia let the flame in her hand grow significantly, and then she blew it hard inside the room. The place was completely filled with fire. The creatures began to scream desperately and to look for a way out of that place. They found a path out through a small window located in one of the walls and jumped through it without giving it a lot of thought. They didn't even notice Olivia's presence, and they left a rotting smell behind, making it hard to breathe. Once she was in the room, she noticed that the phookas had been guarding a trapdoor.

She pulled the metal handle, and there was Trevor. His hands and feet were tied up.

"TREVOR!" yelled Olivia, running downstairs to the dungeon and untying the boy quickly. The two friends hugged.

"I was trying to understand what was happening up there. How did you get rid of the phooka?"

"I set the place on fire and they ran. They're not very brave, apparently. When they find themselves at a disadvantage, they run away like scared prey."

"They're not very smart either. In between the annoying laughter, they let it slip that Lars hid the Book of the Portals in his favorite room, the large one underground."

"Do you know how to get there?"

"No, but at least we know where to look. Olie, are you OK?" asked Trevor, finally seeing that Olivia's clothes were all covered in blood and her face was full of small cuts.

"Yes ... Bran was not really Bran." Trevor looked confused, and she continued, "It was Baltazar Fletce. We fought and I'm here now ..." finished Olivia, her stomach turning once more by the thought of Baltazar dead on the floor with her sword into his chest. Could she ever forget that?

"I wish I could have helped you."

"I know. I really do ... Let's find the Book of the Portals and get this over with. It's about time," said Olivia, walking toward the old wooden stairs that provided access in and out of the dungeon.

Trevor grabbed his bow and arrow, which were lying next to the trapdoor. Olivia and Trevor ran through the corridor to the mirror room, and Baltazar's body wasn't there anymore. There was only blood everywhere, wreckage and a huge hole on the floor, right in the middle of the room. She hesitated for a moment, wondering what could have happened to the man.

"Olie?" Trevor called, noticing her confusion.

"We must run, Trev! We're not alone in here."

They ran hastily through the house, trying to remember where they came from and how to get to the main room. The way was still tricky and inconsistent. They hurried across both wide and thin corridors. Sometimes they would recognize a small detail on the walls or the ceiling, other times they felt that they had never seen the place they were in before. Olivia and Trevor were scared; they had been inside that mansion for hours now, and the place seemed to be getting into their heads, making them feel more confused and insecure. Less like themselves. They couldn't lose any more time. Their destiny was hanging by a thread.

The two friends kept going, sometimes slipping on the overly polished floor. The gloomy hallways seemed to have no end, until they finally saw a pair of black doors. Olivia and Trevor looked at each other and ran toward it, opening them to find the large main hall. They walked in and across the room, a huge set of red double doors was leading to the east wing of the house. As they opened them, a beautiful dining room was revealed. The place seemed ready for a sophisticated party. The tables were set with red linen and shiny silverware. In the corner, a piano didn't quite fit the rest of the place, which was so impeccably and carefully decorated. The instrument was crooked, and the bench had fallen onto the floor.

Olivia and Trevor exchanged a meaningful look and got closer to the piano. The weird position of the bench told a story. Something had happened there, and they were pretty sure of what that was. They tested the floor, knocking it incessantly until it made a different sound. It was a hidden passageway.

"He must have been in a hurry. He must have forgotten about the piano and that we would check here eventually," whispered Olivia.

"Olie, there's no handle to open it. You need to do something."

"Er—let me see," said Olivia. Trying to remember something that could be useful now.

"Hurry, Olie! We don't have much time!" Trevor's voice was urgent, but his tone was very low. No one appeared to be around, and they wished to keep it that way.

Olivia managed to glue her hand to the icy cold stone that the floor was made of and pulled it up hard at once. The door opened without much resistance, showing pompous marble stairs leading to a basement of some sort.

Olivia and Trevor went downstairs, entering an impressive room. The walls were decorated with fancy wallpaper; on the floor, a symbol touched almost all the edges of the room. A symbol Olivia had never seen that resembled an eye. In the middle, there was a pedestal and a Book resting on it. The Book of the Portals.

Once again, it looked as though they were alone in the place. There was no sign of Edmund Lars or his allies. However, they had learned before that looks could be deceiving. They should be prepared for the worst; at any time now there could be phookas or trolls or who knew what else attacking them.

The Book of the Portals seemed to call Olivia and Trevor, and as they got closer to it, the whole room vibrated as if they had passed through a force field.

"Be careful, Trev," said Olivia, her eyes locked on the Book.

Trevor closed the Book and his fingers went numb. He felt as though he was touching years of history, sadness, fighting, loneliness. The Book was heavy with meaning, with expectations. Olivia and Trevor were waiting for something to happen as soon as they touched the Book, for someone to attack them. But nothing. The room was still empty.

"Let's go!" urged Trevor, hugging the Book of the Portals tightly and walking to the stairs they had used before. "I don't believe that we've been through all this and won't even be able to put a face to a name."

"I believe it's better this way."

They ran up the marble stairs very fast and crossed the dining room like a hurricane. The place seemed to have stretched. And as they were so eager to get out of that house, they felt like it was taking forever to get to the dining room doors. When they were finally about to go through the doorway, the doors closed, making a loud noise that echoed inside the room.

Olivia and Trevor turned away slowly, and there he was. Standing in the middle of the room was a tall, skinny man, hair as red as blood and straight, falling over his shoulders and delicately framing his features. The man had a tranquil look on his face. The tranquility of someone who knows exactly how something is going to end. Someone who is sure of victory. Olivia and Trevor knew before any introduction: They were seeing Edmund Lars for the first time.

CHAPTER TWENTY-FIVE

THE EXPECTED JOURNEY

"I bite my tongue," cursed Trevor as soon as he put his eyes on Edmund Lars.

Olivia and Trevor didn't know what to do or what to say. They just stood there, looking at Lars. Trevor held the Book of the Portals tightly in his arms, trying to decide what to do next.

As Olivia stood there, she studied Edmund Lars' face and found him disturbingly normal. He would easily pass unnoticed in a crowd. He would easily blend in anywhere. He would easily be someone else.

"So, what are we waiting for?" said Edmund Lars in his grave, penetrating voice, breaking the silence. The expression on his face didn't change a bit. It was almost calming.

He didn't give Olivia and Trevor much time. As soon as he was finished talking, he threw a giant flame at the two friends. The fire quickly spread out and took over the room completely. Tiny salamanders came out from it, full of life and scintillating, dancing on the ground. Olivia's and Trevor's eyes burned from the fire, and the smoke scratched their insides as it entered their lungs. They both coughed frantically. Trevor threw the Book of the Portals closer to the doors and began to shoot arrows at Edmund Lars, who didn't seem to care.

Olivia was now thinking about how she could extinguish the fire from the room. And before she even noticed, she was making water fall from the ceiling, like an artificial rain. The fire weakened, and the salamanders disappeared one by one. The tables that had been so beautifully set before were now burned, and there was only wreckage scattered across the room.

Trevor was moving around throwing arrows relentlessly and protecting himself when Lars sent more fire and blasts of wind at the boy's direction. Olivia lifted what was left of some of the burned tables by waving her hand and then throwing them at Lars. He could almost too easily defend himself and would stop them in the air, breaking the tables into a thousand pieces, turning them into dust on the floor. Trevor tried to take advantage of the moments in which Lars defended himself from Olivia's spells. He would fire more arrows at the wizard, in the hopes that one would eventually strike him and do some kind of damage. However, nothing seemed to alarm him. Nothing that Olivia and Trevor did get even close to touching his skin.

They kept trying, and their movements were now synchronized. Trevor jumped lightly from one side of the room to another, resembling a bird playing between the branches of a tree. His movements were agile and coordinated, but even so, his arrows were never fast enough to touch Edmund Lars.

The evil wizard had barely moved during the whole fight. He was still there, practically in the middle of the room, waving his hands and making Olivia and Trevor believe that there was something, a sort of invisible shield protecting him. His face was unchanging; his eyes even seemed peaceful. Olivia saw no hesitation, no surprise, and even no hate there.

Edmund Lars seemed to be invincible. At some point that was the only thing that Olivia and Trevor could think. He was so skilled in magic that all the things around him seemed to be at his will. And Olivia even wondered if that wasn't the case for herself and Trevor too. Had this all been part of Lars' plan since the beginning? Were she and Trevor fighting just the way Lars intended? He appeared to know every step they would take, everything they would try against him. He was always prepared and protected.

The room was now almost completely destroyed. The wreckage from the dining tables and chairs were transformed by Lars into long snakes that crept in Olivia's and Trevor's direction. Trevor jumped back fast, getting closer to Olivia, who was trying to think of something that could save them.

"Get behind me!" Olivia yelled to Trevor, who quickly obeyed.

Olivia got down and touched the floor, making it shake like in an earthquake. The movement made the snakes lose their form as the small wood pieces separated. Olivia's powers came from nature, she needed the element's assistance to do her magic. She thought about water, and she asked for its help. Moments afterward, a rush of water washed over the floors, making the fake snakes completely disappear.

Olivia searched Lars' face and found a discreet smile. This was the first time during the whole battle that the man had moved. He began walking toward Olivia and Trevor, who quickly got into their attack positions once more. But there was something about Edmund Lars that made them slower. They got a bit hypnotized by him, and they just stood there, ready for battle but doing nothing.

Suddenly, there was a bang, and the two red doors opened at once. Through them came Belenos, Alegra, and Orion, who quickly joined the fight. Belenos got to Olivia and Trevor and grabbed them urgently by their arms.

"Let's go! Let's go! We must go!" he said, almost yelling.

"But–what about Alegra?" said Trevor.

"There's no time. She's strong, Trevor. You must trust her," said Belenos, guiding them to the door. Trevor got down on his way out and grabbed the Book of the Portals from when it had landed. The thing was intact, even after the fire, the rain and everything else that happened inside that room, as though it was unaffected by it all, or even indestructible.

They ran outside as fast as humanly possible. All that Olivia saw around them was a blur, and she didn't even have the time to enjoy leaving that terrible place. Belenos guided them to the side of Edmund Lars' house and kept running until they were inside the black forest. After hurrying blindly into those creepy woods, they finally saw Cordella and Alavro.

"Oh! Blessed be!" said Alavro, relieved.

"Come on, come on! There's no time." Cordella used the same tone that Olivia and Trevor had the pleasure to know on the first day they arrived in Tartae. They were close now. The end was near.

"We need to be fast. Lars is on the move," warned Belenos. In the black of the forest, his face still had a glow. However, he looked worried and stressed.

The forest around them was dark and sinister. Once again, the emptiness of that place was palpable, nature appeared to be lifeless. There was a nasty smell all over, and something seemed to be lurking and plotting. It was a dreadful place, and Olivia wished she were somewhere else.

On the forest floor, there was a series of symbols and a drawing that reminded Olivia and Trevor of a tree and a flower, very similar to one of the paintings they had seen in Cordella's house when they arrived in Tartae. Around it, there were twelve Keys of the Portals lined side by side, forming a perfect circle.

"Olivia, the Key." Cordella reached for it. Olivia took off her necklace and handed it to Cordella. "No, keep it in your hand. And you, Trevor, take Olivia's hand now." Trevor gave the Book of the Portals to Alavro and took Olivia's hand, and Cordella enveloped their hands inside of hers tightly. The key pressed against her skin, causing some kind of twinkling in her palm. "You two can't let go of the Key at any time. You keep holding it." Cordella looked deep into their eyes.

The five of them formed a circle around the Keys that were laid on the floor, and Alavro opened the Book of the Portals solemnly. Olivia couldn't read what was written on the page he chose, but an almost suffocating agony grew in her heart. She held Trevor's hand tighter, and he did the same. The energy was expanding and vibrating.

Cordella, Alavro and Belenos closed their eyes and voiced some unintelligible words. A yellow light bloomed from the forest floor, delineating a circle around them, forming a spiral and enveloping them in that golden, glistening light.

"It's time," whispered Cordella solemnly. "Repeat after me." And all of them began to say the words in unison after the witch.

"From rupture, peace is born;
From destruction, salvation blooms.
To Nature we plead:
May we close the gate.
May each world be limited to itself,
May there be again a limit in itself."

A brilliant light blinded Olivia, and a strong force pushed and pulled her in all directions. The whole place was swallowed by a white light, and her hand was still glued to Trevor's, like they were one.

When she was finally able to open her eyes again and look around, she recognized the City of Leve. And everything was the same. Crickets were stridulating, and a car honked in the distance. Olivia and Trevor hugged each other. They didn't say a word. There was not much to say after all that had happened. When they finally let go, they only exchanged a meaningful look and headed home.

Olivia walked inside her grandmother's empty house. No one had even noticed she was gone. The house was dark and quiet, and she found everything strange: the smells, the corners, the shadows. She went to the bathroom and turned on the fluorescent lights. Seeing herself in the mirror made her give a baffled scream. She was covered in dirt and cinders; her face was cut in multiple places, and there was blood everywhere. However, from everything she saw in her own reflection, something intrigued her more than the rest. Her eyes were different. They shone with a different light. The green in her irises was now deep and electric, and it hypnotized her for a couple of minutes.

Although she was now *home*, she felt like a stranger. She could only think about how it all happened so fast during those last hours in Tartae and wonder what had happened to her friends. What had happened to Bran? What destiny did Tartae have?
Olivia splashed some water on her face and emptiness took over her heart. Tartae was left behind.

CHAPTER TWENTY-SIX

BACK TO WHERE IT ALL STARTED

"**D**o you want some popcorn, Olivia?"

"Yes. Extra butter, and I also want chocolate, please."

"Of course!" answered Lara casually, getting ready to order.

It has been a year, four days and eight hours since Olivia got back to the City of Leve. And she was counting the minutes. The decision to travel back to her world was abrupt and beyond herself. However, it was the only thing she could have done, the only option she'd had. She made the best out of being back, trying to enjoy every little thing her world had to offer. She made constant trips to the movies and found ways to get lost into those adventurous–although inoffensive–make-believe worlds. All of that to try and forget Tartae. Life seemed to be back to normal, and nothing was altered. Not even her battle wounds were noticed by anyone in Leve. They gradually healed and then disappeared. As for her eyes, they regained their usual color in no time, unfortunately.

Her grandmother was still cruising around the world, living her own version of an adventurous life, Olivia believed. And Olivia didn't even know if the woman would notice if Olivia were gone forever, since Mrs. Halin barely called and was very much invested in being far away.

In order to heal completely from the physical wounds she got in Tartae and recover her emotional stability, Olivia asked Mr. Fildor for two weeks off, and he granted it without asking any questions. "Oh, everybody needs to take a break. I know it very well," said the man with an honest smile, only to break into the same complaints, "I sure need a lot of breaks—you know, my back hurts, my feet hurt ..."

And as for school, Olivia and Trevor were lucky enough to be almost at winter break when they arrived.

They took a while to recover from the pain, the trauma, the fear they had been through. Even sleeping on their beds was hard for a while. They spent some time sleeping with their lights on, waking up with every sound, searching in the night for their weapons.

Unlike Olivia's grandmother, Trevor's father had been about to call the police when he had arrived home on that Sunday early in the morning. Such a stunt was not like Trevor, who would never test the limits that his father had imposed. Trevor knew how much his father worried about him, especially after he lost his wife.

Harder than explaining why he was home so late was explaining why his clothes were in that pitiful state and why he was wearing something that his father had never seen before in his life. Trevor did his best to explain using facts that wouldn't lead Mr. Meris to believe that his son had gone insane. Trevor told his father that he was part of a play and that he didn't say anything before because he wanted it to be a surprise. Mr. Meris didn't seem to buy it, but he let Trevor get away with it. The boy looked more tired than a marathon runner, and the man simply let it go. After that, Trevor had to sign himself up for the drama club so his story would be at least a bit convincing.

Olivia and Trevor kept thinking that they would someday laugh about all of this, but that day hadn't arrived yet. A year had passed, and they were still having nightmares about Tartae. The last hours they were in there, the battles, the fire, the way those phooka creatures laughed. Olivia could still feel the disturbing sensation of her sword's blade perforating Baltazar's Fletce flesh, and Edmund Lars' look longing for her death. She still woke up in the middle of the night searching in the shadows for something that she didn't wish to find.

As the time passed by and the wounds went away, Olivia tried to adapt to her ordinary life in the City of Leve again. Her job in the bookshop was still boring, and high school had come to an end. She was now finally getting ready to go to college. She had a talk with her grandmother, who had just won some good money on a casino cruise, and the woman agreed to pay for her studies.

"At least for a while," she said. Her life was getting back on track and her future was not a faint promise anymore.

But with every nightfall, and every time she looked at the sky and didn't see the two Tartae moons, Olivia missed that place. From time to time, her heart would go back there almost uncontrollably. It would take her back to the forests, to that constant feeling of flirting with the unknown. She would remember how much she had learned and how fascinating things were. It was hard to be back in Leve.

Olivia and her friend Lara entered the movie theater and sat down in their places. It was a movie about a couple who were soulmates, and they found themselves in different moments in history. As if the two souls were traveling through time together. Olivia wasn't very excited about the plot, as it wasn't her kind of story, but Lara had seen too much of Indiana Jones lately, and Olivia was in debt with her.

"Lara, I need to go to the restroom before the movie starts," said Olivia quickly. She didn't want to miss anything during the movie, and the trailers were already on.

"Don't get lost," joked Lara, not looking away from the screen.

Olivia opened the door to the restroom, which was completely empty. The sound of water dripping echoed, and the stall doors trembled due to the powerful sound system in the theaters that shared walls with the restroom.

Olivia had a weird feeling. Something was out of place. Something inside her was struggling, trying to free itself, and it was fairly uncomfortable. She examined the restroom, looking for something uncommon and, *drip, drip, drip*. There was only the sound of the water.

As she stood in the middle of the restroom, she turned to the mirror, and then she knew.

"Someone's here," she whispered to herself. As though she were talking to her reflection or searching for a confirmation inside of herself. She spent some more seconds pondering, deciding if she was right or imagining things. After months without the adventures and adrenaline of living in Tartae, this could be nostalgia. A desire to reclaim something that was lost. "There's someone here."

Olivia looked around the room and exploded in a scream:
"SHOW YOURSELF!"

For a split second, she thought that nothing was going to

happen. That she was imagining things that didn't exist. For a moment, the world stopped. And then, the restroom floor trembled and the stall doors slammed madly, making a deafening sound.

"SHOW YOURSELF!"

Olivia gathered all the strength she had, remembering all she had learned in Tartae. If there was anything she was proud of, it was that she was better now. A better fighter, a better witch. However, she had no idea if her magical skills would work properly in Leve. How strong she would be here.

Finally, after minutes that seemed to pass too slowly, a pale figure came out of one of the stalls. A short, muscular man, with gray hair and big, dark circles under his eyes. With him, a number of phookas bounced out. They jumped from side to side and made the water from the toilets splash all around, flooding the bathroom and making a complete mess.

Instantly, Olivia was taken by only one thought: Edmund Lars was not defeated. The Portals of Tartae were open again.

ABOUT THE AUTHOR

Marcia Soligo grew up avidly reading fairy tales and watching The NeverEnding Story movies. Creating worlds and stories was an important part of her childhood that led to an interest in fantasy literature and myth, which she has continued studying until today. Marcia was born in Brazil and majored in communications and journalism. She currently lives in Chicago with her husband and their dog.

Made in the USA
Columbia, SC
10 December 2021

50694130R00119